DANCING WITH DANGER

ACES HIGH MC - DAKOTAS
BOOK 1

CHRISTINE MICHELLE

ABOUT THE BOOK

He's a biker with an attitude.
She's a dancer on the run.

What do you do when your husband is a beloved football
superstar who is trying to get an insurance settlement in exchange
for your demise?
You get kidnapped by a well-meaning family friend you knew
nothing about. Then you're forced to run away when he fails to
show up again. You might even dance in questionable strip clubs
so you can stay under the radar and survive another day.
That is exactly the path that I took, only in the end, it not only led
me to a motorcycle club in the Dakotas but to a family I never
knew I had.
I'm not sure if I trust them to keep me safe or sane. Rage, their vice
president, is the first man to gain my interest in a long time, and
he blows so hot and cold that I'm not sure if I should stick around.
I brought trouble to his doorstep and in return, he brought safety

and passion to mine. If I can survive what my ex has in store, then maybe, I'll be able to fall for the right man.

Romantic suspense
Other woman drama
MC Romance
Small town
Action and adventure

TRIGGER WARNINGS

- Strong language
- Violence
- Attempted Murder
- Murder
- Death of loved ones
- Other woman drama
- Drug/alcohol use
- Kidnapping
- Contract killers
- Family betrayals
- Sexual situations described on page
- More potential triggers not listed here

AHMC DAKOTAS

1

Charlie & Rage

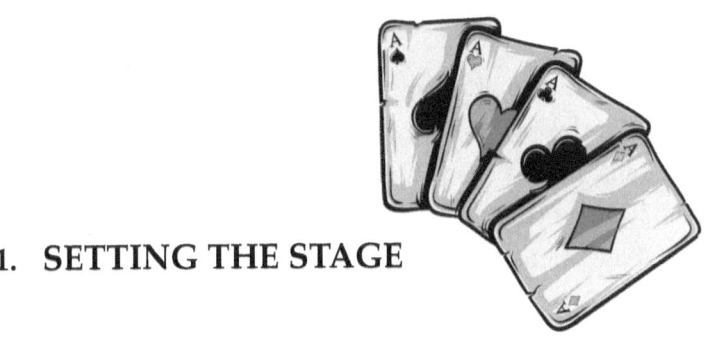

1. SETTING THE STAGE

"CHARLIE COOPER IS THAT YOU?"

I cringed inside when I heard my real name shouted out by the drunken idiot who I once attended high school with. Savion, one of our bouncers who played bodyguard for the dancers, was on him before he could slur another word. The damage was already done though. I never acknowledged whether the asshole was correct, but Savion's quick interference didn't go unnoticed by the crowd of my usual fans who were now grinning greedily with the knowledge they had just been gifted.

My name was indeed Charlie Cooper, but up on the stage I always went by Shadow. That's where I was hiding after all, in the shadows. At least I had been hiding there until just about five minutes ago.

I finished my set and sashayed my ass off stage to go settle up with Harry, the owner of this fine titty-bar establishment I found myself working in. Yeah, yeah, titty-bar wasn't politically correct, but guess what sweet-cheeks,

I

there's nothing politically correct about shaking your money maker for throngs of horny, sex-deprived men in order to pay your bills. I call a spade a spade and get on with my life. No need to sugar coat that shit.

I had managed six months in this place, and clearly Phoenix, Arizona wasn't far enough away from my hometown to go unrecognized. Now, I'd be forced to move on.

Dave Musher, the idiot who called out my name, knows my ex-husband. Well, for all intents and purposes, my still-legal husband. Not many people knew what went down with us, so I'd put money down that good old Dave was doing Joshua Cooper a solid right about now and telling him exactly where he saw me and what I was doing.

When I pushed open the office door, Harry glanced up with a dismal look on his face. "I heard," he muttered. "Fucking hell, I'm losing my best dancer, because that asshole couldn't keep his trap shut." Harry shook his head. He knew why I was here, and what it would mean that I was called out publicly. "I'm guessing you're here to settle up and get gone as soon as possible?"

"Yeah," I heaved out the single world with a giant sigh of disappointment. It wasn't like working for Harry as a dancer was the best job I ever had, but I'd felt safe here. The guys knew my history, and they'd been looking out for me since I landed at Harry's place. I knew I would be damn lucky to find some place like this again, especially since I had to stay off the grid and work under the table.

Damn Joshua Cooper to hell for what he tried to do. Damn me for ever trusting him to begin with, and damn that whore who got in his head with her little plan.

"Are you sure we can't help with your situation, Charlie? I hate to see such a good girl on the run. You know other places like this aren't going to be like mine. There are plenty of places where you could get hurt, or-"

"I'll be fine, Harry. I appreciate the concern and thank you all for keeping me safe all these months. I know how to spot the good places. How do you think I found you?" I winked cheekily. At that, Harry grinned, stood, and came around his desk to give me a hug.

"Sure am gonna miss you around here. If things ever turn around for you, you're welcome back anytime. And not just as a dancer. I could use a good manager too so I can get a vacation one day."

"I promise, you'll be the first call I make if I ever get clear of their little plot, Harry." I started for the door before Harry called me back.

"Here, take this," he explained as he handed me a well-worn business card. "An old friend owns the place. It's not totally on the up and up, but you won't be forced to do any of the dirty deeds that go on there. It's strictly on a voluntary basis. If you find yourself near St. Louis, tell him I sent you." He smiled brightly then. "For fuck's sake, do not tell him why you're running though. The man can't keep his damn mouth shut to save his life, or yours. He wouldn't rat you out on purpose, but if Cooper's name came up in conversation for some reason, he'd start running off at the mouth like he had diarrhea."

With a laugh, I took the card, wished Harry well, and called a cab to get me to the closest bus depot.

2. LANDING ZONE

THREE MONTHS AND FIVE SHADY ESTABLISHMENTS LATER, I HAD
made my way northeast to the Dakotas. It was at the second
strip club along the way, the one in St. Louis that Harry told
me about, where a fellow dancer named Macy filled me in
about a little town near Sturgis that had some bikers who
were easy to work with. She thought they might also be
willing to offer me protection if I could get the gig.

When I asked why she no longer worked there if it was so
great she explained that they had a strict policy against
taking money for sex. She had gotten caught doing just that
and was turned out immediately. I hadn't been sure about
working for a biker gang, club, or whatever they called themselves, but the fact that they fired her for whoring changed
my mind.

That's how I found myself standing outside of a place
near Spearfish, South Dakota named Renegade Rosy's. I
wondered how the men came up with the oddball name for a
strip joint. I was grinning up at their rather inventive sign of

a woman pole dancing around an exaggeratedly large rifle when a male voice called out to me.

"You going in sweetheart?" The deep baritone reverberated from just over my shoulder. No flinching required on my part, I had seen him approaching in the reflection on the blacked-out window in front of me. A woman should always be aware of her surroundings, after all, especially one who was running for her life.

"Yeah, just pondering over the name of this place," I explained, cool as a cucumber.

He snickered a bit. "That so? Why would you wonder something like that? Some sort of vested interest in strip club names?"

I shrugged. "I was hoping for a job, actually." It also hadn't escaped my notice that he was wearing the kutte of the Aces High Motorcycle Club. They were the guys who supposedly owned the place.

"And what makes you think we're hiring?"

"I'm just here on a hope and a prayer," I answered honestly. He tilted his head and gave me a quizzical look before moving past me to snatch the door open.

"Well, come on in then, darlin'. Let's see what we can do for one another." In any of the sleazy joints I'd hopped through before landing here, I would say that was innuendo for what I'd have to do to get the job. This guy's body language didn't match his tone, though. I had a feeling I was being tested.

"Hopefully that means you need a dancer and I need a job, because pretty much anything else is out of the question," I warned him, figuring the up-front approach was my best bet. He turned, his laser-focus eyes taking me in from the front for the first time before a cheeky smile produced the sexiest dimples known to man on his lightly stubbled face.

"Alright then, let's head back to the office. I'll get Spinner on board with this impromptu interview."

I knew from Macy that Spinner was the guy who fired her, and he did it in a very gentle manner even though he was pissed about her extracurricular earnings. He even had a bus ticket out of town printed off for her before she made it to the office.

I followed the man I had met at the door, taking in his appearance as he walked ahead of me. He had long, dark hair that brushed his exceptionally broad shoulders. Shoulders that tapered down a muscular back to a tight, fine ass that his dark jeans were hugging in all the right ways. Just as I was taking note of that spectacular ass, he turned his head, looking back over his shoulder at me with a knowing smirk.

"See something you like, sweetheart?"

I shrugged nonchalantly. "You have a nice ass, it's not a crime to check it out, is it?" His grin ramped up to high beam status for a moment before disappearing as he began to give a spiel about the rules. "If you work here, the brothers are off limits to you. Just something to keep in mind."

"Okay," I agreed readily. I was not in any hurry to hook up with anyone anyway. Hell, even if my husband hadn't blown away our vows by cheating and trying to have me killed, I wouldn't be able to start something with anyone until I knew that horrible horror story in my life was over. Actually, I wasn't sure I would ever trust another man. Ever. Which made it a damn shame that I wasn't into women. The man's quirked up eyebrow showed he was surprised by my quick response as he opened a door down the hall we had traversed and stepped aside to allow me entrance.

There was a beautiful mahogany desk off to the right with what looked like the Lamborghini of desk chairs behind it. The damn thing had a control panel that made me wonder what kind of tricks it was capable of. I didn't get long to ponder the question though, because another man moved into the office space crowding the room. He was every bit as large and imposing as the first man who brought me here. Where the first man was smiling darkness personified, the other was broody-blond goodness. His looks reminded me of California surfer dudes trying to make it in the modeling world, only harder-edged instead of metrosexual.

"You're not from around here," the new man spoke as if he knew what he was talking about. I shook my head in the negative and started to speak. He held up his tanned, calloused hand to halt my words. "It wasn't a question, lady. I already know you're not from Spearfish, so what you're going to explain is why you're here, why you thought you could get a job with us, and what it is you want?"

His narrowed eyes let me know he was waiting for me to lie to him about something. I'm not sure who exactly they thought I was, but their suspicions almost made me back right out the door. Almost. Desperation kept me rooted in place though, because I was going to be running short on funds if I had to hightail my ass out of South Dakota to somewhere big enough that I could get lost.

"I trust my information will not go beyond the ears in this room." He looked taken aback for a moment but agreed.

His word wasn't the only one I'd be getting though. I turned to tall, dark, and panty wetting to get his agreement as well. He gave it, also barely masking his surprise at my insistence.

"Okay then, my name is Charlie Cooper. I met a girl in a club in St. Louis that used to work for you guys, and I liked what she had to say." They both appeared to be on edge as I told them. "I knew her as Macy, but she said she worked here as Sweetie-Pie." The blond bristled immediately at the mention of Macy's stage name.

"If you know Sweetie-Pie, then you know she was fired, and for good reason." I nodded. "And you'll also know we wouldn't consider her a good reference."

"Ah, but you see, *I* was the one who considered *her* a good reference when she told me why she was fired." The blond cocked his head, curiosity written in his baby blue eyes.

"Why did she say she was fired?"

"She was turning tricks on the side, and she said that was a definite no-no." I smiled and leaned forward, placing my hands flat on the surface of the desk. "Look, I just need to work for a place where I don't have to worry about some shady asshole trying to sell more of me than I'm willing to give, and all I'm willing to give is my dancing. My body belongs to me. If I decide someone is to touch it, it damn sure won't be because money was exchanged for the honor." Blondie's eyes flickered back to his darker counterpart who was standing too far behind me to see his reaction.

"Why are you in Spearfish?" The blond asked.

"I needed to get as far away as possible from my old life."

"What happened in your old life that required you to

run?" His eyes were narrowed suspiciously again. I started to answer, but he held his hand up again, while taking note of something that popped up on his computer screen. "Before you answer, you should know, we will run a background check on you before we hire you. So, let's not start bullshitting about things now."

I blew out a frustrated breath. "Well, I won't be working for you then. Sorry to waste your time today." I lifted my hands from the desk and turned to go.

"Do you want to try explaining why you can't have a background check run?"

My shoulders slumped in defeat when I realized they probably already had someone doing it the moment I said my name. "You already started it, didn't you?" I glanced back to see a look I couldn't figure out pass between the two men. "He'll find me now," I huffed as I pulled the door open to leave. I had only taken one step out when a large hand tucked in around my waist and pulled me back into the room.

"Get your hands off of me!" I'd like to say I sounded confident and empowered, but really, I just sounded like a screechy shrew caught off guard by the brute force.

"My apologies, but you need to have a seat and tell us why pulling your information was a mistake, because it's already been made, and we won't be held responsible for putting someone in unnecessary danger."

I sighed as the man released me and I flopped into the chair he'd placed me in front of. "Almost a year ago, my husband tried to have me killed so that he could collect on insurance policies he had taken out on me. It was done at the behest of his side piece. The man they hired to do the deed was an old Army buddy of my dad's, and instead of killing me, he hid me away. He never came back to get me after he went to tell my bastard husband that I was dead.

"About three months ago, I was working in Phoenix and someone I went to high school with happened to be at the club, and outted me by name in front of everyone. I've bounced between five different clubs since then. Club number two, in St. Louis, wasn't so bad, and that's where I met Macy. I figured South Dakota was pretty far, and I could be off the grid here, so I worked my way north in the hopes of keeping a low profile."

"How would a former NFL player know someone ran a check on you?"

"His cousin is in the FBI. I'm pretty sure he's already called in that favor since he had me listed as a missing person. He was hoping I was dead and would be found, but after his buddy saw me in Phoenix there's zero chance of him believing that anymore."

"Why didn't you go to the police initially?"

"Because I didn't want to out the man who saved my life. He was a friend of my dad's. They served together in the military way back when. Besides, I know Josh has friends in the Vegas PD. They don't exactly notice things when enough money is exchanged."

"Your father's friend was apparently an assassin." It was a statement, but it sounded a lot more like a question.

"So? He explained he never took jobs like the one to kill me. He only signed on to do it because he recognized my picture in the request."

"So, you refused to turn him in for murder for hire, then he hid you away, the man never came back after offering your husband some sort of proof that you were dead, and you ended up on the run?"

I nodded my head.

"Then some asshole you went to school with, who also knew your ex – sorry, your husband – saw you stripping, and called out your name in public so you ran again?" Blondie continued with the recap as I forced myself not to roll my eyes.

"Yeah, then I ended up here hoping I was far enough away to coast under the radar until I figured out what to do."

"You're listed as missing and endangered in the system," blondie explained. "I'm assuming he initially thought the hired killer took you out and was just trying to fleece him for more money to tell him where the body was. A person has to be missing for seven years before they can be declared dead."

"I think it's a shorter time period in Nevada, but still takes years," Mr. darkly sexy interrupted.

"Okay, so at any rate, assuming he was desperate for money, he wants proof you're dead rather than having you go missing for so long. He can't collect until a death certificate is issued."

"Most likely," I managed to choke out. "Look, I appreciate the recap of my shitty life, but honestly, I need to get on the road as soon as possible..." I started to say as I got up and backed toward the door again, keeping my eyes on both men in the room.

"Do you have any experience behind the bar?" Blondie asked.

I tipped my head up and down indicating that I did. "It's what I did when I moved to California in between dancing gigs."

"Perfect. We can't hire you here at Rosy's, because we can't have possible violent trouble rolling up here to find you. Since we ran the check here, they'll come looking."

"I understand," I stated calmly, even though I felt like my last bastion of safety was being ripped out from underneath me.

"But," blondie continued, ignoring my obviously rising stress levels. "We can have you tend bar at the clubhouse. We'll give you room and board plus $200 a week for expenses. You won't be expected to do anything beyond serving drinks and cleaning your station. If anyone tries to touch you, or gives you shit, you will let one of us know immediately. Understood?"

"Not really," I sputtered. "You're giving me a job, just not here?" I asked.

"Our club, Aces High M.C.," he pointed to the patch on his kutte, "has a clubhouse where all the members hang out. We have a bar, and it just so happens we are short a bartender. So, again, you can take that job and let us help figure this shit out for you, or you can be on your way to..." he left the words hanging, knowing full well my plan had been to find their club to begin with. I didn't have anywhere else to go.

"My plan, beyond this not working out, was just to keep moving," I sighed, exhaustion settling in my bones like an old friend at the thought of having to get back out on the road with dwindling funds.

"Look, I feel bad that we may have blown your cover after we promised we wouldn't repeat your name. Take the job. We'll try to help get your life back as our penance for fucking things up."

"Okay," I agreed. What else was I going to do? I could keep running and eventually end up on a news story about a body someone discovered somewhere while my husband played the grieving widower for the cameras.

"Okay," he tossed back. "By the way," he started to say as he stood and reached his hand out in my direction, "I'm Spinner." I shook his hand, and he tipped his head back to indicate the man still standing behind me. "That's Rage. He's going to show you to the clubhouse."

"All right." I moved closer to the door while side-eyeing Rage. "Your name doesn't seem to fit with the dimples," I stated, completely filterless. My lack of an internal thought to spoken-word filter was sometimes the bane of my existence. Spinner tipped his head back and bellowed out a laugh. "Don't laugh," I teased the blond biker. "I honestly would have pegged you for Rage, or at least Grumpy, before you told me your names." Rage's lips twisted up at the corners.

"Give it time, Darlin'. You'll see why you are all kinds of wrong on both counts," Rage informed me while the dimples in question remained on display for me.

3. CLUBHOUSE BLUES

RAGE GLANCED AROUND IN THE PARKING LOT AND THEN BACK toward me before something seemed to dawn on him. "You didn't come here in a car?"

"Nope. When B-um-the man dropped me off at the safe house he took the only car with him. He was planning to tell Josh the deed was done, but like I said he never came back. I'm not sure what happened to him at this point."

"I get that, sweetheart. We'll try to find him too if you want us to."

I shook my head. "I don't think he'd like that. He told me more than once he was a ghost who disappeared when needed and snuck up behind the enemy when they least expected it."

A flicker of recognition passed over Rage's face quickly and then was gone. "So, how did you manage to get here?"

"I bussed it to Spearfish and took a cab over here from there." He inclined his head a little bit and then glanced back at the most badass bike I'd ever seen. The base was black with chrome detailing, but the thing that captivated me was the custom paint job. Done in both bright and subtle greens there were what looked like souls being ushered from the front of the tank to the back and the same could be said for the rear fender where it ended with the souls being sucked into the mouth of what appeared to be a skeleton in a top hat with an Ace of Spades sticking out of it.

"Okay, well, the clubhouse isn't too far away. You think you can hang on to me for the ride, or should I wait and call for a pickup from a cage?"

I rolled my eyes at the man. "I have been on the back of a bike before. I'll be just fine with the ride over on two wheels, thanks."

Now, it was his turn to look shocked as he swung his long, muscular leg over the bike and got comfortable. "Well, hop on darlin' and we'll see what you remember. Lean with me when I do, and don't be afraid to hold on tight."

I was giddy with the anticipation of sitting on the damn bike, let alone getting to ride on it. I quickly threw my leg over, popped my feet where pegs, and slid in close to the man who smelled of leather and some woodsy cologne I couldn't quite place.

"I haven't ridden since my daddy was alive." The words tumbled from my mouth before I knew what was happening. Rage reached back and gave my thigh a little squeeze before he started her up and took off startling a yelp from me thanks to his quick departure. I felt Rage's shoulders and chest move with his laughter, rather than heard it.

We had already been on the outskirts of town at Renegade Rosy's, but we literally took off further out of town to get to the clubhouse. I'm not going to lie; I had a moment of worry that I had done the wrong thing by hopping on the back of this man's bike and taking off into the middle of nowhere with him. I just told them that people essentially thought I was dead and/or missing, and that my husband had millions riding on proof of my death. They could try to sell me to him, or... I stopped that train of thought right where it started. I didn't get that vibe from these guys. Then again, I married a man who later tried to have me murdered, so I wasn't entirely certain I could trust my own judgment anymore.

Instead of dwelling on the horrible possibilities, I chose to take in the surrounding area and appreciate the scenic views of the black hills off in the not too far distance. It was still late summer, and the leaves hadn't started turning yet, but I imagined in another month or two they would make this place look spectacular. As the thought occurred, I wondered if I would still be here in October. That was just under two months away. I must have tensed at the thought because Rage squeezed my thigh again, and then opened up the throttle and we took off flying down the road for a few minutes.

I suddenly remembered the feeling of freedom while gliding down the roads on the back of my dad's bike years ago. I wondered what he would think of the mess I got myself into. For that matter, I wonder if he would have warned me away from Josh or approved of him. He probably would have shot him. My dad had been an excellent judge of character.

I tuned back into the ride as our speed started decreasing. There still wasn't anything around that I could see until I noticed the little obscure roadway that seemed to lead even deeper into nowhere. Again, a quick flash of panic hit that maybe this man didn't have the best of intentions.

As if he could sense where my mind had gone, Rage squeezed his hand down on my thigh for the third time to reassure me that all was well. We travelled beyond a place in the road that was lined thickly with trees on either side and after about a mile we broke through to see a large compound in front of us. It had fencing surrounding it, and a gate to go through to get in. Inside the gate, I could see a massive parking area and just beyond that a giant building that looked like it may have once been a small hospital or something of the sort.

The large, mostly rectangular building appeared to be at least 20,000 square feet from the outside, but I couldn't accurately judge the depth. It was a two-story structure without including the possibility of subterranean levels, that much I was certain of.

"Holy fuck! Rage has a bitch on board!" Someone shouted as Rage pulled into the lot after one of his brothers let us through the gate. I stiffened, and Rage no doubt felt my fear through the movement. As he cut the engine, I noticed he was glaring at the guy who had yelled.

He pointed at the man and snarled, "If I needed you shouting my business I would have called ahead. Get the fuck inside and clean all the damn bathrooms."

"Oh shit," muttered the man, who I now noticed also wore the patch that said 'Prospect" on his leather vest. I took that moment to plant my hands on Rage's very sturdy shoulders for balance while I dismounted my shaky legs from his beautiful bike. As Rage also got off the incredible machine I just stood and stared.

"It's a work of art," I mumbled to myself.

"Thanks, Mikey did it for me," he explained looking a bit sheepish, and not seeming to realize I had zero clue who Mikey was. "Let's go get you introduced and set up with a room so we can stow your shit." He stopped short then, no doubt realizing for the first time that I didn't have any shit to stow. "Where are all your things, darlin?"

"Well, I only had the one bag, but it didn't make it when I had to transfer busses in Denver. I basically have my wallet at this point and the clothes on my back."

"Fuck me!" Rage snarled. "You could have mentioned that before we traveled the opposite direction of town."

"Yeah, I guess, except I was in a bit of shock about the fact that a couple jackasses just blew my anonymity all to shit."

He sighed and then snatched my hand out of thin air with his own. "Let's go." He tugged gently and I followed, because honestly, what the hell else was I going to do? We made it to the front entrance of the slate gray, mostly non-descript building and I watched as he punched in a code. Well, I tried to watch, but he hid it well as he worked the keypad.

"You guys expect trouble a lot? You sure do have shit locked down out here."

He snickered. "Haven't had trouble in years. Least, none until you showed up with trouble stamped all across that cute little ass of yours."

Well, shit.

Once inside, we were in what looked like a tiny square room where the only thing other than the door we just came through, and the opposite door before us, was a bank of cameras. Rage looked up so his eyes directly connected with one that was panning over us.

"I have a guest. Spinner should have called ahead about her." A buzzing sound lit up the room and the door in front of us opened with a slight groan before we moved beyond it.

The tiny room opened into a spacious place that looked like a young man's wet dream. There were couches along the walls, round tables and chairs scattered willy-nilly about the place, and several pool tables. A butt load of bikers and more scantily clad women than I'd seen on a good night at any of the strip clubs I'd worked in over the past year were also lounging around here and there. I was taking it all in while Rage continued to move us forward toward a bar area that took up an entire corner of the ridiculously open-space we were in.

"Rabbit," Rage called out and a man that looked very much like Spinner glanced over from behind the bar. "This here is Charlie. She's going to be working the bar with you for a while. She'll be staying here too, but she is not up for grabs. You feel me? You see anyone touch her, and you let me or Spin know immediately." Rabbit's eyes went wide, but he agreed with a tilt of his head.

"Good to meet ya," he said as he stuck his giant tanned hand out to greet me. "You any good at slinging drinks?"

"I used to sling them on the Sunset Strip, so I'd say I could probably handle this place." I glanced around, assessing what kind of liquor they had on the shelf. "I'm guessing everyone keeps it simple here anyway."

He laughed. "You got that right. Come on back here, and I'll show you the ropes a bit while Rage takes care of some business." Rage nodded approvingly while looking completely distracted. He still pulled tight on my hand, in an attempt to gain my attention, as I started to walk away.

"I'll be back in just a bit. I need to go let our Prez know what's up, firsthand. Then I'll make sure the girls get a room ready for you. We'll pop an off limit sign up on the door too so no one mistakes you for one of the BRATs."

"Okay, sure." I glanced from him to the man he called Rabbit then simply waited.

Rage turned from me as Rabbit lifted a hinged piece of the bar up for me to get through to the other side. "Listen up," Rage yelled out. "We have a little extra help at the bar. Name's Charlie, and she's off limits. Anyone touches her, gonna get touched by me... and not in a nice way, you feel?"

There was a raucous cry of catcalls, affirmations, and general teasing tossed about, but no one questioned what Rage said. I smiled and waved a hand in the air quickly before turning my attention back to Rabbit. Then I eyed him for a moment, taking in his name embroidered on the chest of his kutte.

"Two questions," I stated. "First, what is a BRAT, exactly; because I'm guessing it isn't being used in the way people describe unruly children? Second, how does one get a name like Rabbit?" I asked nonchalantly.

He chuckled good-naturedly. "The BRATs are the club whores that hang around. Bitches Relinquishing Ass and

Tits. Most clubs call them club whores, sweet butts, or party girls." He shrugged his shoulders. "We just got a little more inventive with naming them one day since the title tends to fit their attitudes too. They're all here willingly, and they get to stay on site, and are taken care of in exchange for being available for any brother on the premises."

At the incredulous look I didn't bother hiding, he reiterated, "They're here willingly, and free to go whenever they choose." He waited to see if I had a problem with that. I didn't. To each their own. So long as I was never mistaken for a BRAT, I would be just fine ignoring my personal issues about them. "How does a chick get a name like Charlie?" he hit back without missing a beat.

"Well, mine is short for Charlotte," I cringed as I offered the name I'd hated since kids kept calling me "spider" in grade school after the children's book about the spider and pig.

"Well, mine is short for likes-to-fuck-a-lot," he deadpanned until he watched my eyes widen in surprise and then we both doubled over laughing. It was just the icebreaker needed to relieve the tension that had built with being thrown into an entirely new world than I was used to. I wiped a tear from my eye when Rage walked back over to the bar, glanced between the two of us, shook his head and asked what was so damn funny. "Just getting to know one another, right Charlotte?"

"Sure thing, Likes-to-fuck-a-lot!" We both dissolved into incredibly immature giggles as Rage rapped his knuckles on the bar, shook his head once again, and tried to hide the grin that was attempting to spread on his face.

"Seems we put you in the right place after all," he said before walking away once more. Rabbit held his fist up and we bumped ours together before a throat clearing caught our attention. An older man had bellied up to the bar watching our interaction with interest.

"Shot of Jameson and a draft," he tossed out gruffly as he ignored me in favor of Rabbit. It didn't matter; I was already pulling the draft as Rabbit poured the shot. Teamwork at its finest. "About time we got some new ass in here." He locked eyes with me as I slid the draft his way. "You'll be riding my dick tonight, sugar."

"The fuck I will!" I snipped indignantly as I slid the beer towards the asshole. I took great pleasure in watching as it sloshed over the sides a bit.

He moved to grab hold of my wrist, but Rabbit caught hold of his hand before he could by slamming his down on top of the man's. "She is off limits. She's working behind the bar, but she ain't a BRAT for the taking. Rage brought her in." He shut the man's next question down with that simple statement. "You have a problem with things, you take it up with him. You fuck with Charlie here, in any capacity she's not comfortable with, and you deal with me too."

"What the fuck kind of shit is this?" The man groused loudly. "You takin' up for a bitch over a brother?"

"Word has been put out that she's off limits. That means you obey the word of your brothers, or you find yourself no longer able to be a brother," another older man stated simply as he walked up to the bar with Rage at his side. His eyes were glacial blue, just light enough to have a hint of color, but subtle enough to almost be mistaken as eerily white. He glanced in my direction and tipped his head in greeting.

"I'm Iceman, sweetheart. I'm the President of the Dakota's Chapter of Aces High. Rage has informed me of your situation, and he will be the one updating you on the progress. He's also the one you go to if you have a problem. Seems you can also lean on Rabbit when needed. That's good. I don't anticipate too many issues, but some of our older brothers folded in from another club a few years back, and they ran things a little differently there. We still have some growing pains to adjust to."

While Iceman was talking, I noticed Rage was busy glowering at Beaver, the guy who had just been giving me a hard time. Beaver noticed too, and slammed his shot back, picked up his beer and swaggered away as best he could with the beer belly he was sporting. Gross. I couldn't believe he thought I would ever entertain the idea of having sex with him, but then again, from what I was gathering a BRAT wouldn't have any qualms about it. I wasn't sure if they got paid in the traditional sense, or what, but I also wasn't certain I wanted to know the full mechanics behind that situation.

A shiver ran through me at the thought of being here and open to having sex with any of these men. Some of them, granted, were people I might have had a one-night stand, or more, with in a different life. But the others were a big old hell no.

When I peered back over to Rage he was smirking. "Feeling a little judgy sweetheart?" he asked snidely as if he'd been reading my mind.

"Nope, everybody has their own limits. I know what mine are, but I honestly could care less where other people's reside. I am curious though," I started.

"About what?" Iceman asked as he narrowed his eyes on me.

"If you have these girls here for sex, then why was Macy – er Sweetie Pie – canned for doing basically the same thing at Rosy's?"

Iceman laughed. "I'm gonna let you take that one on, Rage." He tapped Rage on the shoulder twice and then sauntered off while throwing a "Good luck with that," over his shoulder.

Rage sighed heavily. "The girls here provide a service in exchange for room, board, and protection. It's one they readily agree to. They also undergo testing and must comply with using a birth control method we can verify. We make sure the girls are kept safe that way as well as the brothers. The girls who work at Rosy's are hired to be dancers. Whoring there is illegal, and we run that business clean. We also can't guarantee the safety of the women, brothers, or club guests when it comes to STDs or pregnancy, because we aren't able to have the same sort of employment contract there considering it's a public establishment and must stay legally above board." Everything he stated was done so in an almost clinical manner. I was half amused and still very curious.

"So, do you ever pull from the dancers to bring in more BRATs?" I tossed my hands in the air at his quirked brow. "I'm not judging; it's an honest question. I grew up in Nevada for Christ's sake. Whore houses are legal near where

I used to live with my dad. A couple girls I went to high school with went to work for them as soon as they were legal, so I know how it works for them. It's not a stretch for me to be curious about the differences in a place like this." By now a few other brothers had saddled up to the bar and were waiting to be served as Rabbit had been entertaining himself with our conversation too.

"How about concerning yourself with YOUR job instead of how everyone else's works?" Rage glanced over to the members currently waiting on their drinks.

"Nah, it's okay. I'm highly entertained by listening to you describe our world to a newbie," one of them chuckled.

Rage ignored the comment as Rabbit started dropping beers on the bar in front of the guys. I assumed he knew their usual orders. Rage once again rapped his knuckles across the wood of the bar before he spoke. "You have a cell on you?"

I shook my head. "Nope. My savior assassin took my original phone and told me not to bother replacing it. Didn't really bother me, because honestly, I had no one I could contact who wouldn't go running back to Josh anyway."

He nodded his head as if he completely agreed. "I'll be right back," and with that he was off in the direction I'd seen Iceman headed when he'd departed the main area too. Sadly, me watching him go put a whole other bit of drama in my view. There was a woman bent over one of the pool tables, and she was taking it hard from one of the brothers right there in front of everyone. I was not a prude, but some things could not be unseen. Gross.

"So where are you from?" Rabbit asked me after all the guys were served. There were a few still seated within hearing range though. I looked at them and back at Rabbit a couple times before he caught on to why I wasn't saying anything. "Something you'll learn about us really quick, Charlie, is that every man wearing that patch is loyal. They've been made aware you're under our protection, and they won't go blabbing their mouths to anyone outside of our club."

I gave him a hesitant nod, but still answered him as quietly as possible. "A small town near Vegas, although, I was living in Vegas before I had to run." The guys seated at the bar seemed amused that I had spoken quietly enough that they couldn't hear me over the thrashing guitar sounds coming through the speaker system. It was one thing to talk about growing up in Nevada. It was another to be linked as the adult Charlie Cooper from Vegas that disappeared almost a year ago.

"Did you bartend in Vegas?" he asked, and respectfully, he kept his voice down too.

"No, I was one of the dancers in a few shows there. The last one I did was Dirty Dancing before I had to go."

"No fucking way! You were a showgirl?" he damn near shouted.

I groaned audibly. "Seriously, Rabbit?"

He cringed. "Sorry," he stated quickly. "But for real? You were a showgirl?"

"Yeah, I was, but in the way you're thinking, only briefly. I've trained to dance my whole life. I've been in a few music videos, a few plays, and a couple shows in Vegas." I shrugged. "It's not really a big deal. Judging from the others' reactions it really was though.

I just hoped like hell they really were able to keep their mouths shut. Not that the damage wasn't already done with the background check, but at least that would lead anyone looking for me to Renegade Rosy's. By the time they got that far it would appear as if I didn't get the job or protection from the club and had moved on.

My hackles raised a bit as I noticed one of the older gentlemen staring at me as if he knew me. I made eye contact and didn't back down until he started speaking. "Said your name was Charlie?" he looked thoughtful as I nodded my head. "Your dad Marcus Kinkaid by any chance?"

My jaw dropped. I stood there doing what had to be a spectacular impression of a deer in the headlights. Yeah, I grew up near Vegas, but I never had a poker face to speak of. "How?" Was all I could get out as I tried to process the fact that this man, in this far away place, had associated with me with my father in less time than it took a grown-ass biker to down a beer.

He smiled warmly at me, as if he knew how uncomfortable he had truly just made me. "Kinkaid and I served together. He was a good man." He tipped his beer up, almost lost in thought for a moment.

"The best," I added.

"I don't think you remember, because you were a little thing when your momma was lost, but Marcus was a member of Aces High MC when he was younger. We patched in together in Cedar Falls, West Virginia when we both left the Army." I couldn't be more stunned if someone just told me that my father was the real Santa Claus. The man nodded as if he understood.

"He went nomad, and mostly inactive after your mom's accident. Took off for his hometown in Nevada, and I only saw him a few times after that on runs. He never brought you around anymore though. Said he promised Luanne that he would keep you clear of the life, or something like that." The man laughed then. "Looks like maybe an angel sent you our way, girlie."

Cue the tears. I knew it probably wasn't smart to show weakness in front of a room full of burly tough-as-nails bikers, but this man sitting before me just insinuated that my dead father was the angel on my shoulder looking out for me. Considering it was my dad's friend who caught the murder contract, and his biker club that took me in, maybe the stranger in front of me wasn't far off from the truth.

"What the fuck did you do to her, Shameless?" Rage's deep baritone reverberated through the place causing goose bumps to stir across my skin. The man who was just talking about my father held his hands up in surrender.

"Charlie and I should probably head back to Iceman's office with you right about now. If you didn't feel obligated to help her out before, you will once you hear what I have to say."

"Yeah? Why's that?" Rage asked, clearly skeptical, his eyes darting almost comically back and forth between the older man and myself.

"She's one of our long-lost club princesses, son." Rage's head snapped around toward me then, anger flashing in the deep dark pools that now seemed to bleed black instead of the warmer brown I'd noticed earlier. "Calm down, she had no clue." Sensing a longer story, Rage tipped his head toward the office as a slack-jawed Rabbit lifted the partition in the bar for me to get by.

"You're just full of surprises tonight, Showgirl!" Rabbit called out.

"Stop it with the showgirl stuff," I demanded.

Rabbit grinned. "Nah, I think you just earned yourself a road name since you're a club princess and entitled to one and all."

"I have no clue what you're talking about," I stated stiffly and followed behind the two men leading the way to the club president's office.

4. HIDDEN TRUTHS

Iceman glanced up the minute we entered his office, frown firmly in place as he took in everyone's anxious demeanor. "I knew we were anticipating trouble, but this quick? Do we need to have a lesson in how to behave around the brothers prior to her working like I suggested?"

Now, I was pissed and narrowed my eyes at Iceman like he was the enemy I was about to pounce on. Rage's knowing smirk also caught my attention, and he quickly made his way up to the top of my shit list with his boss, president, or whatever the hell Iceman was to him. "I was doing just fine out there, thank you," I huffed.

The man Rage had called Shameless stepped forward then, drawing everyone's attention. "I wanted to bring it to your attention that I know Miss Charlotte Kinkaid, personally."

"You told us your name was Cooper." Iceman stared at me, waiting for an answer to his statement as if he had asked a question instead.

"I was born Charlotte Kinkaid, and then," I let out a dramatic gasp, "I got married and changed my last name."

He rolled his eyes at my dramatics; Shameless gave me a cheeky grin. "Not surprised she's sassy, her daddy was a smartass, for sure." That proclamation had ears all around the room perking up and taking note.

"Explain." Iceman commanded.

"I served with Marcus Kinkaid, and then we prospected together in Cedar Falls, were inducted together, and stuck by one another until he went nomad, and mostly inactive after his wife was killed."

"Kinkaid," Iceman tested the name on his tongue to see if it triggered a memory of the man.

"You probably know him as Brazen." Both Iceman and Rage snapped to attention then. I did too, but only because that name triggered a memory for me.

"I thought that was just the name he gave his bike..." I murmured out loud while fishing backwards in time through my memories.

Eyes flipped back toward me. "This is THE Charlie?" Iceman asked, and I was once again taken aback by his seeming familiarity with my name.

"That she is. I figured you needed to know before you ended up making any more decisions concerning her."

"Why in the hell didn't this information come up in our own systems when we ran a background?"

"Well, I'm assuming because she gave you her married name, and Marcus probably wasn't around to update it after her wedding."

"He passed on two years before I got married," I confirmed.

"Son of a bitch," Rage muttered.

"Well, sweetheart, here's the good news. We were going to do the bare minimum to keep you safe here while we investigated your claims and figured out if you were too much trouble or not." He waited for my reaction, but got none from me, because honestly, I hadn't even expected that much. I simply needed a job to earn cash to get somewhere else if it didn't work out here. He nodded his head at my lack of response and continued. "This information changes things though. You are family, and we take care of what's ours."

That's about the time my knees buckled and Shameless helped guide me to the couch that was up against the wall opposite Iceman's desk. "I'm sorry, I just... this is a lot to take in. You say you know my dad, and that I'm family, but before I married Josh, I didn't think I had anyone else in this world. Apparently, I didn't even know my dad as well as I thought. When Josh tried to have me killed, I thought I had the rug pulled from underneath me, but this..." I sighed. "This is like having my own history re-written before my eyes."

Iceman looked at Rage. "Put in a call to Ghost. He's probably going to want to come up here for this. He and Brazen were tight before what happened to Luanne." Then he switched his focus back to me. "I allowed you to keep your assassin's name private before, because I didn't think it would be important, but now I'm going to have to ask that you tell us."

"Jake Bishop is what he told me, and my dad had talked

about Bishop before, and had pictures too. It was definitely him, only older."

"Son of a..." Rage stopped as he was headed out with a cell phone to his head. "Yeah, it's Rage. I need you to get Ghost on the phone immediately." With that, he left the room and my focus turned back to the other two men that were still there with me. Iceman had a ghost of a smile on his face and Shameless looked as if he were wiping a tear away.

"I take it you know him too?"

"Bishop served with your dad and me. He came on with the club a couple years after we did since he signed up for another tour after us. We haven't heard from him in a couple years. You just gave us hope that he's still out there."

"But I just told your other guys that I thought he was dead. He took me to a safe house, left to go throw Josh off my scent, and never returned."

"You met Sweetie Pie in a strip joint in St. Louis, right?" Iceman asked.

"Yeah," I answered quickly wondering what she had to do with anything at this point. "I'm assuming if she worked there, it wasn't a very high-class establishment," he continued. I winced knowing what they must think of me.

"I did not do what the other girls did there. I ONLY danced," I emphasized.

"I have no doubt about that, but why do you think sleaze-ball strip joint owners would be willing to let you work under a different set of rules from their other dancers?"

"Because I'm an amazing dancer, and also Harry referred me there when I was first outed in Phoenix." I answered.

Both men laughed.

"Seriously? I'm fucking awesome! I trained most of my life..."

Iceman cut off my tirade. "I'm sure you're the best dancer ever sweetheart, and that means jack-all to club owners. You had an angel over your shoulder looking out for you. Seems Bishop has been one step ahead, as usual."

"He let me work at those places, knowing who I was?" The shrillness in my voice made it evident that I disapproved of the way the man had apparently been looking out for me.

"He kept you safe and undercover. He played it smart, and I'm assuming he had a long game he was playing in doing so. He didn't get to keep his last name as his road name for no reason. It fit, being as it's a chess piece and all."

"Bishop was a hell of a tactician in the Army, and he's used his skills for the club more than once," Shameless confirmed.

"Why did my dad take me away from the club if you guys are all so great and ready to protect me?"

Shameless huffed out a long breath and a sadness settled in like a weight on his shoulders. "Your mom, she was in an accident that resulted in her death. I don't know if he ever told you or not, but she was also about 6 months pregnant at the time." I felt sick to my stomach. I had never known I was going to be a sister. "She lived, for a while, and they tried to save the baby too, but she threw a clot, and the baby was just too early. Neither of them made it.

"Luanne swore the truck that hit her had a man wearing a patch belonging to an enemy club of ours at the time. She made your dad promise that if anything happened to her, he would get you away from the club. He kept that damn promise." Shameless' chagrinned visage took me by surprise. "I always thought she meant for him to keep you from The Tribe, the other club, but he took it to mean any of them for some reason."

I felt the warm wetness as tears tracked down my face. My head shook back and forth without my permission, trying to dispel the truths that were flying free from these men tonight. Everything I thought I knew about my family was adding up to a pack of lies and I didn't know how to feel about it. I loved my dad with all my heart, but right now I felt so betrayed by him.

He took memories from me. He took knowledge that I should have had. He took experiences, and an entire family of people from me all because my mom thought she saw something when she was in a car accident. I just couldn't wrap my head around it all.

"I, um..." I just stared down at my fingers as they clasped together harshly in my lap. "Um, could someone show me to my room? I just... I, um, I need a minute to process all this. I'd rather do that privately if it's all the same to you guys." I glanced up with pleading eyes focused on Iceman and he simply nodded his head.

"We'll get you taken care of, Charlie, I promise." I just nodded my head as he picked up his phone and called someone to meet him in his office. He glanced up at me. "You comfortable with Rabbit getting you settled?" I nodded my agreement again. "Figured a friendly face would help." Another two minutes and Rabbit was there, helping me to my feet, and then rubbing his hand up and down my lower back, all the way across the clubhouse, up a set of stairs, and down a long hall, two doors from the end.

"This is your room, Showgirl. If you need anything, you scream your fucking lungs out 'till I show up." He pointed next door. "I'm right in there, okay?"

I nodded again.

"You have an en-suite bathroom, so you don't have to share. It should be stocked with the basics, but you can let me know tomorrow if you need anything special."

"Thanks, Rabbit." He tapped the frame around the door and backed away so I could shut the door.

"Hey, Showgirl, make sure you engage that lock." He pointed to the slide lock at the top of the door. "Most of the guys here are good ones, but I can't vouch for someone who may get drunk and try to wander into what they thought was a vacant room, you know?"

"Sure, thanks again." I know my words came out sounding as flat, but I also knew that he stood on the other side of my door and waited until I did as he said. Once I turned the door lock and slid the top lock in place, I heard the heavy, booted steps that indicated Rabbit was walking away. Only then did I turn to really take in the room that had been given to me. I was probably too numb to fully appreciate the comfort that surrounded me after living in fleabag motels for the past few months.

Directly across from where I was standing was a set of large double windows that looked out over the back side of the compound. It had grown too dark for me to see much out there, so I focused on what was right in front of me. The windows were draped in heavy, dark blue curtains that seemed to have a thick lining on them. Most likely they were blackout curtains, which made sense for a group of men that no doubt kept the party fires burning long into the night.

Between where I stood at the door and the windows was what appeared to be a queen-sized bed with a deep blue comforter thrown over what looked like a freshly made bed. The wrought iron headboard rested just off the beige wall and to each side of the bed were gorgeous metal and wooden nightstands that looked like they fit the biker-trendy vibe perfectly. On the opposite wall from the bed were two doors separated by a wall that a long dresser and mirror sat in front of. The doors, I found as I walked over, opened to a smallish walk-in closet that had built in shoe racks, another set of racks and drawers at about waist high, and the typical bar across the top to hang clothes from. A comfy, overstuffed Navy-blue chair took up the space in the corner just to the left of the closet door.

I spun toward the last door and went to take a look at the bathroom beyond. To the left of the door there was a large, singular sink with plenty of counter space, a medicine cabinet with mirror facing me, and a toilet in the corner. Off to the right-hand side was a linen cabinet that housed navy blue and white towels, wash clothes, and hand towels as well as extra toilet paper and a smattering of hygiene items.

Next to the linen cabinet was the spacious shower that had a massaging showerhead plus a rain shower attachment coming down from the ceiling. Everything was spotless and not at all what I thought I would be walking into. This room was gorgeous. Walking back out into the bedroom, I noticed that underneath the windows was a long desk-like surface.

On one end there was a mini fridge where the other side held a cabinet with pullout drawers. In the middle was a desk chair so that someone could look out over the back yard while completing whatever business brought them to the desk in the first place.

Hell, I probably would have been in love with the room if it weren't for the fact that I was damn near numb at this point. What had just happened to my life? It was already in shambles, but now I felt like I couldn't trust anything I thought I once knew. Not about myself, my family, where I came from, or...

Ah, damn. The tears were streaming again. Apparently, I wasn't as numb as I thought. Seeing no point in taking a shower since I didn't own any other clothes now, I moved to the bed, turned the bedding down, and climbed in fully clothed. I did manage to kick my shoes off before the fluffiest pillows in the world managed to lull me into a sleep that was sorely needed.

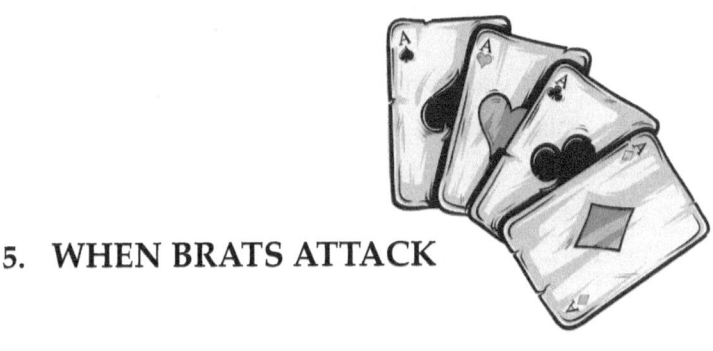

5. WHEN BRATS ATTACK

A LOUD BANGING ON MY DOOR WOKE ME FROM THE MOST PEACEFUL night of sleep I'd gotten since I'd been on the run. I'm not even sure what the hell made that possible considering everything I'd learned in the previous twelve hours.

"If this whore doesn't get her ass up, I'm not going to be responsible for what I do to her shit," a snide female voice called out to a tittering response from another female. I rose from the bed at that and walked over to my door.

After flinging it open, I was greeted by some barely clothed women. I raised an eyebrow in question. When neither spoke, and instead only gaped at me, I had enough. "You banged on my door loud enough to wake the fucking dead, so I'm assuming you had a good reason for that?" I knew I didn't start work until later this evening, because it was something Rabbit had gone over with me prior to the multiple revelations about my life last night.

"Who in the fuck do you think you are? You don't talk to us like that!" Skank one informed me. I ignored her original

39

question since it was obviously none of her business who I was. Sure, I might have been tasked to trust the brothers, but I grew up in Nevada where rule number one was to never trust a whore.

"You think you're too good to answer Jezzie?" The other woman questioned me.

"I don't know what the hell a Jezzie is unless you meant lezzie. In which case, no, I just thought it was a stupid question, and not worth my response, because you don't need to know who the hell I am."

"Listen up you fucking whore," she paused for affect, clearly thinking calling me what she was would bother me. It didn't. "We are the top ladies here." I scoffed at her use of the word ladies. She carried on, oblivious. "You follow my lead, you come when I say come. You back off when I tell you to, and you stay the fuck away from the men I tell you to. Understood?"

"I don't know who **YOU** think **YOU** are, but I don't bow down to anyone. I'm certainly not taking orders from a whore who doesn't know how to do makeup, over accessorizes, and wears hideous fucking shoes. I will definitely never take your cues on whom I can and can't talk to. So, yeah, that should make us all pretty fucking clear about where we stand."

The skank raised her hand to strike me. I was ready for it, having experience with plenty of her type in both the professional and exotic dance worlds. It turned out I didn't have to prepare for a fight though. Rabbit showed up and grabbed her wrist out of thin air, like magic.

"You so much as lay one fucking finger on this woman,

and I will have you both out on your asses and banished quicker than you can draw your next breath. We clear?"

Skank one startled with eyes going wide as she gasped at Rabbit's words. Skank two puffed up her over-inflated chest. "What the hell Rabbit? We were told to see to the new girl."

Rabbit narrowed his eyes on her. "Who told you to see to her, and what exactly did they say to you?"

"Rage caught us when he was on his way out this morning. He said to take the new bitch to go get some clothes, so she'd be ready to work later." She pulled a black credit card out of her cleavage to wave back and forth in his face.

Rabbit snatched the card from her. "This here," he pointed at me, "is family. She's not some club slut, hang around, or BRAT. You will treat her with the respect due an old lady or a princess. You ever raise a hand to her, and I'm gonna follow through with my promise." He glanced at my angry visage and added, the last touch. "That will be after I let her have her pound of flesh."

The skank duet glanced nervously back and forth between Rabbit and me before nodding and scampering off. The one who fancied herself the leader of the sluts turned after a few steps though. "We were supposed to go shopping though."

"Did Rage say anything about getting yourselves something?"

"Um...." I could see by the shift in her eyes she was thinking of lying. Lucky for her, she was just smart enough to see that the narrowing of Rabbit's eyes meant he wouldn't tolerate it. "No. He just said to get her stuff for work."

"Right. I'll handle that. You two go do your job. Clean out the main bathrooms this morning."

"That's a prospect's job," the other skank whined.

"Not today it isn't. We'll call this penance for the fact that you were going to spend Rage's money on yourselves without his consent, and the fact that you treated Charlie less than respectfully."

"We didn't know who she was."

Rabbit took several menacing steps toward them, closing the distance all-too quickly. "And If I ever hear you treating the new club girls like that, I will personally see to it that you both are escorted out in front of the fresh meat. No doubt, I just found the reason we can't keep a new girl beyond a week. You better believe I'll be talking to Iceman about this shit later. I suggest you make the bathrooms spic-and-fuck-ing-span clean out there while he decides if you're used up cunts are worth the amount of attitude you've been throwing around."

The girls moved quickly down the hall and out of sight as Rabbit turned back toward me. "Sorry about that. If I had known Rage was going to throw you to the wolves like that, I would have gotten up earlier to head them off." He glanced down at my bare feet. "Go grab your shoes, and we'll head out for a little shopping trip."

"Are you sure? I can probably call a cab and go on my own. I still have a little money on the side."

He moved closer. "First of all, we don't allow cabs up to the property. Secondly, you will save your money. This is on the club, because we should have been protecting you from the beginning, and because some of our guys fucked up yesterday when they didn't take precautions while running that check on you. Thirdly, and this one should go without saying, but I'm going to reiterate it anyway. It's not safe, Showgirl. I know you've been running on your own for a while now, but we just tipped whoever may have been watching off to your location. We have to assume someone is going to come looking, and when they do, we aren't giving them an easy target. You feel me?"

I nodded in agreement, because what else could I do? "Okay, let me go grab my shoes then." There was no use in arguing since he was right, and besides I figured Rabbit might be able to give me some insight while we went to the store together.

Once I got my socks and shoes back on and made my way out the door, I realized I couldn't lock up, because I didn't have a key. After a moment of staring at my door I sighed as I realized I had nothing that belonged to me in the room anyway. "I'll get you a key when we get back."

"Yeah, I just realized it was pointless now, because I don't have anything." My shoulders hunched in a bit as I spoke. Rabbit put his arm around my shoulder and pulled me in close. He kissed the side of my head and then whispered in my ear.

"It will get better, I promise." I smiled up at him as his longer-on-top wavy blond locks flopped into his eyes. His smile creased the sides of his mouth and formed the slightest wrinkles near his eyes letting me know it was genuine. Where his actual brother by blood, Spinner, had bright blue eyes Rabbit's were a startling mix of green and gold that could no doubt hypnotize a woman.

It was almost a damn shame I'd just sworn off men forever, because I imagined he was one of the good ones. At least I did until the door across the hall opened and a scruffy, messy-haired younger man stepped out sans shirt with pants unbuttoned to the point that it was pretty obvious where his happy trail lead.

"Damn, Rabbit, you didn't get your name for nothing, huh? Already tapping the new chick?" I stifled a giggle as Rabbit dropped his arm from my shoulder and bore down on the man across the hall.

"I'm not tapping that, and you will remember to treat her with respect. She's family." At those last two words the man straightened up, zipped his jeans, and looked sheepishly at me.

"Sorry, Charlie. I didn't mean to offend you."

"No worries," I stated nonchalantly. I completely understood everyone's misconceptions about the new woman who showed up the previous night seeming to cause some drama in her wake. Those that weren't around for Rage's initial "hands off" message, were probably still waiting to get word through the grapevine, or possibly playing ignorant to get more information about me. Again, I couldn't blame them for the latter. It's probably something I would do too.

We stopped by Iceman's office so that Rabbit could let him know about the skank twins, but he wasn't in. Rabbit texted the man instead, and then he grabbed the keys to a truck so that we would have somewhere to put whatever I bought. "You know, I don't need much. Whatever I get should fit in the saddle bags."

"You have literally nothing but the clothes on your back,

44

correct?" I nodded. "Okay, then we will be getting enough shit that it definitely won't fit in the saddle bags." When I looked like I was going to argue he hushed me. "We're family. You may not get the importance of that statement yet, but you will. You will also get that we owe you. We owed your dad. You will let us do this little bitty thing for you."

I didn't know whether to laugh, cry, or fall to my knees and thank this man. Not with a blowjob or anything. I definitely wasn't a club slut. You know, just a groveling, thankful gesture, because I hadn't seen a whole lot of kindness from people in a really long time.

"Thank you," I told him as he shut the truck door on me. When he climbed in the cab on the driver's side, he grinned wide as possible before speaking.

"Thank Rage. We have his credit card to use!" He laughed as I sputtered, about to decline that use. "Nah, he deserves your retail therapy being charged to his card for sending the BRATs to deal with you. I can't believe he'd trust them with his card, or with you." He glanced in my direction. "Don't know what he was thinking," he grumbled. "And hey, don't feel too bad for him. Those bitches would have completely abused the card. You could go spend happy at the shops today, and he'll still be getting off easy. The idiot!"

"Well, in that case..." I rubbed my hands together in a greedy little gesture.

Rabbit laughed a full-on head tilted back, full-bodied laugh. "That's the spirit!"

"You know I'm kidding, right?" I said, dashing his hopes. He just shook his head. "I'll get a few things I need," I started to tell him.

"You'll get a few things you need; plus a few things you want. We're coming up on the end of summer real soon too. So, you'll need clothes for cooler weather, probably some boots, a jacket, and..." he cut himself off when he saw the look of horror on my face. "Not a shopper?" he asked.

"No, not really. This is going to take all day," I grumbled.

Again, Rabbit laughed at my expense. "Damn, you really are the perfect woman, aren't you?" he shook his head as if to clear it. "Okay, well, don't worry. I'll be your personal shopper. I've already got a list of shit going through my head, so we'll just make this as painless as possible. You supply sizes, I'll pick shit out, and you tell me if it's your style or not. If it is, we buy it. If not, we scrap it. No big deal."

"If you say so," I told him and then proceeded to watch the scenery pass us by outside the window.

THE SHOPPING tally ended up being something like this:

A pair of leather biker boots, a pair of classic black heels, a new pair of tennis shoes, and some hiking boots. I cringed just at the thought of how much that cost on its own. Rabbit assured me it was fine.

Then we went to another store where I was embarrassed on a whole new level as he held up all sorts of undergarments asking, rather loudly I might add, if this was my style or if that was my style. When I wouldn't acknowledge him, he held up the biggest pair of granny panties he could find, and yelled, "So, then these must be your style since you're nixing all the sexy shit. It's okay to admit you love granny panties, Charlie!" All the women in the store loved Rabbit and snickered behind their hands at my expense. Some of the women openly laughed, rather loudly, much to my chagrin.

Finally, I relented and purchased several panty and bra sets, again the final total of which I could not stick around to see. I let Rabbit handle the transaction while I wandered away and sniffed the various fragrances on display. When we left there, he took me to a clothing store, purchased me an entire new wardrobe, just as he had threatened. We also went for a trip through the local department store to pick up the hygiene products I normally used, a regular toothbrush, instead of the travel one I was currently using, and a set of earplugs which thoroughly confused me until Rabbit explained the walls could get thin in the clubhouse when the bitches were auditioning to be porn stars. Ugh.

The day continued in much the same fashion, until we entered a leather shop, and Rabbit had me fitted for a new riding jacket and some riding leathers. I wasn't about to turn them down if I was going to find myself on the back of a bike in the coming days, weeks, or months.

When we finally finished up, I was dragging ass, and ready for some food and a nap. I hadn't realized it until then, at damn near three in the afternoon, but I hadn't eaten at all, or most of the previous day for that matter. Just as I was about to inform Rabbit of that fact, my stomach grumbled out an ungodly noise that startled us both.

He frowned over at me as I watched the lightbulb go off in his head. "Shit! Damn it, why didn't you say anything before we left? I forgot you probably hadn't eaten yet. Okay, we're going to grab some pizza and head back. I promise we'll feed you better after this." I think he mumbled something about being a dumb ass under his breath.

"It's not a big deal. I could have spoken up sooner. Honestly, this morning I just wanted to get away from the Skank Twins, then we were too busy, and it didn't even occur to me that I was hungry until about a minute before my stomach went on a rampage."

"No need to make me feel better," Rabbit tossed out indignantly.

"Trust me when I say, I'm not the placating type. I'm also a big girl capable of speaking up for myself. If there's blame to place, it's my own for not telling you I needed to eat sooner."

"Fine, but can we keep the 'me starving you' incident on the down low, because I won't feel as justified for calling Rage out on his prickish behavior if my own hasn't been saintly as hell." He batted his thick, dark eyelashes at me while adding an angelic grin to the mix. Dear lord, the man was sexiness personified even when he was being goofy. I could think of more than a few girls I'd worked with over the years who would love to get their hands on him.

"Saintly as hell seems like an oxymoron," I mentioned.

"I can't ruin my rakish reputation completely," he offered with a wink. "Saint in the streets, devil in..." My laughter must have been infectious because he couldn't even finish that statement without busting out into man-giggles.

We were high on pizza and caffeinated drinks after the low from shopping on empty stomachs when we walked into the compound and through the secure tiny front room. I had been telling Rabbit about a misadventure I'd had with an older showgirl who was lubing up her thighs so they wouldn't chafe. She swore it was an old trick, but I think someone pulled her leg into believing it would work. Unfortunately for her she didn't wipe all of it off her hands well enough so when we pulled a maneuver that had our hands on the floor before we pushed up and used the momentum to take us into the next move, this woman's hands slid, and she plummeted face first into the stage.

"No fucking way," Rabbit threw his head back to laugh as the door opened allowing us entrance into the main part of the building.

"Yeah," I laughed right along with him as the memory of seeing it happen in person hit me. "But that wasn't the end of it. Remember she'd lubed up her thighs too, so she tries to get up, and the girl who attempted to help steady her legs pulls her hands back, horrified that there's some weird substance on them, just as Gerry slipped again. Her shoes were gliding on what was left behind on the floor from her hands. Another face plant and Becca was shrieking in the background about her hands being covered in nasty old-dancer-hag vag-juice." Rabbit and I had both dissolved into laughter at that point and were completely unaware for a moment that everyone had stopped what they were doing and were staring at us.

"Vag-juice?" Rabbit huffed the words out like it was a question, which served to egg on our laughter. "Oh shit! I really need to hang out with you in Vegas someday."

"What the fuck is going on?" A loud voice called out over our hysterics. It was only then that we both sobered up enough from our mutual belly laughs to realize we had literally every person in the clubhouse's attention. My eyes widened in surprise, and I suddenly became very nervous about the purchases that were made earlier, thinking that's why Rage just bellowed his question at us.

"Um," I started.

"What's with the attitude, bro?" Rabbit asked, his face turned into a veritable mask of indifference.

"What's with the attitude? Why the fuck are you with her?" Rage stabbed his finger into the air in my general direction leaving me a nameless "her" as he chastised Rabbit. I saw the moment Rabbit's mask slipped a bit and his own fury became evident. I also noticed, out of the corner of my eye, that the Skank twins were enjoying the show immensely. Maybe they fuck Rage on the regular and that's why he sent them to me this morning and trusted them with his card. I really didn't know shit about any of these people or the dynamics involved between them all.

"Why the fuck am I with her? Well, let's see," Rabbit tapped his chin with his finger for effect. "I was woken up by bitch one and bitch two over there trying to bang down Charlie's door like they were the DEA raiding the joint. Then they started throwing attitude her way, telling her that they would pick her 'working clothes' and would inform her which men she was allowed to touch and which she wasn't. That was all before that one," he pointed to skank two – the girl now known as Jezzie, "tried to slap her when she attempted to set them straight about NOT being a goddamn BRAT. Oh, and just for you to file away for later, they were also making big plans for their own personal spending on your account since you were dumb enough to trust them with your card in the first place."

If eyeballs could spit fire, that was what Rage's were doing as he turned smoothly to face the direction of the now cowering dipshit duo. "You did what now?"

Rabbit ignored the question being asked of the girls. "I believe they said you told them, and I quote, 'take the new bitch to get some clothes so she'll be ready to work tonight.'"

I couldn't help the snarl that ripped free, and I lost the little bit of guilt I had about the shopping spree I'd just been on with Rage's card. His attention had solely been focused on Rabbit again as my new best friend laid everything out for him, but the minute he heard the unhappy noise I made, his eyeballs were back to spitting fire. It was a fire he quickly turned the on the two girls who royally fucked up today.

"That is most definitely not what I said," he growled between clenched teeth. "You dared to try to lay a finger on family today? You disrespected family? Treated family like a common whore? And let's not forget tried to tell a new girl who she could and couldn't sleep with?" Rage looked over his shoulder at Iceman who had stepped in when the commotion began. "I think we know what the problem was with all the new girls that have been run out of here so easily."

"Rabbit brought it to my attention earlier. I was waiting for him to get back to get details and address it with the brothers. We need a majority." Iceman stated the last as if it pained him to say it. "I'll call for that in a moment though. Let's address the situation with Charlie first so there are no more miscommunications. Get everyone the fuck in here right now. If someone is off site, get them on speakerphone. I need everyone to hear this, and I'll send out a head's up to all the other chapter presidents later too."

Everything grew quiet, with just a few whispered conversations making a hazy cloud of noise in the room while others trickled in from various hallways and rooms that dumped out into this main space. Finally, Iceman seemed satisfied with the turnout and climbed onto the table nearest him so he could be seen and heard above everyone else in the room.

"Listen up," he looked around the room, scanning to make sure he had everyone's attention. "This young lady here," he pointed to me and crooked his finger for me to come stand with him. I did as he asked, of course.

"This is Charlie. She is NOT, I repeat NOT a fuckin' BRAT. This lady is FAMILY!" Wide eyes all around the room greeted me. A prideful smile came from Shameless as he looked on with arms crossed over his broad chest. He nodded an acknowledgment when he noticed I was watching him. "Charlie here is the daughter of our late brother, Brazen."

"Holy fuck!"

"No kidding?"

"Well, fuck me sideways!" Those were just a few of the round of astonished statements that greeted that announcement.

"Charlie is gonna stay with us for a good while, maybe permanent if she likes it here, and she'll be working the bar here at the clubhouse for now. She is to be treated with all the respect you would show an old lady or a club princess. If I hear otherwise, you will answer to me directly."

"And me," Rage added loudly.

"Add me to that ass kicking detail," Rabbit called out.

"You'll also deal with me since I'm officially her Godfather." Shameless added, gifting me with a little more information than I had before about my past. I smiled at him and tossed a look that promised he needed to tell me more later. Again, he nodded at me.

Iceman tipped his head once in acknowledgment of the responses, then beamed at me with pride in his eyes. "You okay with everything, sweetheart?" he asked me quietly.

"Yes," I stated quickly.

"Good. Here, let me help you down now." And he did just that as he took my hand and held me steady until my foot hit the floor. Before the other could join it, my hand was transferred to Rage, who held me until I was steady. Then he pulled me closer to him by way of his warm hand sending zinging electrical pulses up and down my skin where my shirt had parted ways with my pants and left bare the skin near my right hip. His thumb busily trailed over the expanse of skin as Iceman continued with his spiel.

"Now, these two," he called out as he motioned for someone to be brought forward. Rabbit sauntered up with each of the skanks at his side. "What do you two have to say for yourselves?"

They both started talking at once so Iceman shut them down. He pointed at the one called Jezzie and told her to start. "I didn't want to be mean to her, but Tallie keeps telling me it's our job to haze the new girls to make sure they're tough enough to hang with you guys." She held up her hand indicating the bikers that filled the room. In all honesty, I could understand the logic behind that. "I really didn't know that the girl was family. We thought from the dismissive attitude Rage had this morning that she was just another BRAT in training."

"It isn't your job to 'think' you know what's on a brother's mind. If you are unclear about directions given, you ask. Am I understood?"

"Yes, Iceman, I understand," Jezzie offered with her lips poked out in a pout while her stick-straight blond hair moved as a silky screen around her shoulders.

"And what do you have to say?"

"It's true," the other woman stated with a cold indifference. "I was hazed by Carla when I started, and I thought I had to carry on that tradition. I wasn't aware," she tossed what she thought was a hidden glare my way. "That **SHE** was anything but a trainee."

"That's interesting," a man closer to the bar spoke up, and then moved forward so that everyone could see him. "Because we heard the announcement Rage made last night. You even made a comment about how it was weird that Rage had a bitch from the outside in here." He smirked as the girl visibly shrank back from his words. "It was right before half the damn club watched me bend you over the pool table, Tallie. So, yeah, you knew she wasn't a club slut or meant to be a BRAT here. Not only did you know, but you just lied straight to our President's face."

"No, really, I wasn't paying attention last night. I thought..."

"Can it," Iceman called out on a raised voice. "Here's what we're going to do. Jezzie, I know you were out with Rico last night, so you didn't hear the announcement. I'm going to give you the benefit of the doubt that you didn't know. You will still be on probation with us for the next month. Step out of line even once and you are done."

Then Iceman turned to Tallie. "I was going to leave your fate up to a vote of the brotherhood, but considering you just lied to my face, I can't keep you around. You are no longer loyal to this club. Not only have you driven away prospective club girls, but you also disrespected our family, our principles, and me personally. You are hereby banished. You will wait outside by the gate while a prospect packs your room out. Once he's done, he will take you to the bus stop and drop you off. If you choose to stay in town, you are to have zero interaction with any of the brotherhood, their families, or affiliates. Any of the Aces High Club members caught having interactions with this woman from here on out will face discipline, and possible expulsion from this club. If anyone present thinks this is unfair punishment, speak now, or my ruling stands."

"Please, no. There's nothing out there for me," Tallie begged. Iceman crossed his arms over his chest and scowled down at her while he gave it a moment for someone to speak. Tallie looked around wide-eyed and desperate before the realization dawned on her that no one was going to speak up for her.

She turned on her heels quickly, finding me in the crowd standing between Rage and Rabbit. "You did this! I will make sure you get what's coming..." and Shameless had her tipped over his shoulder and was carting her toward the security door at the front of the room faster than I could blink.

"You say one more fucking word that sounds like a threat toward my Goddaughter, and I will make sure you never see another sunset again." I heard him say to her as he punched a button near the door that made it swing open for him. He also turned and called over his shoulder, "Mech, get her code removed from the doors."

Some red-haired guy with an amazing beard and a tablet in his hands glanced up from typing something into the device and offered, "Already taken care of, Shame." With that Shameless was out the door with Tallie, and I was apparently back to being a curiosity.

"We need to get some of you out recruiting to make up for the deficiency in entertainment around here. Check with the girls over at Rosy's and see if any want to swap houses," Iceman called out. "You're all dismissed for the night. Get back to what you were getting to before this impromptu meeting." Then he hopped off the table and made his way over to us. "Rabbit, that all her stuff from today?" He pointed to the two bags each that we were still clinging to.

"Nope. She definitely has a bit more out in the truck," he offered with a knowing grin in my direction.

"Okay, have a prospect go unload for her and take the stuff to her room."

"Oh, you don't have to do that. I can get my own..." I started to say but was promptly cut off when Rage pulled me tight to his side again.

"Shh," he corrected me. "It's the prospects' job to do things like that for us. Let them prove their worth. Besides, I'm pretty sure you need to get ready for work. You start in an hour, yeah?"

I glanced over at a clock on the wall. "Damn, I didn't realize it was so late." I turned toward Rabbit. "I totally blame you. You should have been a girl as much as you like shopping." The room grew quiet, and I realized I'd just inadvertently insulted Rabbit in front of a room full of his badass brothers. Shit. He didn't sweat it though, thankfully.

"Come on now, Showgirl, we were shopping for underthings, and whatnot. Aside from your granny panty fetish, I gotta say that store was the tits!"

Laughter boomed through the room. "Oh, for the love of…"

"Granny panties!" He finished my statement for me – though not with the words I was going to use – while grinning widely. "I know. Would you get over the bloomers already, babe?" he spit out his retort amidst his own hail of laughter.

"Damn you, Rabbit. Karma is a bitch!"

"Damn straight, I fucked her once. Was it my fault I picked up her sister the next week? Nah, but Karma still slashed my fucking tires." One of the younger guys called out, and suddenly everyone was laughing at him and his bad luck with a stripper named Karma and her sister. It did not escape my notice that Rage had let go of me during my banter with Rabbit and moved his ass over to the bar without so much as a backwards glance.

6. GUT PUNCH

Since the shopping trip, pizza stop, and impromptu meeting left me little time to get ready, I chose to toss my damn near waist-length, strawberry blond hair up in a messy bun on top of my head. Despite the shopping extravaganza we'd had today, I opted to pair my new boots and body-hugging jeans with an Aces High MC support shirt that someone left in my room while I was gone. I realized it was a tank top once I unfolded it. It was black with the red and white logo. The same skull and top hat that graced the tail end of Rage's bike was also present on the shirt. Instead of sucking souls the logo had a skull smoking a joint, or something.

Despite me trying to tell myself that I didn't have a need to impress anyone, since I was still obviously married to a murderous cheating bastard, I found myself applying a little eyeliner and mascara that made my hazel eyes pop brighter than before. For some reason the eyeliner that I always carried in my little purse brought out the green hues in more abundance than the warm cinnamon brown that usually dominated the odd kaleidoscope mix I had going on.

Still, I knew what I was doing. I was making myself pretty for Rage. Hell, I didn't even know his real name. I still didn't understand his crazy hot-cold reactions to me either, but there was no denying that feeling that zinged through me with his every touch. I would have to be blind, or a fool, to deny the attraction too. His protective streak was something I enjoyed immensely. My soon-to-be, I hoped, ex-husband had never felt protective of me a day in our relationship. The man tried to have me killed for money rather than just divorcing me, to say I hadn't felt protected by him was an understatement. I guess protectiveness would have to be an important attribute for any guy that found his way into my future as a result of my past.

I glanced down at my boots one more time as a knock sounded on my door. I knew better than to break boots in when I had to stand on my feet for hours, but I honestly wasn't sure when else I'd get the chance. Today, I'd been allowed out in town with just Rabbit along, but somehow, I figured that would change now that a little time had passed, and it was possible that Josh knew where I was. Another knock brought me back out of that scary scenario and I crossed my room in a few strides to open the door. Rabbit stood there grinning like a loon.

"Well, Showgirl, aren't you a sight?" he cooed before stepping back out of the way and dangling something on a silver chain. I reached out and clasped it in my hand, but Rabbit pulled it back and ended up looping the chain over my head. At the end was a silver key. "To your door. This way, you don't lose it."

"Thanks, Rabbit. How did you know I was prone to losing things?"

"Well, considering you came here with literally nothing, I figured it wasn't a bad guess."

I sighed. "Extenuating circumstances forced that, but yeah, I was notorious for misplacing my phone and keys before everything." I stared at the worn carpeting in the hallway. "At least I was in my old life. I became very vigilant about that stuff when I was hiding out in shit-bag motels for a while."

"Jesus, I wish you had known to come straight to us. I wonder why Bishop never told you about us?"

I shrugged. "Maybe he was trying to honor my dad's wishes? I don't know. I wish he would have though. It would have certainly saved a little bit of my dignity, and a lot of my sanity." Rabbit gave me a quick side hug, and then pushed me along in front of him.

"Let's get to work and take your mind off all your shit by listening in to these idiots' gossip like the true hens they are. I swear, they're worse than my grandma and her Bridge Club." I laughed at Rabbit, because I couldn't imagine him with a gossipy, bridge-playing granny in his life.

When we got to the bar there were already more than a few bodies waiting to be served and the prospect tasked with doling out drinks looked harried with the job.

"Hey there," I called out to him as I ducked under the bar and swung into position, immediately pulling a draft for someone who had shoved their mug forward for a refill.

"Hey," the prospect gruffed back.

"You have a name?" I asked.

"His name is Prospect," a deep voice, that sent a shock of gooseflesh rippling across my arms and up my neck, answered. I glanced up and gave Rage a sweet smile that made him cock his head to the side, looking a little mystified.

"You have numerous prospects though. How do you tell them apart when you're yelling at them if you only call them all prospect?" I thought it was a logical question, but apparently not judging by the many grunted responses I received.

"Well, when I yell Prospect, they all come running, unless they're tasked with a job they've been told not to leave except in dire situations. The first one to me gets the new job, and the jobs get shittier as the day wanes. So, you want to be the one to respond. If I called out their names to assign jobs, I might show favoritism. Plus, we get to see who is the most motivated to get the job done this way."

"Okay, I get it." I pulled three more drafts as he had been explaining how things worked to me.

"Get me a double shot of Jack and a YingLing, girl." A scrubby looking dude called out. I could see the motor oil staining his hands still, and the creases in his brow that showed he'd had a rough day.

"Sure thing," I called back as I started pouring.

"She has a name," Rage admonished.

"Well, that's all well and good, but I don't know it," the guy shot back.

"No worries," I said in an attempt to diffuse the very unnecessary tension. "I'm Charlie." I pushed his drink order to him as I said my name and the asshole responded with, "Thanks, girl."

"You little shit," Rage growled while heading toward the man.

"What's shakin', Showgirl?" Rabbit asked as he sauntered over having noticed a potential problem. I just pointed at the guy who was obviously a mechanic. "This guy wants to call me 'girl'. That one doesn't like it," I added pointing to Rage. "I don't know what the etiquette for that type of thing it is around here, but it doesn't bother me. I've been called far worse, and little better, while bartending in LA. So, it's no big deal to me." I moved on after making myself clear, and received appreciative glances from some of the older crew that were bellied up to the bar. Apparently, they liked my reaction. So, noted.

"All right, Rage, you heard the lady. You can stand down now," Rabbit told his buddy. Then he hopped up on the bar, leaned over and swatted the mechanic in the back of the head. "And Junior, you need to learn some respect!"

"What the fuck, man? Not like I called her a slut or a bitch or something. I just called her girl."

"Yeah, after she told you her name, numb-nuts."

"Fucking hell," I cursed. It didn't stop me from pulling drafts and pouring shots. I was blind to anything more going on, until the BRATs arrived for the night.

It was during that time when Rabbit explained the difference between a BRAT and a club slut. The BRATs were basically given room and board while some had their education paid for, and others just procured a check for services rendered. They were not to say no to the club brothers, with a few acceptable safety measures thrown in for their sakes. They had to maintain health checks and birth control too.

The club sluts were hangers-on brought in by club members or friends of the club who were down to fuck anyone, at any time, in the hopes of either landing an old lady spot, or the job of a BRAT. According to Rabbit, they all seemed to think that the road from BRAT to old lady would be an easily accomplished thing, although it rarely happened that way. In the infinitely wise words of Rabbit, "Who wants to claim a woman that all of his brothers have fucked?"

After that little lesson in how the hierarchy of club women worked, I got too busy to even process what I'd been told. Thankfully, for a while, I was also too busy to notice some of the activities going on, because more than a few of the sluts and BRATs had lost their clothing somewhere along the way.

I was inundated for about a good steady hour before drink requests slowed a bit. It was then that I looked up and noticed Rage was standing in the corner with a very familiar blond head in his hands as his mouth attacked her neck. Jezzie. My heart sank at the sight, and I didn't even understand why, but that didn't stop the feeling from making itself known. I also didn't miss the look of complete triumph on Jezzie's face when she saw me watching. I guess a message was being sent after all. I received it loud and fucking clear.

"Charlie," Rabbit called to me rather brashly from his position on my right. I wasn't sure how long he'd been standing there staring, but it sounded weird to hear him call me by my real name rather than the ridiculous Showgirl nickname he'd given me.

"Huh?" I answered before tacking on the rest so it wouldn't look like I was completely heartsick for no good damn reason. "And not that I'm complaining, but why are you suddenly calling me by my actual name?"

"Showgirl," he smirked as he drew the nickname out slowly. "I've been trying to ask if you're ready for a break for the past five minutes, but you were too busy sightseeing to tune into your best buddy behind the bar."

"Sorry, I was lost in thought." I betrayed the exact thought by glancing in Rage's direction once more before putting myself in check. Rabbit's eyes followed mine, and he mumbled out a string of cuss words before he pulled himself back together.

"Damn, that dumbass," he muttered before turning to me. "Go take a break, sweetheart. Bathroom for us is right through there," he tipped his head to indicate the door in the back of the bar area where I'd noticed the prospects barbacking from. "You can catch some food from the kitchen back there too, if you're hungry."

"Thanks," I told him as I turned on my heel and took off like a bat out of hell. Fuck my life. The only guy I have felt an attraction to, and if I'm being honest with myself, more of a connection with than I ever had with my own husband, and he was with one of the two girls who treated me like absolute shit this morning. Just great. Apparently, I was right about the pep talk I had given myself just the other day. I did have the worst damn ability to judge a person's character in the history of ever. I would have to remind myself of that whenever my hormones tried to run rampant again. Full-body shivers, meaningful glances, and impromptu touches from a sexy man didn't mean anything more than the bastard was probably horny and down to fuck. None of it could be trusted.

7. SILENCE IS GOLDEN

GROGGY DIDN'T BEGIN TO EXPLAIN HOW I FELT AFTER WAKING UP AT noon when the festivities last night didn't settle until closer to four in the morning. It also didn't help that it took far too long to get to sleep, because I was unfortunately very aware of the make-out session Rage was having with Jezzie most of the night, and then I took note when they both disappeared upstairs and down the same hallway where my room was. Oh, that I wished the hallway up there wasn't open to the floor below up to a point, but it was. Unfortunately, I saw far too much of what went on between them before they managed to disappear into a room together.

After showering, reading a book I found in a drawer, and tossing and turning a bit, the last time I looked at the clock before now was around 9:30 a.m. I had to assume I had been asleep since shortly after that, so that made for maybe two and a half hours of sleep. Beautiful. I needed coffee. I jumped up, tossed on some shorts and a tank top along with some fanged bunny slippers that Rabbit had insisted I "must have" during our shopping spree, and opened my door to head out in search of some food.

Unfortunately for me, I happen to possess the absolute worst timing on the face of the earth. I'd just cracked my door when Rage and Jezzie came spilling out of the room across the hall and down one from my own. Jez was leaning all over Rage, and he was pushing her away a bit. Neither noticed me yet as my door was only cracked. "Stop, Jez. I'm really not in the mood for your shit this morning."

"You were in the mood for plenty last night though. I was afraid you wouldn't want to talk to me again, but you did so much more than that." Her lip pouted as she grabbed hold of where his cock must have been in his still unbuttoned jeans. "I just want to thank you for your loyalty to me," she cooed.

"Thank me for my…" he seemed baffled by her statemennt. "What the fuck ever, Jez. You need to get out of here. I don't do this clingy bullshit, and you know it."

"Fine, but you know where to find me when you've had a chance to wake up and stop being Mr. Grumpy Pants again." Grumpy was said in a baby voice that came out more like Gwumpy. I cringed. Eww, the creep factor was real. Jez bounced off and I was about to close my door to give Rage a minute to get gone too before I went for food, but a clapping sound from further down the hall where I couldn't see pulled me up short.

"What's that about?" Rage balked.

"Well, you fucking idiot, it's about the show you put on last night. I don't know what you're doing, or why you suddenly decided to push my new bestie away, but she deserved far fucking more than to see the bullshit stunt you pulled."

Was he talking about Jez, me, or someone else altogether? Damn it, Rabbit, spell it out for the eavesdroppers in the place.

"Really don't know what you're on about, Rabbit. If you could get to the point, I am in desperate need of some fuckin' caffeine this morning."

"Okay, sure. I'll spell it out for you. Her husband cheated on her and tried to have her killed. I'm sure that leaves a person with serious fuckin' trust issues. But then, she finds out in the past forty-eight hours that her life, her family's life, has been some big lie in a way, and damn if that probably hasn't damaged the woman's trust even further. Not to mention the fuckers she's had to deal with on the road to get here while bouncing between strip clubs to survive, and what she most likely had to fend off all on her own as a result. Then she has the vibes you've been throwing at her that are fucking hot and cold at the drop of a dime. I imagine that's got to fuck with a person who has trust issues as deep as hers must run." Rabbit stated.

"She seemed plenty cozy with you, so what's the problem?"

Rabbit laughed. "I'm her buddy. I'm her coworker. I'm the asshole who rescued her from the shit show you set her up with yesterday instead of taking care of her yourself. But let's get this straight right now, that's all I am. Damn if I don't wish there was a little more than buddy chemistry between us, because she's fuckin' perfect, dude. But that's not how it is, and anyone could see that if they didn't have their head implanted firmly up their own ass." Rage looked ready to kill Rabbit with that comment, but Rabbit wasn't done yet. "But you didn't stop with the shit show for some reason. You were all touchy-feely with Showgirl last night during the meeting, only to go cold again moments later and walk away just because she and I made a couple jokes to lighten the tension in the room.

"So, then what do you do to the girl with the massive trust issues? You go to the one mother-fuckin' woman left in this joint who taunted her and participated in the previously mentioned shit show of that morning, and you paste yourself to her for the night in plain view of my new buddy. I'm not even gonna tell you what her face looked like when she saw you eating at the diner of Jezzie in the common area, but man, when she saw you take her upstairs her knees actually buckled."

I didn't think anyone noticed that little slip up on my part. Damn it. I just knew I played off dropping that hand towel when I felt like I'd been stabbed in the gut with jealousy and something else. As I watched the verbal smack down Rabbit was laying on Rage, the man's face contorted in a way that made it impossible to read the emotions swirling there.

"She watched you choose her tormentor after sending her signals that you wanted to be with her. It must have felt a little like history repeating itself considering her husband cheated and tried to have her stabbed in the back in the most literal sense possible. Oh, and we'll put the cherry on the top of that betrayal with the look of triumph on Jezzie's face as she noticed our girl watching. And the icing with the cherry...

you just let Jezzie 'thank you' for being loyal to her, by choosing her over Charlie last night."

"What the fuck?" Rage growled at Rabbit, clearly not understanding that last bit.

"She didn't just thank you for choosing her over Charlie, but for flaunting that shit in Showgirl's face. You fuckin' idiot! How do you think Jezzie's going to act out there now when no one is around to witness and check her behavior? Hell, you may as well have given Jez your word that she was your old lady, and you're too fuckin' clueless to realize what's up. Normally, I wouldn't care and would leave you to sort your own shit out, but I happen to like Charlie. Everything you're doing is biting her in the ass and fucking with her trust even more. And that is something I won't fuckin' stand for, asshole. So, get your shit together!"

"Fuck!" It was said quietly, but not lacking for passion.

"Yeah, that about sums up your colossal fuck up."

"I didn't even think about who it was. I just grabbed the first blond I saw. It didn't even click, man. I was seeing fucking red when you were..."

"When I was being her buddy?" Rabbit asked sarcastically. "Seriously dude, go get your head removed from your ass, and so help me, if you hurt my friend again, I won't care that you wear that VP patch. I'll take it to your ass anyway."

Rage nodded and disappeared back into his room while Rabbit strolled off down the hall. I pulled my door closed as quietly as possible and went to go throw some cold water on my face. Coffee could wait a minute, because the heat in my face from the embarrassment, and the anger brewing, needed a bit to settle.

Rabbit had hit the nail on the head with his assessment of how that whole scene made me feel. It started out with confusion and disbelief before wandering straight into me feeling betrayed yet again. I had, in fact, contemplated leaving in the wee hours of the morning when I couldn't shut my brain off to get some sleep. Let's be real though, where was I going to go? If I stepped out of this frying pan, I was probably going to land straight in the fire about five minutes before I wound up dead.

"Arrrgghhhhh!" I screamed my frustrations into the air around my bathroom. Part of me wanted to just rip something apart, another wanted to curl up in a ball and cry my heart out. This could not continue to be my life forever. I didn't want to be trapped in a prison of desperation, and that's the fine line I'd been riding for almost a year now.

A knock at my door sounded. "You okay in there?" It was Rage. He'd no doubt heard my little act of frustration. I made sure to slam the bathroom door closed and lock it since I wasn't sure if I re-locked the bedroom door after I eaves-dropped on him moments ago. Nope. Definitely didn't lock it if the heavy footfalls from a pair of boots outside my bathroom door were any indicator. "I asked if you were okay in here. I'm gonna need an answer," there was a jiggling of the locked doorknob. "Like right now, or I'm kicking the fuckin' door in."

"Piss off, I'm busy!" I yelled.

"Busy doin' what, darlin'?" he asked in his put-on charming voice. Yesterday morning, that would have melted me in a way. Today, not so much. I knew it to be as fake as the man himself.

"I was assured I wouldn't have to entertain anyone in my room if I stayed here. I'd appreciate if you'd leave my damn room right now!"

"What the fuck?" He banged on the door once, twice, then stomped away only to stomp right back up to the door. "Seriously, what the fuck is that supposed to mean? I'm not here for..." He hissed out a string of expletives and then continued with his fake concern. "I heard you yell, and just wanted to check to see if you were okay."

That was it. I hit my breaking point. I tossed the door open and stared the man down hard even though I had to crane my neck back to look up at him considering the size difference.

"Let's get this straight right now, I don't want you here. I don't want you anywhere near me. I don't trust you, and I sure as fuck don't want you helping yourself into my room. Me yelling isn't your concern. Me being frustrated with my situation isn't your concern. Me feeling trapped inside my own life, that sadly doesn't feel like my own anymore, is NOT YOUR CONCERN! I need you to leave me the fuck alone and get the hell out of my goddamn room before I completely lose my shit, you sorry ass excuse for a fucking man!"

"I think it's time for you to get going for now, son." A familiar, soothing voice called out from the doorway between my room and the hallway. Rage looked stricken by my words. His pallor turned ashen, and the horror of how he'd changed my opinion of him in one night was etched in every line and curvature of his face.

His hand started to reach out, no doubt ready to brush

away the tears I was only now aware were free falling down my face. I flinched back before he could make contact.

"Charlie," there was so much pain contained in my whispered name, but I would not allow that to affect me. He had crushed me. No, we weren't together, and I couldn't be mad at him for pulling a fuck buddy into his room or making out with someone in front of me, but the fact that it had been her... I could definitely be mad about that.

"Rage," Shameless called out again, closer now. "You need to go." Rage turned on his heel, took one look at the seriousness in Shame's eyes, and nodded his head.

"Take care of her," he told the man who was apparently my Godfather.

"You bet your ass I will, and you better believe you and I will have words later about the stunt you pulled last night, too. Don't think for one minute that shit went unnoticed by anyone, son."

"Fuck!" he hissed again before continuing out the door.

8. FATHER FIGURE

"Come here girly," Shameless called to me, and I obeyed, because something about him reminded me so much of my own dad, and I needed him right now. I went willingly into his arms and that's when the dam broke and the sobs started.

"I just want my life back," I cried into his shoulder. "I want to dance again for the art of it, not because I need dollars thrown at me." I felt the flinch in Shameless, but he continued to hold me as I wailed out my troubles. "I want to be free to go places without having to look over my shoulder and worry that someone has found me, that today's going to be the day that I die. Why?" Sobs racked my body.

"Why did he do this to me? Why did any of them do this to me? What is it about me that makes me people lie to me, and betray me, and take away everything that is me? I'm no one now. They took it all. Changed it all. What do I have now?" The sobs continued while strong arms held me up and gentle hands continued to brush my hair back from my soaked face. He let me cry it all out into his shoulder before he answered any of my questions.

"You have me, Charlie, and I promise you that I will earn your trust if it's the last thing I do. I signed on for that the day you were born. I promised to look out for you for the rest of your life. You were a little misplaced for a while after your dad died. I got the news later, because I was out on a run we did across the border, but the minute I found out about your dad I went looking for you."

"I went to California. I couldn't stay there. My heart hurt to see all the memories of my dad everywhere."

"Yeah, I think we're getting that picture, sweetheart. We realized too late that you were working out there under a stage name."

I nodded my head into his chest, and then pulled away. "C.K. Sawyer," I confirmed. "My initials for Charlotte Katherine, and mom's maiden name. I used it whenever I was working on a production that I thought daddy would disapprove of," I offered sheepishly. "I guess it didn't matter once he was gone, but old habits, and all."

"Nothing wrong with that." He pulled me, gently, over toward my still unmade bed and sat down on the edge of it with me. "I know this is shitty timing, but could you walk me through how you ended up married to this Cooper guy? Did your dad know him before he passed?"

I scrunched my nose up trying to remember if my dad had ever met him before. "I don't think so. We went to high school together. He was two years ahead of me. We never dated in school, but we hung around a lot of the same people. So, when I was working on a music video in LA, one of the casinos was out there scouting for dancers for an upcoming show, and Josh had come with the scout, Brighton Miller, who was his best friend. When they saw me on set, it was like a big reunion, and Brighton got me signed under contract. The rest of the next two months was like a whirlwind. I had a job that would last a few months, paid well, and Josh was the perfect charmer.

"You have to understand, before him I was a good judge of character. I swear it. I know I had been. I was also a little lost and lonely, and not the least bit guilty for having some of my dreams come true and having the audacity to live them, and enjoy them, when my dad was gone. He was the last of my family," I started to say before I saw the hurt look on Shame's face. "The last that I knew of at the time," I corrected.

I sighed and then continued. "Anyway, I was kind of starved for affection, and Josh was there to give it to me. Little did I know, when he left me to go take care of business during the day he was really off screwing his long-term girlfriend from back when they went to school together. She was older so she was out of school before I started there. She was a dancer too, but a bum knee due to an injury made it so she couldn't work anymore. At some point the two of them cooked up this scheme to take me out for the insurance money. I think they did it before I was ever with him, like I was targeted for it from the beginning."

Shameless looked at me in surprise then. "I didn't know when it was happening, obviously, but Bishop told me before he took off. Apparently, the entire relationship, the marriage, all of it was some big sham insurance scam. They thought I made an easy target when I was signing the contracts with Brighton and couldn't give him a next of kin contact in case anything happened to me during production. The girl with no one to care whether she goes missing, or dies suspiciously, is always an easy target, right?" I asked rhetorically.

"Apparently not, since you're still here," Shame said with a smile.

"Yeah, well, I can thank Bishop for that, because I was too damn blind and stupid to save myself."

"Don't beat yourself up over that too much. It's a hard thing predicting when people are being insincere. It's in our nature to want to trust and believe that someone else is being forthright with us. Do me a favor and let that guilt you're carrying go, because it's doing nothing but weighing you down needlessly. You did what you had to do when you realized you were a target. You're still here, fighting your ass off a year later. That means something. You didn't give up, and just breakdown. Hell, you even showed exceptional loyalty to Bishop by not going to the police and trusting him to handle it. That is a quality we can all get behind here."

"Why do you think he lied to me?"

"Because he's a fuck-nut psychopath?" Shameless offered completely straight-faced.

I huffed out a half-hearted laugh. "Not him. I meant my dad."

"I wish I had a good answer for you. I can only assume he thought he was protecting you by not telling you he was part of the club, and truth be told, the past ten years of his life he wasn't much a part of it anyway. He'd only do one or two runs with us a year. He did just enough to keep his active, nomad status, and nothing more." Shameless heaved out a heavy sigh. "I know Lulu's death hit him hard, especially since he lost his son too."

"See, that's what I'm talking about. I never knew I had a brother to mourn with my mom, you know?" I sniffed back the emotion that was threatening to send new tears streaming down my face. "Why didn't I remember she was going to have a baby?"

"You were young, sweet girl. You were five, and they'd been trying for about two years to give you another sibling, but it just wasn't happening. Lulu kept claiming it was stress from worrying about Brazen going out on the road so much, but damn if I didn't get the feeling there was more to it then. I even talked to your dad about it once."

"What do you mean?"

"When your mom came to, after the accident and before the blood clot, she told us that she saw someone in a Tribe kutte that day. She kept saying, "He was coming for me. I chose wrong." Shameless looked lost in his own thoughts for a moment. "We thought she was just confused because of the head injury, but I couldn't let it go, even when Brazen told me to do so. I did some digging, and found she'd been sneaking around with a member of the Tribe for quite some time. She'd been mad at your dad for not cutting back on the runs, and..." he shook his head. "I hate having to tell you another ugly truth, but I think you need to know to understand."

"Okay," I stated while trying to absorb what he was telling me.

"It wasn't the first time your mom had cheated. Brazen

forgave her the first time, because there was you. He had a test done to prove he was your dad," he added quickly to make sure I knew my dad was at least who I thought he was.

"But that didn't stop the man from the Tribe she'd hooked up with back then from trying to lay claim to you so that he could start a war. They wouldn't take no for an answer. The crazy bastard swore the DNA test had to be faked or some bullshit too. I know that it wasn't, because I was there to hold Brazen's hand, so to speak, when he had it done. Anyway, those claims resurfaced after Lulu's death. Everyone was pretty sure the kid she was carrying hadn't been your dad's, even though he was hell bent on claiming it no matter what." Shame shook his head. "That man was loyal to his vows to a fault, I tell you." He patted my leg then and continued. "With the threat of constantly having to deal with those jokers trying to lay claim to you, he put in for nomad status, and hightailed it to the west coast where the Tribe had zero foothold.

"Your dad stayed out west after that. He settled in and only came around about a year later when he could get you into a summer camp where he knew someone always had eyes on you."

I laughed then. "Damn him, and here I had been begging him for those camps, and he played it like they were a burden on him," I rolled my eyes. "That sounds just like something he'd do."

My stomach, once again, decided to break up the party with yet another biker. "Sorry," I grumbled after my body decided to make so much noise that I could no longer ignore the hunger pangs.

"Nonsense. Let's go get you some food." He really took a good look at me then. "You're too skinny. Has anyone even told you where to get meals from around this place?"

"Um, I assumed the kitchen behind the bar."

"Fucking morons, the lot of them. No, Charlie, that's where you can get a snack while on your break when you're here working. We have better facilities to accommodate our large numbers in the east wing, just beyond where all the pool tables are in the commons area."

"Oh, I haven't really had a chance to look around," I explained quickly.

"Do me a favor, and don't go exploring around here without someone like me or Rabbit by your side. I trust ninety-five percent of these guys with my life, but we had a few questionable patch-overs from another club that fell apart a few years back. I still don't know about them."

"How did they get voted in if you still think they may be shady?"

"Well, it's a majority vote, and I was not in the majority that time."

"Okay, well, I'll be careful."

I'm an observant person. It comes with the territory when someone is out to kill you, so you better believe I took notice of Jezzie and another BRAT as we passed through the main common area of the clubhouse while headed to the kitchen. They had already been seated in a corner far from where Shameless and I headed. So, color me not so surprised when, after getting our meals and settling into a little nook seating area in the kitchen, I saw the two women parade into the kitchen in search of refills for coffee that was still visible in their cups.

"I'm telling you, Crystal, he rocked my world All. Night. Long." She over emphasized the last three words, probably in the hopes that I would overhear her. I kept my face a mask of indifference as I continued eating, but I noted Shameless' expression changed a bit. In fact, he took out his phone, and started toying with it as I continued eating.

"Oh, tell me all about it. He doesn't often get with us BRATs. I'm still waiting to try him out," the other girl panted breathlessly. She was acting as if just the thought of getting with Rage was about to cause her to orgasm. Nasty.

"Oh, I know, but I've been one of his regular go-to girls for ages, and last night just proves how he feels about me. Our fuck-fest was a slap in the face to you-know-who."

"The new princess, sure," the bimbo with Jezzie confirmed. Jez, for all her stupidity smacked the girl in warning.

"Anyway, so besides giving me a proper seeing-to with his fingers when we were in the common rooms, he took me back to his room last night!" She squealed giddily.

"He never allows the girls in his private room!" The other one squealed with her.

"I know! Obviously, the shit that went down with Tallie and that new whore really put things into perspective, you know? Plus, he had me in every position imaginable last night, and never seemed to tire of me. I think this is it. I'm moving up to old lady soon. Rage is going to be mine!"

She kept gushing while I continued to shovel food in my

face, and Shameless simply held his phone out in front of him just bit while he looked like he was about to burst with anger. It was only a couple seconds later that what sounded like a hoard of thunderous boots came crashing into the kitchen area. In an instant it became far too crowded for the big bodies that were taking up all the space, along with all the oxygen.

One of those bodies, judging by my strange hyper-awareness of him, was Rage. I still refused to look up to see what was about to go down around me.

"Calm down, brother," my buddy, Rabbit said. Followed up quickly by Iceman's statement. "We'll get this taken care of, man."

"What the fuck do you think you're doing?" Rage bellowed into the room only to be greeted by an echo of his angry question. I still didn't look up, because I was obviously eating and minding my own, so he couldn't be talking to me. I did however note that Jezzie had a shit-eating grin on her face as she stared at me.

Unfortunately for her, staring at me made her miss the fact that Rage was yelling at her, not me, until her little friend tapped her arm to get her attention. Then the smirk dropped off Jezzie's face in quick order.

"I asked you a question," Rage demanded of her.

She finally clued in and started to look worried. "I don't know what you mean. Crystal and I were just getting some coffee."

"Is that so? Looks like you were already topped off before you came in. Otherwise, how would it look so light when you don't have milk or cream out?" Iceman interjected.

"We were just topping off before we headed to do

chores," she gulped while trying to look as innocent and small as possible. Crystal apparently wasn't as stupid as I thought she was, because she started to slowly distance herself from the other woman.

"What the fuck were you just running your mouth about in here?" Rage questioned again.

"Crystal and I were just talking about what an amazing night the two of us shared together," she cooed as she reached over to touch his chest with a familiarity that made me cringe.

If ever I thought Rage had been about to blow his top before, I had been wrong. His face literally started changing colors. The knuckles on his balled-up fists turned white, and his chest began to heave with labored breaths as he stalked a little closer.

"Yeah? Let's clarify for everyone here what our night entailed, shall we?" He moved another step closer while knocking her hand off his chest as she began to squirm. "I used you to make a show of something in public last night. Then I took you to my room too. It was my mistake for grabbing you to get that message across, because it sent the wrong one. But once we got to the room, what exactly took place between us?"

She glanced around nervously, and then threw a vicious look my way. "We bonded in our own special way," she offered up vaguely. His fist went flying and smashed into the cabinet right beside Jezzie's head. She screeched and flinched away.

"The fucking truth! Right now!" He ground the words out

between such tightly clenched teeth that they had to be doing damage to his molars.

"You sat in a chair reading while I fell asleep," the girl finally answered with a pout.

"Did I fucking touch you once we were behind closed doors?" Rage asked, and I had honestly had enough of this show. I stood quietly and started for the kitchen door only to be blocked by Rabbit, who shook his head and motioned for me to wait.

"Well, when we first got upstairs, before we went into the room," she started, but cut herself off when she noted Rage's growing impatience. "Not again until this morning," the girl answered on a shaky voice.

"Clarify how I touched you this morning!" He spewed the words at her as if the very use of them were a venom, she was about to become infected with.

"You shook me awake, grabbed my arm, and hauled me out of your bed while you told me I had to get gone," she complained. The confusion, hurt, and anger at being used in the manner he was suggesting, rather than the one she tried to lead everyone else to believe, made her voice wobble with emotion.

"So, what part of any of that had me fucking you in every position all night and ready to claim you as my old lady?"

My back was turned to the fiasco, as I'd been about to make my exit through the door, but I saw her humiliation play out in the glass cabinet fixture to the right of Rabbit.

"That fucking cock tease ratted me out?" she yelled. "Hey, you fucking cunt, I know you hear me talking to you!" My shoulders stiffened, but I refused to acknowledge her.

Instead, I tipped my head back, glanced at Rabbit, and the look I gave him communicated efficiently that it was time for me to go before I lost it completely on everyone in the fucking room.

"She didn't need to. You're on probation as of last night, you stupid whore!" Shameless bellowed. "I called him up and let him listen for himself. He just happened to be with these two when the call went through."

Shame, no doubt, meant Rabbit and Iceman. "You were settled in the commons when we walked through. You came in here purposely to start shit with my goddaughter," he spat out. "Then you lied about shit that went down between you and a club brother. You think one of us wasn't going to call your behavior out?"

"I didn't mean..." she started to say, but Iceman cut her off.

"I've heard more than enough already. Get your shit packed. Congratulations, I gave you a second chance, and you managed to fuck it up in less than a day. You may now enjoy the same banishment your friend Tallie earned herself last night."

Finally, Rabbit moved out of my way so I could get the fuck out of the caustic environment. "Wait up, Charlie," I heard Shameless call, but I couldn't wait. I was just done with this whole thing.

"This is the shit that keeps rolling downhill from your poor judgment last night," I heard Iceman say from behind the closing door of the kitchen. "I let you play your stupid hand last night, because I honestly didn't think you'd take it as far as you did, but I hope you realize there isn't a whole lot of coming back from the kind of damage you inflicted. That thing we talked about moments ago in the office seems a bit moot at this point." The door closed again, effectively cutting off any response that may have come. Shameless was beside me by then, and I just couldn't deal with another person.

"I'm going to go organize all the things Rabbit and I got yesterday. I'll see you later," I told the older man, as I started moving quickly to get away from him.

"I'm letting this go for now, because I think you need time to yourself to process, but you know I'm here if you need me. Give me your phone really quick, Charlie."

I stopped and huffed out an exasperated breath. "I already told Rage that I don't have a phone. I haven't had one for damn near a year since Bishop took mine. Who was I going to call? The only people I knew before might have gotten me killed by telling Josh they'd heard from me, and you know what? Every single one of them would have done it too. They wouldn't have believed that the NFL star could possibly do something like that. It doesn't matter anyway. I'm doing just fine without one."

"Fucking Christ," he muttered. "I'll be up to check on you in a bit."

"Great, can't wait!" I snapped before storming off in the direction of the stairs that would take me to the room I'd been given to use. Sadly, I would only get a small reprieve away from everyone since I was due back to work by eight. Stupid weekend. Stupid bikers. Just fuck my life to hell and back already because I was more exhausted from the past eighteen hours than I had been in all my time running from my cheating, murderous, fuckwad of a husband.

The whole time I spent on my own in my room, I couldn't help wishing for a change in my chemistry. Clearly, I had been attracted to the wrong kinds of men for a while. I knew my screwed-up reasons for settling for Josh, and somewhere deep down I always knew I was doing just that – settling. He never made random gooseflesh pop up on my skin. He never set my heart to fluttering either. He was just a comfortable person to have around so that I wasn't trapped in a vortex of having no one to care about me.

There was knee-weakening, goosebump inducing, heart-thudding, excitement-driven chemistry between Rage and me though. Sadly, I had to find a way to turn that shit right the hell off, because I couldn't deal with it. I just couldn't go there with someone who was no longer capable of being a person I could potentially trust.

I finally had everything from the previous day's shopping excursion put away when there was a knock on my door. I hesitated in opening, because honestly, depending on who was on the other side, I wasn't certain I wanted to open up.

"It's me, Charlie," Shameless called out. Well, I couldn't exactly refuse to open the door for the self-proclaimed father figure that had stepped into my life. Unfortunately, when I did relent and open it, I got a good glimpse of Rage sitting against the wall on the opposite side of the hall. I stepped back to allow Shameless into my space and ignored the pleading look Rage threw my way before I shut the door on him.

Shameless immediately held out a small black flip phone. "I know it doesn't look like much, but it's an untraceable pre-paid. We need you to have it in case of emergency so that you can contact us, or we can contact you. I glanced through and saw that most of the top echelon's numbers were already programed in, including Rage. Then I opened the texting app and saw a blast text there to all the guys informing them that this was my number. I slumped in defeat.

"I promise no one will use this phone to harass you for any reason. So, if that's the reason for your sad face, you can just wipe it out now." His demeanor was stern, and it made me glance up to see the hard look on his face. "Sit down, girl. We need to have a talk about how things run here."

"Okay," I murmured tentatively. Knowing that if he was about to tell me I had to suck it up and deal with Rage treating me like shit, or anyone else doing so, I was going to have to find a way to get free of these people. I wouldn't trade my safety for my free will. I might as well be dead in that case.

"I want you to just listen and absorb some things before you try to interrupt me, got it?" he asked. I nodded my agreement. "The thing about biker clubs is that they are chock full of alpha males. These are men who don't play by the rules, ones with very dominant personalities, and sometimes those personalities tend to be a bit possessive. That possessiveness can come off as overly aggressive or even stupid decisions when they think what belongs to them is being threatened."

He must have seen the concern in my eyes because he held out a hand to still me. "Now, don't misinterpret 'aggressive' as meaning harmful. That's not what I meant. It's just," he hesitated, seeming to think through what he was about to say next. "The thing is, and I'm not going to beat around the bush here. I'm going to jump right into the actual matter at hand, so we aren't misunderstanding one another. That man, the one sitting out in the hall moping like a little boy who had his lunch money stolen, he has never, in all the years I've known him, been taken with a female in any way that matters." Oh boy, I started mentally packing my bags.

"Don't check out on me yet, Charlie. Listen." Again, I simply nodded and waited for him to continue. "He's never had to deal with jealousy before because he simply didn't care. You don't care when you're not connected to someone. You just don't give a shit when there aren't feelings, or some pretty undeniable chemistry, involved. That's why the club brothers are able to share the BRATs and club sluts without issues, despite how dominant and possessive every one of us can be." I wrinkled up my nose at him.

"Come on now, no judging. Everyone lives life their own way. Some of those guys use the girls – who sign up to be used for what they get in return – because their wives have died and while they have physical needs, they don't want to give their heart to anyone else. Some are young and sowing their oats. Others just can't be bothered to keep it in their pants despite their vows." He grumbled out the last a bit disapprovingly.

"Doesn't matter why they do it, that's their business. It runs smoothly, for the most part, though because no one really has a vested interest in those girls beyond a good time."

"What about the girls though? They're giving time to you all that they can never get back, and from what I've seen they're just hanging in there for the chance to become something more to one of you."

"They don't see it that way, sweet girl. They see it as an adventure. Some of them are sowing their oats too in a place where they know they're safety is paramount, the worry of sexually transmitted bullshit is low, and unwanted pregnancy is almost negligible. Some are here for protection from ex-boyfriends or families who abused them. Others are here to have a good time while soaking up a free education that we offer to pay for."

He smiled at me before shaking his head. "Like the men in the club, the women all have their reasons, and the minute they no longer want to be here, they are free to go, and we give them a decent severance to send them on their way safely. The only exception to that last bit is when they betray us in some way. Then they walk away with their possessions, memories, and not much else. Everyone has freedom to choose here. No one is forced to do a damn thing they don't want to do." He looked at me pointedly then as if he'd been reading the fear I'd had.

"So, with that bit cleared up, we'll move back to the issue at hand. Rage fucked up. I get your anger and you feeling betrayed. Hell, I don't know what the fuck that dumbass was thinking by grabbing that skank out of all the girls that would normally clamor for his attention. I seriously think she put herself close to him on purpose, and he just grabbed the first warm body when he felt threatened by your closeness with Rabbit. I know good and well he's out there regretting the hell out of his stupid, impulsive actions, especially after Rabbit set him straight about how completely off base he was."

Shameless blew out a breath before looking me in the eye

once more. "Now, I'm not saying you have to hook up with him or even be friendly to the man. You can even attempt to forgive him in your own time. One thing you will need to remember is that disrespect of our members isn't tolerated. Not even by family. So, think about that the next time you go yelling things, or speaking in anger at the man who stands as our current Vice President of the Dakotas Chapter, okay?"

"Okay, so what happens to me if I lose my temper on him in front of people? It's not like he didn't deserve it!"

"Oh, we all know he did. Doing so in future, now that you've been warned though, will lead to you either being sequestered to your room like a petulant child when you're not working, or you made to move out of the clubhouse altogether and being banned from coming back in. That's normally what would happen with family behaving disrespectfully. The problem in your situation is that we can't turn you out, because your life is literally in danger outside of this compound. I don't want you to ever feel imprisoned here. And if you need to vent frustrations, yell, scream, or whatever... just dial my number, and I will come serve as your whipping boy, so you don't find yourself in trouble for that sassy mouth of yours."

"I feel like Alice trapped in a crazy new world with no good way to turn," I admitted. "I don't..." I started to say and hesitated. "I'm tired, Shameless. I've been running, and before that I wasn't exactly happy, and on top of everything else, I come here and find out pretty much everything I ever knew about my family was a goddamn lie. Then the first few people I meet and choose to trust... well, you saw what happened there. I can't forgive him, because you explained he was jealous, and jealousy is new to him. I'm having to wrap my brain around my life changing in drastic ways once again, and the last thing I need is some crazy bastard trying to mind-fuck me because of a perceived slight that never happened. Honestly, despite our chemistry, the last thing on my mind right now is adding another man in the mix of my messed-up life.

"I'm still married to the one who tried to have me murdered, and I don't know how to rectify that since I've been in hiding. I never thought Josh was the love of my life, but how do you wrap your head around being a disposable payout for someone? How do you even begin to understand that your life meant far less than the anticipated payday to someone you've known since high school?" I swiped at the angry, confused tears that fell freely down my face.

"Most of all, the thing that keeps me up at night, is that I didn't realize what was going on. I didn't know. I didn't get a weird feeling, or tingly sense of imminent danger. How do I ever trust my judgment with another person again? Rage just proved to me that I was completely right in feeling that way. His actions embodied everything that has gone wrong in my life since my father died, and apparently, long before that too."

"I'm so sorry, baby girl." Shame pulled me into his arms and held me tight. "I'm so damn sorry I wasn't there for you sooner. I'm fucking pissed at that idiot outside in the hallway too for taking away the little bit you were starting to get back. How about this? How about you take your time learning to trust people again, and anyone who fucks with that trust will answer to my fists!"

I giggled a little at that image. "You're going to beat everyone up who lies to me?" I asked.

"You're damn straight I will. Lie to you, step on your toes, put you down, whatever their sin... I'll be their judgment day. And if I think you're trusting the wrong person, I'll be completely honest with you, okay?"

"Okay, although, maybe take it easy on the people who legitimately just step on my toes by accident. I'm not sure they deserve your fists of fury for being less than graceful."

He chuckled a bit. "Noted, sweet girl." He squeezed me tight one more time before adding, "I know I'm not your dad, and I can never replace him, but I am here for you as he would be if he hadn't been taken from you. So, anything you need, you just ask. Don't hesitate. If it was something you would ask of him, or talk to him about, I am now, and forever more, at your service."

"Thank you," I whispered over a lump of emotion. "I don't know why I immediately felt so comfortable with you, but I'm really glad that I do."

"It's because your heart remembers me, sweet girl, even if your mind isn't able to." With that he stood and moved to leave.

"I like that," I said to him before he opened the door.

"What's that, Charlie?"

"That my heart remembers you. I like that a lot."

"Me too, baby girl, me too." Shameless saw himself out, and I was once again left to my own devices.

9. BAR DRAMA

AFTER CONTEMPLATING EVERYTHING FOR A BIT, THE PERSPECTIVE Shameless offered in Rage's defense made sense. That didn't mean I had it in me to simply move past it. His behavior was a small blip in the great big scheme of it all, but it was like the tiny straw that finally broke the camel's back. At some point, my shoulders just decided they couldn't carry any more without breaking. I needed to give myself time to heal, and to try to lighten the burden I carried around before adding anything more to it.

I got ready for work, and ended up heading out about thirty minutes early, even though it was in the same building. It was Saturday night, there were a lot of voices bouncing around in the hallway before I even finished getting ready, and I wanted extra time in case Rage was still spending time in the hallway waiting for me to come out.

He was not in the hallway any longer when I finally emerged from my room. Instead, I was treated to some young guy I'd noticed from my first day here. He had a different girl pinned against the wall opposite my door. His pants were bunched up under his ass, and her dress – or was it a shirt – was pushed up and out of the way. I so did not need to see two people fucking in the hallway today. If this was going on at 7:30 p.m. I could only imagine how the rest of the night was going to go in the commons area. I sped past, trying to ignore the couple, when I heard him snicker. "Hey there, princess, what's the rush?"

"Apparently, some of you need to get drunk to fuck in public, so I have to go do my part. Good to know I don't have to worry about saucing you up before you bang your bitches against a wall. One less beer I have to pull tonight," I slung back over my shoulder with a wink. The guy nearly dropped the woman he'd been pounding into the wall as he threw his head back and laughed heartily at what I said.

"Oh, fuck!" He laughed as I continued down the hall. "You are going to be so much fucking fun to have around here, Showgirl!" I tossed him a one-finger salute for the Showgirl nickname and continued around the corner and down the steps.

"Wait up!" I heard Rabbit's voice call from behind me, and I stopped immediately with my foot on the second step down. When I turned to look, he was standing there with Spinner, the guy I'd met originally at Rosy's. "You remember my brother?"

"Of course. Nice to see you again," I told the man who seemed to have trouble holding onto his stoic demeanor from the club the other day.

"Don't mind him, he's trying not to lose his shit after you just put Flint in his place back there."

"Flint?" I asked.

"The guy who was banging the chick up against the wall," Rabbit explained.

"Ah, yeah, well, I went easy on him since I got a lecture about respecting assholes even if they piss me off first." That brought a frown to Rabbit's face. "Don't worry, Shameless just explained how I could be 'jailed' in my room for being an asshole in public to you guys."

Rabbit came closer and grabbed my arm gently to get my attention. "If you need me to step in and pound some face, you just name names or point fingers. Don't worry about those stupid rules. I mean, don't get yourself in trouble, but you know it's okay if we boys pound on each other."

I laughed then. "Jesus, what is it with you guys and your offers to deploy your fists of fury?"

"Fists of fury?" Spinner asked.

"Yeah, Shameless told me almost the same thing earlier, only with a little more graphic detail thrown in. I think my dad would be proud of his protective stance," I said without thought. The minute the words were out though, it was like a kick to my heart. I flinched at the soothing pat from Rabbit. "Sorry, still kicks me in the ass sometimes to talk about him without even realizing I'm doing it. Like he's still here, but not." I shook my head to clear it. "I haven't really had anyone else who knew him, or of him, to talk to about him since he died. This is a new experience for me."

Surprisingly, it wasn't Rabbit who responded. It was Spinner. "We get it. We lost both our parents about ten years ago. A trucker who was too stupid to pull over and catch some sleep hit them. I think we've both had moments like you just did, so you never have to apologize for that."

"Thank you, and I'm sorry about your parents. I guess we're all members of the orphan club then?" I don't know why I said that, but its something I'd felt over the past two years since my dad died. I felt like an orphan, despite the fact that I was an adult already. Having no one will do that to you.

"Yeah, I guess we are," Rabbit agreed. "Come on, let's go sling those drinks. These guys have bitches to bone in public, you know?" Spinner laughed out loud at that which made me smile even bigger. Then I wondered if either of them was the 'bone in public type', and figured I'd get that shit out of the way.

"How about you just throw a heads-up my way so I can look away if either of you happens to partake in that shit. The last thing I need is to be able to identify every fucker in here by how hairy his ass is, or how his crack looks peeking out from his jeans."

Both guys boomed out laughter that had people from downstairs glancing up at us. "Man, I wish I had known you were this much fun that first day," Spinner told me before he walked down the rest of the stairs chuckling and shaking his head. "I can see why my brother is so taken with you," he added as Rabbit slung an arm around my neck and gave me a noogie.

"Ugh, seriously, Rabbit?"

"What? You've got one of those messy bun things in, I was just funkin' it up a bit more for you." I rolled my eyes at him as we moved downstairs and crossed the wide expanse of the common area to get to the bar. We both ducked behind the bar while the prospects greeted us with thankful expressions.

"It's not even eight," Rabbit stated. "Are you telling me that you can't handle these guys in the early hours? Maybe I need to make you switch shifts with Showgirl and I next weekend."

"No, it's been fine," the smaller of the two guys said immediately.

"You know how it is with us. They call out the wrong order, and..." the smaller kid elbowed the guy in the stomach to shut him up. I sensed trouble. I wasn't exactly sure what just happened, but Rabbit's eyes were alight with mischief over whatever the prospect had been about to spill.

My newly appointed bar-buddy rang a bell at the back of the bar that got a lot of people's attention. "Did you guys hear that? Apparently, some of you have been giving the prospects wrong orders." A bunch of growls of dissent rose through the ranks.

"Oh shit," the prospect with the big mouth groaned as he finally realized his mistake. The other prospect's shoulders drooped as he glared accusingly at his coworker. I assumed they would both take the hit for what was said.

"Do we make mistakes when ordering our own drinks, brothers?"

"Fuck No," was the yelled response.

Rabbit put his hand to his ear and called out again. "I couldn't hear you! Do. We. Order. Our. Drinks. Wrong?"

"FUCK NO!" The roar of all the deeply male voices rever-berated through the very bones of the building. I felt it through the floor as the sound traveled to my feet in waves, and it made me smile. These big burly men were becoming my family in short order. Some had been my family once already when I was a little girl, and I think this was one of those moments where my heart recognized them, because I felt a warmth and a security settle over me that I hadn't known in years.

With a wide grin plastered to my face, I turned to ask the man who sat at the bar in front of me what he wanted. Unfortunately, it was Rage who was seated there. The smile fell from my lips, and I just quirked up an eyebrow in question.

"Can I get a draft, darlin'?" he asked so quietly I almost didn't hear him. I snagged a glass, pulled the draft, and set it down in front of him all without saying a word. Then I moved on quickly to top off some of the other brothers' drinks and fill a couple orders for shots.

Rabbit sent the prospects, who were supposed to be relieved of duty for the night when we got there, to clean the bathroom stalls in the large public bathrooms off to one side of the commons. I hadn't been in them, and from what I was told, I was missing absolutely nothing. I kind of felt bad for the guys, but then again, they signed on for the abuse to be a part of this special place on a regular basis. The more time I spent here, the more I saw the appeal of it.

Over the course of the next hour, Rage had me refill his draft three times. Not once did I speak to him. Not once did I smile for him. Not once did I acknowledge him longer than it took to pass him his drink. Not once did he get frustrated and leave his perch in front of where I was working. I saw him watching me out of my peripheral as I tended to the many men and some of the women who came up for drinks. As I passed by his spot again, he reached out and gently tapped my hand.

"Charlie," he spoke my name so softly that I would have missed it had he not touched me. I turned to him and went to reach for his empty mug only to see it wasn't exactly empty. "It's about time for your break, right?"

I stared at him, saying nothing. It was time for my break; I had just finished topping everyone on my side of the bar off to help out Rabbit while I was gone to grab some food in the kitchen really quick. When it became evident that I wasn't going to respond to him, Rage let out a defeated sigh and then moved his hand away from me. I turned on my heel and called out over my shoulder to Rabbit that I was going on my break.

Rabbit shook his head as I walked away, and I heard him taunting Rage. "Oh yeah, you fucked up bad, dude!" That was the last thing I heard before the door slammed shut behind me.

It took me a minute to gather myself before I moved beyond the stock area heading back toward the little kitchen the bar area used as a break room. Heavy breathing met me the closer I got, and as I moved into the kitchen space I saw the nasty older biker, Beaver, with one of the club sluts up on the counter going to town on her. She didn't look entirely into the situation, but she wasn't exactly pushing him away either. I think she thought she was paying her dues to get picked up for a coveted BRAT position. More power to her, but the thought of having to cover through Beaver to get it made me cringe.

"We prep food here," I stated as I pulled out my phone and started texting Shameless and Rabbit at once.

> Showgirl: Beaver's fucking some chick on the kitchen counter in break room behind bar. Please, tell me this isn't the norm or I'm never eating here again.

"Unless you're offering to join in, I suggest you mind your damn business and get the fuck out of here," the man snarled at me.

"This is my designated break area, and I'm on my break," I retorted. The man roared, pulled out of the girl, turned to face me with his rather unimpressive cock still hard, and now pointing in my direction, as he moved quicker than I would have anticipated toward me. His hand was around my throat and jacking me into the wall before I had even a second to respond.

The girl who he'd just been doing on the counter behind us screamed as I struggled for breath all the while trying in vain to get my feet to touch the floor again and relieve the pressure from my neck. I just knew that my throat would never be the same as the pain gripped me. When I was just on the border of blacking out from lack of oxygen, as my head was slammed once more into the wall behind me, the asshole's surprisingly strong grip tightened even further on my throat. Just when I thought all hope was lost, the door crashing open registered distantly before the man in front of me was tackled to the floor causing me to fall as well.

A flurry of fists set to work on my attacker as someone else pulled me up from where I had sprawled out on the ground during my fall as I attempted desperately to get air back into my lungs. Whoever was there tried to talk to me, but all I could hear was static in my ears as my blood flow slowly resumed in places it never should have stopped. I choked a harsh breath, sending fire shooting through my throat as I did so.

The moment things started coming back into focus, I noticed all the bodies spilling in through the doorway of the kitchen. A few headed toward the commotion off to the side where someone had tackled the asshole. Others in the group of men came directly over to me. Shameless was one of them. He pulled me close to him and inspected my throat.

"Get Doc in here, now!" He shouted. I tried to tell him I was fine, but I couldn't make the sound come out. It was then that I really started to panic. My eyes bulged wide, my breathing picked up, and I couldn't catch my breath after a moment. I couldn't talk. Oh god. What if he'd damaged something permanently? Jesus. Had I ever been safe here? I swear, every time I had a feeling of comfort, something or someone was there to snatch it right back out from underneath me.

"It's okay. Calm down, sweet girl. It'll take a minute to get everything back in working order. Don't panic. Breathe. That's it. In real deep..." I coughed violently when I attempted the deep breathing. "Fucking mother fucker..." Shameless snarled before he looked at someone standing behind me. "I hope you got a few in for me too," he stated before turning his attention back to me. "Okay, let's try shallower breaths, Charlie."

I got myself back under control when Shameless pulled away a bit. "I need to know something. Just shake your head for 'NO' and nod for 'YES', okay?"

I nodded. "Did he touch you?" I nodded again, and then pointed to my throat as if to say, "Obviously."

"I meant did he touch you inappropriately?" I gave him my best, what the fuck do you consider inappropriate look, and again pointed to my throat. "Sexually?" he finally whispered so that only the two of us would know what I was truly answering. I shook my head, and he seemed to breathe easier then.

"I got your text and came to make sure everything was okay in here. What the hell happened in the few damn minutes from when you left the bar to when we found you?" Rabbit asked.

I gave him a desperate look, tried to speak again, and not a damn thing but pain and torture happened in my throat. Motherfucker! If I didn't get my voice back, I'd kill that bastard myself. Another man came running in the room then, and immediately went to Beaver, who was lying on the floor, out cold, and covered in blood. And gross, his cock was still hanging out of his pants though it was limp, smaller if that was possible, and useless now. I wish they'd let me up so I could stomp on it for good measure.

"You will not touch that fucker until you see to her first," I glanced up to see Rage pointing at me. His knuckles were torn and bloody, chest heaving, and the look on his face promised death to anyone who disobeyed him.

"Okay," the new guy said as he backtracked to me across the small space. "Well, I guess I don't have to ask what happened here." He reached out to touch my neck, and when I pulled back, he looked me in the eye before explaining who he was. "They call me Doc. I'm medically trained. Is it okay to touch you so I can assess the extent of the damage?" As the words his left his mouth something smashed into a far wall as an anger fueled roar filled up the room.

"Everybody not directly involved needs to get the fuck out of here and make room, right fucking now," Shameless yelled the order, making sure everyone heard him.

The girl who had been in the room when I first entered tried to leave, but Shameless yanked her back. "Nice try sweetheart, but you're going to tell us what we need to know since she can't talk right now. And when you're recounting what happened, remember she might not be able to speak right now, but her hands ain't broken, and she sure as fuck can write it out for us."

Doc moved in as Shameless asked her questions. Surprisingly, she answered honestly, and every once in a while, Shame would glance in my direction to see if I agreed with what she was saying. I simply nodded when needed as Doc continued to look in my mouth, gently examine my neck, and ask random questions about my breathing. Luckily, I was breathing okay even though it also caused me some pain to do so.

Finally, they let the girl leave the room, but not before getting her information and promising to check in on her too. She seemed happy with that, and I was going to put in a good word for her becoming a BRAT if she passed their background check, because she was honest with them to a fault. And that was something they valued here.

"What's the verdict, Doc?" Iceman finally asked as Doc dug through one of his bags. I hadn't even noticed Iceman was in the room until then. Doc looked up and glanced between Iceman and me a few times.

"Honestly? Her inability to speak and pain level concerns me. She's breathing fine, so no worries about the trachea. If there were any fine cracks near the larynx damage to her voice could be lasting, so I'd rather get her checked out in a hospital where I can see for sure. There are things we can do to fix or prevent damage, but when left too long, it could become permanent."

"Then take her to the fucking hospital!" Rage roared from across the room.

"You know good and damn well it's not that simple. She looks like a battery victim. Worse, she's listed as a missing person in the databases. The minute she walks in there, she runs the risk of law enforcement becoming involved, and then whatever you guys have planned to get her out from under a contracted hit is going to be for nothing."

"FUCK!!!!" Rage shouted again.

"I can check to see if Sonya can get us the portable ultrasound tomorrow morning. That should be good enough to check the chords for any damage that might be lasting. Until then, I can get her a shot of something to help with any swelling and alleviate the pain she's feeling. I'd also like to have someone on standby with her all night. She's going to need to have that neck iced fifteen minutes on, fifteen off for an hour and then plenty of rest. The meds are going to knock her out anyway, but someone will need to monitor her breathing throughout the night."

Three people at once said they could do it. Shameless, Rabbit, and Rage all volunteered for the honor of babysitting duty. A tear slipped past my defenses, but it had nothing to do with the pain and more to do with the fact that I had three people volunteering to care for me. I wished I could express my gratitude for that.

"You okay with them taking shifts to watch over you, Charlie?" Iceman asked and I nodded, then winced, because I attempted to nod far too vigorously.

"Okay, I'm going to wait to give her the shots until she's settled in her room, because she's going to fade quickly once I do. Charlie, are you allergic to any meds?"

I shook my head, and mimed writing on something. Rabbit pulled his phone from his pocket and handed it to me with the texting app open. I typed out:

> I'm not allergic, but I have a really low tolerance for medicine. As in, I can be knocked out from taking over the counter allergy meds, painkillers, and stuff. So be careful with your dosages.

When I was done, I held the phone out for Doc to read what I'd written. He smiled at me and chuckled a bit. "Okay, lightweight, I have you covered." I attempted to scoff at him and winced because it hurt like a motherfucker. Doc turned to face everyone else in the room. "Who goes next? The dickwad on the floor or Rage?"

"Rage, obviously," Iceman stated simply as he leaned over the dickwad on the floor. The man was no longer knocked out and was staring up at Iceman. "Remember last month when I put you on probation for touching the dancers that we said were off limits to the club members? Then the shit you tried to stir up after we kicked Tallie out? Well, you just hit your third strike, Beaver. I'm sure you know what that means."

I couldn't tell if the man looked shocked or not, because his face was far too swollen. "Before your ass is carted out of here tonight, we'll strip all club logo and paraphernalia from your person and your belongings. You are not to have or claim any further affiliation with our club. We'll go over the rest when we handle that shit in a bit."

"I'm just gonna pop a stitch or two in this one so it heals up okay. Oh, wait, is that..." Doc shined a light on one of Rage's knuckles and chuckled. "Damn, dude, I do believe that is a piece of tooth." He used something akin to tweezers to grip the tooth remnants and pull it out of Rage's hand. Then I watched as he cleaned then literally sewed a hole in that hand closed without so much as using the slightest bit of pain meds or local anesthetic.

I looked down at the phone still in my hands and started typing again.

Sorry for all this trouble. I feel bad about taking my break now.

I turned the phone and showed it to Shameless and Rabbit. Rabbit shook his head and gently patted my shoulder while Shameless tipped my chin up so I was looking at him. "Do not ever apologize for something that wasn't your fault, sweet girl. If anyone should be sorry, it should be all of us for not getting rid of that piece of shit sooner. We knew he was a problem, and we took the long way around correcting that. You get no blame in this fiasco. You understand?"

He blew out a long, hard breath before finishing. "Hell, you did a good damn thing sending that text to Rabbit and me, letting us know he was back here before anything happened. That fucker wasn't supposed to be back here to begin with. We'll discuss that later too, so you know from now on who is allowed and where."

I nodded my head quickly. "Okay, let's get her off to bed so I can get her some pain relief guys," Doc stated.

I glanced over and pointed at Beaver. Doc seemed to understand what I was asking. "His sorry ass can wait. I'm not treating a man who thinks its okay to rough up a woman for no good fucking reason. Hell, for pretty much any reason unless to save someone's life." Doc glanced between the men left in the room. "Who is doing the honors?"

"That would be me," Rage stated simply as he closed in on us.

"Do you really think that's a good idea?" Rabbit asked without sounding like he was bothered by whatever was currently going down.

"Yeah, I do." Rabbit tossed his hands in the air then, but I also saw the smile tipping the corners of his mouth up as he did so. Rage came to stand directly in front of me, then he bent a little and whispered, "I'm going to pick you up now, and carry you to your room. You have a problem with that?"

I nodded and pointed to his injured hands.

"Don't worry about that," he told me as I waited for whatever would happen next.

Rage immediately swooped me up in his strong arms and

cradled my body tightly to the solid, muscular chest I'd been dreaming about for days now. And damn it, but the man smelled like absolute heaven. He embodied leather and a subtle woodsy outdoor scent that triggered a warm, safe feeling. I closed my eyes and leaned in enjoying the lift to my room. I wondered, briefly, if I'd ever be able to finish a full shift at the club bar without some kind of drama going down.

10. BETTER THAN APOLOGIES

My throat ached as I struggled against the pull of the medicine that still tried to hold me under in a fuzzy haze. It quickly became obvious what had woken me to begin with when I heard voices again.

"Are you sure? You were injured too. You should probably take something and get some rest man. Shameless and I can take turns looking after her, I promise."

"I already told both of you that I'm not fuckin' leaving." That was Rage's voice, and while he was trying to keep it down, he was very adamant about what he was saying.

"Look, dude, I get it. You're not going anywhere. Why don't you just hop up there beside her and get a little shut-eye. You'll still be here, and one of us will sit up to make sure she doesn't have any problems while you get some rest."

"I'm not inviting myself into her bed while she's unconscious. That's all I need is to give her another reason to hate me."

I managed to pull myself out of the hazy fog medicine

always left me in long enough to pat the empty side of the bed in invitation. I could hear Rabbit chuckling. "I guess we woke her up, and that looked an awful lot like an invite to me," he added.

"Go on, son." I heard Shameless say. "Get some rest. One or the other of us will be here all night to check on both of you."

"You don't worry about me. Just make sure she keeps breathing and doesn't need any more pain meds."

"You know we will. We all care about her, even if it's in different ways."

Rage grunted, but I felt the bed depress beside me at the same time, and just the scent of him had me moving a little closer without even meaning to, and before I could register anything else I was out again like a light."

UNSURE OF HOW long I was out cold that last time, I realized almost immediately that my face was pressed against a warm, hard wall of muscle that smelled insanely good to me. I did not want to move. Not even to examine why my arm was not only draped over the person's waist, but that I was damn near clutching it in a possessive way. Though I was awake, I continued to feign sleep, because there were far too many voices carrying on in my room, and I was slightly embarrassed that they were witnessing the position I woke to find myself in.

"Beaver is gone. We stripped him of everything and gave

him an escort out of town. We've got eyes on the girl. She doesn't have the best home life, so if we need to step in, I imagine that one is going to want to make sure we do. The girl told on a brother in front of a room full of us to help Charlie out. That had to be intimidating as hell." It sounded almost like Rabbit, but there was something off about the voice too. Maybe it was his brother, Spinner?

"Where are we with the husband situation?" Rage asked and as his voice rumbled through me. I must have inadvertently stiffened, because he began gently smoothing his hands through my hair as if to lull me back into a deeper sleep.

"I tried to reach out to the Modern Saints Prez, Davis Walker. They're out there near Vegas," that was Iceman. "They informed me we'd be on our own for this one, because there were reasons why they couldn't get involved."

"What the fuck?" Shameless asked. Honestly, the same words ran through my head, but then I remembered seeing the Modern Saints stuff around the house once in a while. I also saw the bitch that my husband was seeing wearing one of their shirts when I followed him once. I had to wake up and tell them all what I knew despite my embarrassment over the position I was in.

"I know," the words came out, which made me immensely happy even though it sounded like I gargled gravel and fire all at once. I moved to sit up, but strong arms pulled me tight against his chest again. A round of chuckles went through the room. I just held a hand up like I was writing in air, and someone put a phone in it for me to use.

Josh invested almost all his NFL money in a brothel two coun-

ties over from where we lived in Vegas. It was why he'd ended up so desperate for money because he didn't hold anything back in case the brothel failed. Didn't take off as quickly as he hoped either. He was an investor for what I thought was just a business group. The name was Lovely Saints for Modern Sinners, but there were Modern Saints things around our house too.

"Well, fuck me running. That explains a lot then," Iceman said after he read the message out loud.

Someone laughed, as if that were good news. "What?" Rage bit out.

"Well, it seems if something were to happen to this Josh asshole that Charlie here would be part owner in Modern Saints' latest business venture since she's next of kin as his spouse." It *had* been Spinner speaking earlier. Rabbit wasn't in the room at all.

Shameless, Iceman, and the red-haired guy, Mech, were all present and accounted for though. Great, and they all saw me drooling on Rage's chest. I felt the slippery trail down my cheek now that I was moving around. I was definitely drooling. I wiped my face with the back of my hand and then proceeded to wipe the drool off Rage's chest while everyone was distracted with one more person entering my room. I felt Rage chuckle but refused to look up at his face.

"Sorry, came to check on my patient. Didn't realize a meeting was going on," Doc offered.

"S'ok, Doc. Get in here, and check on our girl." Of course, that had been Shameless, and another reason why I was beginning to love that man.

"She spoke a minute ago, but sounded like it hurt a lot," Rage informed him.

"I bet it did," Doc told him. Then he looked at me. "I have an ultrasound machine coming later today. Earliest we could get it here was around noon. I don't want you trying to talk until then, okay?" I nodded. "If there is damage, vibrating those chords, and straining to make sounds could aggravate the situation. We need to let it all rest until I have a complete picture."

He reached into a bag and pulled a tablet out. "With that in mind, I brought you this. You can use the stylus to write out whatever you need, or you can use the typing feature. I figured it has to be better than doing all that typing using an old flip phone and cycling through letters. That shit takes forever."

I smiled appreciatively at him, because yeah, it sucked since I tended to have a lot to say. I tipped my fingers up to my chin and brought them out to him in the ASL gesture for thank you. I didn't even think about whether he'd understand.

"You're welcome." I glanced up in surprise, and he laughed. "ASL basics help in my field. Don't try to carry on a full conversation with me, but I know enough to recognize 'thank you' when I see it."

Doc waited a moment while I tried to sit up again only to be promptly caged in by some very solid arms that had no intention of letting me go anywhere. Doc chuckled at my helpless expression. "Rage, my man, I'm gonna need you to let go so I can take a good look at what she has going on there."

"Fine, after these chuckleheads get the fuck out. She doesn't need another audience for this shit especially since she's barely wearing anything." He grumbled. I glanced down at myself and realized someone had pulled my shirt off last night and thank fuck I had a camisole on under my shirt instead of a slinky bra or something. Jesus. I frowned and everyone got a laugh out of that.

"Don't worry sweet girl, you did that all by yourself last night. Got hot for some damn reason," Shameless grumbled while throwing a glare in Rage's direction. "He did at least stop you to make sure you had something on underneath before you showed anything off." With that more laughter and chuckling followed all the men out of the room. Suddenly, it seemed like a cavernous space without all their large bodies filling up the place.

Once they were gone Rage helped me sit up with my back against the headboard and a boat load of pillows surrounding me. Doc came forward to check on me once I was comfortable. He gently felt around my neck and commented that some of the swelling had subsided which was probably why I was able to speak a little this morning. He had me open my mouth, and he took a peek inside, which was disturbing on a lot of levels, not the least of which being my morning breath situation, and the fact that Rage was looking rather murderous the closer Doc moved in on me.

Doc glanced at Rage and shook his head while trying to rein in his smile. "Calm down, buddy. I'm doing this as a professional, no one's moving in on your woman." I would have argued that I wasn't his woman, but they both cut their eyes back to me in warning when I got ready to say as much.

"No using your voice, remember? And there's no use fighting it either. It's happening, so wrap your head around that now while you can't talk, and then you can save up all your arguments for when you need to work your voice out." Rage laughed as he said that bit, so I tossed a relatively nasty glare his way but that only made him laugh more.

"Everything is looking good, Charlie. You seem to be a quick healer. That will help you tremendously." He glanced down at his watch and then back up at me. "I'll have an ultrasound rolled in here in about three hours. Until then, no talking. No solid foods. Probably stick to cold drinks to help with any residual swelling. I'll see if someone can whip you up a protein shake with ice cream for breakfast. That should help tide you over until after we get through checking you later."

Again, I responded with the non-verbal thank you, and he tipped his head in response before gathering his things and leaving as quietly as he'd come in the first place.

I took the tablet in hand and wrote out, *'sorry for drooling on you'* and flashed it to Rage. He smiled at me, forcing those dimples of his out of hiding.

"You don't have to apologize for that, darlin'. Never apologize for being comfortable with me."

Being unconscious and being comfortable are two VERY different things. I wrote out as a joke. He stiffened beside me when he read it. So, I finished up by writing, *Joke – laugh.*

He smiled briefly, and then put his serious face back on. "Charlie," he started. I shook my head while I started writing immediately which made him hesitate.

Not now, Rage. Wait until I get my voice back for whatever talk this is. I don't have the energy for serious right now. I just want to forget all the bad shit in my life for a minute.

He swallowed hard and nodded in agreement, so I put the tablet and stylus aside and snuggled back into his chest, because he was damn comfortable. At least that's what I was telling myself. I heard him sigh, "Thank fuck," before he started playing with my hair again. I don't know how long we stayed like that wrapped around one another again, but in too short a time someone knocked on the door and Rabbit walked in with a large glass of frosty goodness in his hands for me. He also had a needle in the other hand.

I pointed to the needle and shook my head. "Calm down. Doc sent this in with me just in case you needed it. He said the cold might help your throat, but it could cause you pain too. The meds are just in case." I tossed up an 'ok' sign and sat up to take the drink. Rage, once again, reluctantly let me go.

I was two sips into the best shake I'd ever had in my life when Rabbit spit out, "So, I hear you two were cozy enough that Showgirl was drooling all over your chest, man." I shot an immediate glare up to Rabbit and signaled slitting his throat to which both men started laughing. I moved my glare between them both, but as I took another sip of the yummy, cold, goodness I ended up rolling my eyes back in my head and just enjoying the smooth icy feeling cooling the fires in my throat. I moaned, inadvertently, at the ecstasy of having any relief there.

"Okay, that's it. Get out!" Rage told Rabbit who laughed but got up to leave.

He placed the syringe on the nightstand closer to Rage and said, "It doesn't sound like she'll need that, but just in case."

11. WOULD YOU STAY

THREE DAYS LATER, AND MY BOYS FINALLY EASED UP ON ME ENOUGH to allow me out long enough to move around and see something other than the walls of my bedroom and bathroom. Granted, Rage did at least bring me a TV and Rabbit thought to download the Kindle App on the tablet Doc had given me, because – and I quote – "Girls like books and shit, right?"

They were too much. Feeling genuinely cared for by everyone left me extremely thankful for my situation. Not the murder for hire part of it but being lead here to these people and this place in time had been a Godsend. I was finally talking a bit more since the ultrasound came back clear. My voice continued to come out a bit gravelly when I spoke, but Doc assured me that would go away with time as long as I didn't over-do the talking.

The guys had gone to Church, which I learned was a closed meeting for the brothers only. This one in particular was only for the officers in the MC though, which pretty much took away all of my guard dogs. I just stepped into the hall when the player who lived across from me stepped out to greet the ridiculously handsome man that was standing there.

"What's up, Steel?" My across the way neighbor, Flint, asked.

"Is she in there?" Steel asked as the other man blanched.

"Wh-" he didn't even get the full three letter word out before Steel was on him jacking him into the wall. I quickly pulled my phone out and typed 9-1-1 into a text to the guys.

"You know who the fuck I'm talking about. Is Jenn in there?"

"Now, listen…" my neighbor started to say.

"We've been stuck together like glue since diapers, Flint, why the fuck would you do this?"

There was devastation laced in Steel's words. That much was clear by the way his voice cracked and his shoulders slumped when he took a step back. Thundering boot-steps came charging down the hall about the same time. Steel glanced over and noticed them all heading in our direction. He seemed to resolve himself to something, and then turned back to my neighbor, who I now knew was Flint, and landed a solid thwacking punch to the other man's jaw that took him immediately down to the floor.

"We're done, man. I can put up with a lot of shit, but fucking my girl behind my back, even if she is a worthless cunt, that isn't one we come back from."

"We fucked after you guys split last time. I was drunk, man." Flint massaged his jaw. "I wasn't going to touch her again, but she kept coming around, and now she's here to tell me that…" he didn't get to finish explaining what she was there to tell him, because the door to his room opened and a hysterical, crying blond slip of a girl came barreling out and slammed into Steel's chest. She immediately wrapped her arms around his waist and clung to him as if her life depending on it.

He immediately shoved her away though. The push wasn't hard enough to make her fall, but definitely enough to make the point that he didn't want her touching him. "Let me guess, she came with the sob story about being pregnant with my baby and me not giving a shit?"

Flint sucked in a harsh breath. "No, she came with a sob story about being pregnant with *my* baby, actually. She says it had to be from the party after you said you were done with her."

"Well, she claims to have fucked me while I was passed out a couple months ago at a party. That party was three weeks later, so that's a hell of a time window to possibly be pregnant by either of us. And just so we are all clear, fucking someone who is passed out is still rape even if the person doing the deed is a woman, if what she said was true." He seethed. Then he turned to the other men who had run up here to witness the drama thanks to my 911 texts.

"So..." Steel turned to Iceman who was standing there with Rabbit, Shameless, Spinner, and Rage. "She probably needs to be banned from the joint for her disloyalty and abuse of members."

"You can't do that," she shrieked. "I'm carrying a baby and it belongs to one of you."

"If it's mine, I'll be going after custody, and you won't need to be here anyway, considering I can have you thrown in prison for your admitted rape," Steel commented as he pointed around to everyone present. "Plenty of witnesses to the fact that you didn't deny saying it, and if you're claiming I'm still a potential baby daddy, that's the only fucking way it happened, or else it would have been so long ago you would already be showing."

"Likewise, on the custody thing," Flint agreed.

"Well, I can't say I don't agree." Iceman said coolly.

"When she's able to have DNA testing done, I want it to happen, but until then I'm asking to transfer to the new chapter in Georgia that Sweet is putting together," Steel stated simply.

"Steel," Flint spoke softly, as if he couldn't believe his friend would choose to move away.

"Fuck you! I have nothing to say to you." He turned back to Iceman then. "We good with that transfer?"

Iceman nodded. "You can file a club grievance against your brother for taking your woman when he knew she was off limits," Iceman started. Steel shook his head violently.

"He's not worth the grievance, and neither is she."

Iceman continued to keep his eyes on Steel alone. "If that's the way you want it to go down, I will honor your wishes and your request for transfer, but you're going to be the one to tell your momma." He huffed out a sigh as he ran a hand over his bearded face. "I'll never hear the end of it from her as is."

"Sorry man, but I can't stay here. Technically, he didn't poach while we were together, but the fact that he went there at all just... I can't fuckin' stomach seeing him daily, and I won't ask that he's sent away. I need a fresh start."

"You got it son," Iceman confirmed. "When are you headed out?"

"Soon as I'm packed. I already talked to Sweet. He said I was more than welcome once he gets the okay for the transfer from you." Steel laughed then. "Apparently the only good bike mechanic down there is a chick, and they've managed to piss her off somehow." All the men in the hallway chuckled at that except Flint. "They can definitely use some skilled hands."

Iceman stepped forward then and hugged the man. "You better stop in and see your dad on the way down, Hopper will be happy for the visit."

"Yeah, it's part of the plan. I'll tell mom I'm going, but she isn't to know anything about this supposed pregnancy shit until I see DNA results. If it doesn't end up concerning me, she doesn't need to go getting her hopes up about a grandbaby in advance."

"You got it. Hey, Rabbit," Iceman called, and he moved forward. "Get this bitch out of here and put one of the prospects on her. We need to make sure we keep eyes on her at all times until we find out whose kid she's carrying, and to make sure she doesn't do anything to harm it on purpose."

Steel turned back then with a wicked grin as he spoke to the woman. "Just keep in mind, statute of limitations on rape is seven years in South Dakota. Keep that kid safe, because if anything happens to it before we find out, I'm exercising my right to have your ass tossed in prison."

Well, damn. Looks like I wasn't the only one bringing the drama to the clubhouse. As much as I felt for the people involved, I was kind of glad I wasn't alone in causing the big scenes. Rage had made his way over to me and squeezed me to him with his arm around my waist. "Thanks for letting us know," he whispered in my ear.

"Flint, we'll be talking in my office later today."

"Just let me know what time," he confirmed to Iceman in a solemn voice with his head hung low.

"Come on, let's go get you something to eat before you get to work," Rage said. "Are you sure you need to go back to work already?"

"Definitely. I love the room I'm in, but if I have to look at those walls for one more day, I'm going to lose my shit."

"Noted," he said as he led me away with Shameless hot on my heels. Rabbit was still back there trying to pick up the blond who was throwing a hellacious hissy fit.

"So, that was dramatic. Does that kind of thing happen often around here?" I finally asked. Both men chuckled.

"That particular brand of bullshit, not really. For the most part brothers won't stick it in a chick that another of us has a claim on, or at least not without express permission from both parties that it's over. That's rarely done though. Iceman and his old lady are one exception. She was with Steel's dad, Hopper, first but they were never really together. Steel was a result of a one-nighter. They tried briefly to make it work when they found out he was on the way, but those two are like oil and water. Their personalities didn't mix at all. Iceman took her in though and has been regretting it ever since." Shameless explained on a chuckle.

"Oh," I stated simply. Rage smiled at me indulgently.

"It's okay to ask questions, we'll tell you if it's personal or not. Just so you know, the clubhouse always has a certain level of drama. It comes with the territory with so many rough, high-strung men, and the crazy bitches they tend to attract. Also, we have a lot of different women in and out of here anyway. Whether it's the BRATs, club sluts, hangers on, or the girls from Rosy's there are always dramatics going on with them."

"Especially when you get any of them and the old ladies in the same place all at the same time," Shameless added with an exaggerated bob of his head.

"I really feel like the time I've spent here so far has been an education into a foreign land. It's strange and familiar all at once though. I guess my dad never left his biker edge, so the way you guys carry yourselves and speak reminds me of him in some ways. Honestly, I wish I could remember what it was like to be around this environment when I was younger."

"Well, you were only at the clubhouse in Cedar Falls on certain occasions so that you wouldn't see a bunch of this shit. Lulu made sure you weren't around when any of the club whores were. One of the things she did right was always being a good mom to you."

"At least there was that" I agreed. "I don't really remember much of her either. So, thanks for saying that. My dad used to tell me stories, but there was always something missing in them, you know? It felt like he was leaving all these parts out of the whole, and I guess I know why now."

"Anytime you want to hear some stories about your past, you just let me know, sweet girl. I have plenty," Shameless told me.

"Thank you." We had reached the bar by then, and when

I realized that we were headed to the kitchen behind the bar in order to get me food before work, I hesitated. A look, one that said they expected my reaction, passed between Shameless and Rage. I sucked up my trepidation and moved beyond the door Shameless held open for me. Rage kept a hand on my lower back the whole time as we moved into the room beyond the storage area. I stopped, like I did that night when I noticed Beaver banging a chick in here, and I looked around taking everything in.

"I don't want to hate this place," I whispered.

"That's why we're here darlin'. You need to know what happened was a fluke. This is a safe place for you, and the only way you're going to associate it that way is to be here, with us, doing normal things." Rage told me as we sat down at the little table.

I stared at the countertop across the way and must have scrunched my nose up in disgust, because Shameless laughed. "Don't worry sweet girl, it's all been scrubbed down and sterilized."

"Well, that's something at least," I murmured. Shameless busied himself preparing something for us to eat, and I wasn't about to ask any questions about their grand plans, so I sat back and shut up.

"Can I ask you a question, sweet girl?" Shameless finally spoke while he stirred whatever he'd put in the pot.

"Of course."

"If we get this situation with your..." he hesitated, catching his words and swallowing them. "If we get this Josh situation taken care of so that you never have to worry about him or anyone he's affiliated with coming after you, what would you want to do?"

"Celebrate!" I called out and both men in the room chuckled at my immediate response.

"Ok, smart ass! I meant, would you want to go back to Vegas? Do you want to go back to dancing and performing in shows there?" I noticed Rage stiffen out of my peripheral, but I didn't dare look his way as I answered.

"I broke a contract in Vegas when I 'disappeared' so my dance days are over there."

"You had good reason though," Shameless stated.

"Yeah, but I'm assuming whatever is done with Josh and his associates isn't going to be something you want to take credit for. It's going to be dealt with quietly, and I won't tell your secrets to gain favor with that crew. So, I'll be black-listed from performing there ever again."

I shrugged, realizing that I wasn't even the slightest bit torn up over it. "Actually, don't laugh, because this is going to sound silly, but when I was on the run, I would choreo-graph new dances and routines for some of the girls in the clubs I worked in, and they always thanked me, saying they made at least double the tips on the nights they used my choreography over the older, tired numbers they'd worn into the ground." I sat thoughtful a moment.

"I was thinking about asking if the girls at Rosy's might be interested in some fresh choreography, but I figured if someone caught on to my background check that they'd be looking for me there, so it was a no go."

I shrugged. "So, I didn't bother asking if that would be something I could do." Shameless turned with the biggest smile on his face then, and before I knew it Rage picked me up and set me down on his lap. His face snuggled into the hair covering my neck and shoulder. "What the hell?" I asked.

"So, would you want to stay here, maybe, when things get cleared up, I mean?" Shameless asked again.

12. GLARING DAGGERS

It took a few minutes, but understanding finally dawned as I processed what Shameless had asked me. They were all worried I would leave to go back to my old life once I was no longer in danger.

"I wasn't happy with my life before. I've told you that. I had no one. I didn't really have any friends, and seriously, dancers are so much like your BRATs with their competitive natures, I'm sure you understand why that was. My dad is gone. Anything I had tying me to that place isn't there anymore." I laughed then.

"Winter might scare me away once I experience that, because you know, I've never seen more than a snow flurry my whole life." I thought about it for a moment. "At least, I don't recall ever seeing snow when I was little, but I have people here that I care about now and I don't know that I could give that up. I understand having to move out eventually, but..." I started before I was interrupted by both of

Rage's arms tightening their hold on me along with a deep scowl from Shameless.

"You will always be welcome here, sweet girl. For however long you need a place, however long you want to be here, there is a spot for you. I know we're all still knew to you, but you were like a surrogate daughter to me when you were young, and I still feel that way now. Don't you ever, for a single minute, think you are anything less than wanted here."

Aw man, these guys sure did know how to make it hard not to cry in front of them. Finally, I sniffed out an "Okay." And all was right again as Shameless put some Fettuccini Alfredo in front of me. I still had to eat softer foods, but man was my stomach feeling ravenous as the smell of the garlic and cheese set my taste buds to watering. The minute the first forkful hit my mouth I was done for. I didn't even come for air until my plate was empty. Neither man said a word to me about my piggish behavior either.

"Sorry, I feel like I've been starving since I've only been eating softer foods." My voice sounded much better these days, but still had a raspy quality to it that reminded me of long-time smokers.

"You don't have to apologize for anything, baby girl, I'm just happy to see you getting your appetite back," Shameless told me with a smile while Rage hugged me into a tighter embrace. He had been doing that a lot lately, since I was attacked.

For two days, he only left my bed to go to the bathroom, get me more food when it took too long for one of the others to check on us, and once to take a call about something happening down in Georgia. That was all I could gather before he stepped out. He hadn't made any moves on me. No kisses. No making out. He was just there for me to provide comfort while nursing me back to health. It was the sweetest damn thing I'd ever seen, not to mention selfless. I was sure he had more important things to do, and yet he was there with me.

"I want you to take it easy tonight, darlin'" Rage whispered into my ear.

"There's nothing wrong with my hands, legs, or lungs. I'll be just fine."

He gave me a bit of a squeeze. "I mean it, you've been laid up for a few days and coming down off some pretty heavy meds. That takes more out of you than you realize. If you need to sit, you park your ass and watch while Rabbit works twice as hard."

Shameless laughed at that, his eyes twinkling brightly in amusement. "I second that. You're more important than assholes being served drinks."

"Those assholes are your brothers," I reminded them both.

"Yup, but your ours to take care of, so they can fuck right off and wait for their drinks." Rage's statement was no nonsense and, if I'm being honest, really freaking wonderful to hear. It had been a while since I was someone's top priority. Shameless sat another, smaller plate of the pasta dish in front of me and told me to eat up just as Iceman ducked his head in the room.

"Shame, Rage, I need to see you both for a few minutes."

He noticed I was there too and quickly added, "You gonna be okay in here on your own for a minute?"

"Sure," I mumbled around the mouth full of food I had just shoveled in. Rage kissed the top of my head, and the men dispersed, leaving me to do my thing.

They weren't gone more than five minutes when a short lady, probably in her mid-forties, and starting to round out in the middle, walked into the break room. Her hair was mostly black but shot through with streaks of silver that added to her beauty rather than taking from it. She glanced around, and then her cool blue eyes locked on mine as she grimaced with disapproval.

"You must be the one causing all the drama around here lately." Her statement rolled right off my shoulders since I didn't know her from Adam. I continued eating, and ignored her, because honestly, how did a person respond to that shit anyway?

"Shit-stirrer and rude as hell, huh? Well, I am the Queen Bee around here little girl, so I suggest you sit up, quit stuffing your face like a little pig, and behave accordingly unless you want to get what's coming to you."

"What in the absolute fuck?" Spinner roared from the doorway. He glanced between me with a forkful of pasta stalled just shy of my gaping mouth and the older lady who was in serious need of a throat punch. He glanced back at me finally and ignored the older woman.

"Sweetheart, the guys have some questions for you, and they can't wait. I came to see if I could snag you before you went on shift. Gotta say, I'm glad as fuck I showed up when I did."

Then he turned pure fury on the wonder-cunt who was still glaring daggers in my direction, thinking he was glad he showed up to see how disrespectful I was being to her. I didn't think that was why he was pissed, but she had yet to clue into the situation.

Her smirk said it all as she continued to stare me down. "I warned you, little trouble making whores get put in their place around here."

The words were spat out as if I had done something to personally offend the woman. I was beginning to think that maybe she was friends with Jezzie and Tallie or something. She seemed a bit old to be a BRAT, but what did I really know about all that? Clearly, I didn't know enough considering I had someone angry with me every time I came into public spaces.

"You better fucking believe Iceman is going to hear about you verbally attacking Charlie in a place where she was just physically attacked only days ago, Carol." It was obvious from his tone that Spinner didn't care for Carol.

It could have just been that he didn't care for the tone she had taken with me for no good damn reason. Personally, I didn't give a shit. I still didn't know whom this Carol woman was, or why she thought she ran the show around here, but apparently someone forgot to clue her into the man's world she was living in.

"Both of you, come with me now."

Carol turned to Spinner then, a stunned look on her face. "I was just introducing myself to the little bitch who has been causing so many problems for the club, and she sat there ignoring me," the woman huffed indignantly.

"Shut. Your. Fucking. Mouth." Spinner annunciated each word with barely contained rage. I simply stood and walked out the door he was standing beside while we both waited for Carol to get herself in gear.

"I don't have to follow your orders, Spinner," Carol snipped like a petulant child.

"Get to the fucking office, NOW!" He yelled in her face, and finally, the bitch cowered while all the men in the common area stood to see what the commotion was. I heard a couple mumbling how it was 'about time' and 'someone's finally putting that bitch in her place' as we walked by. She shook with undisguised anger, as I walked my happy ass to the office knowing I wasn't the one who was going to get my butt reamed for being a complete twat.

As soon as Spinner pulled open the office door and the men inside could see that Spinner and I had a third person with us, Iceman stood from behind his desk. "Why are you here, Carol?" He did not sound the least bit happy to see her.

"Ask Spinner, he just screamed at me in front of everyone to get my ass to the office." I giggled at the fact that she even put on a pout for him, trying to look every bit the victim she wasn't. Her glare towards me when I laughed out loud was not missed by anyone else.

Iceman turned to Spinner; not looking the least bit upset with him, and simply said, "Explain."

"I went to go snag Charlie out of..."

He didn't get far before the bitch interrupted him. "I think I should explain first, because he walked in halfway through our encounter."

"You don't decide who gets to speak. Sit down, shut up,

and I'll get to you when I am good and damn ready." Iceman's admonishment was cold and hate fueled. He then looked at Spinner. "Continue."

"So, I watched as Carol walked in back, but I was still crossing the commons. By the time I got to the door, I heard her voice raised." He repeated what Carol had been saying to me, and every man in the room went immediately on edge and stared at the woman as if they each wanted the opportunity to tear her apart.

"Is that accurate?" Iceman turned to ask me.

"The only part missing was her initial comment to me that I ignored," I explained.

"And that was?"

"As soon as she walked into the kitchen she said, 'You must be the one causing all the drama around here lately,'" I told them with a shrug of my shoulders. "I didn't respond, and that's when Spinner overheard the rest. Iceman tipped his head back, eyes on the ceiling as he seemed to be digesting that information.

"Normally, I'd ask you all to leave so I could handle my old lady in private, but since she can't seem to mind her own fucking business, keep her mouth shut, and out of club biz, attacking our guests…" he stopped listing off her faults to check his anger momentarily. "You all get to watch."

"That's not how…" Carol started to say.

Iceman sat behind his desk, clicked on his computer for a minute, and then turned the monitor around so everyone in the room could see. Then he hit a button, and video played on the screen of me stuffing my face in the kitchen, and a side-by-side view of the door as Carol came through. The woman, not the video version of her, blanched.

"When did you put cameras in there?" she had the nerve to ask.

"After Charlie was attacked the last time," he answered. I watched as Carol's shoulders drooped.

"It's just that you've been so stressed and preoccupied and all I kept hearing were whispers of this bi-woman." She had been about to say bitch until she saw Rage flinch towards her. "I was sick of seeing you stressed, and wondering if she was the other woman that you've had tucked away."

Whoa. This bitch. Her assumptions and airing dirty laundry in front of everyone could not go down well at all. I glanced over at Iceman, and he looked damn near ready to blow his fucking top.

"You stupid fucking cunt. I've told you before, there is no one else. You are fucking headache enough for me to deal with. Wanna see me less stressed? Keep yourself out of my club's fucking business! You know how it works, you've been in this game for more years than you've been my old lady, so don't start acting ignorant now. Club business is NOT your business. EVER. If I wanna fuck around, there's plenty of club pussy here for me to do it with, and I sure as fuck don't have time for a dedicated side piece. You don't have to worry yourself over me looking stressed anymore either sugar, because I'll be staying at the clubhouse until I figure out what I'm going to do about you."

He glanced around at the men in the room who did

nothing but offer him their silent support. "Now, as to the business of you mouthing off to Charlie. Hear me now, that girl," he pointed a finger at me, "just think of her as your better. She is the alpha chick around here. Since I'm pretty damn sure Rage is going to claim her as his, and Shameless already claimed her as a daughter, and she was Brazen's actual daughter before he passed. That means she has more pull in this place than you ever have or will have in the future."

"You're the President!" Carol moaned.

"And you are nothing to me right now." Again, whoa. "You were warned before not to get involved in shit that you didn't belong in. Then you came in here and tried to call both Charlie and Spinner out as liars when I have video proof."

"I didn't know you had video."

"Exactly, which just means you proved to me you can't be trusted. Loyalty and Honor above all. You have it or you don't. This is not the first time you've proven you don't have what it takes to be the President's old lady, but it damn sure will be the last time." He huffed as he sat back down in his seat. "You aren't being banned from the club, but only out of respect for Steel. Your son will be made aware and if you make one more misstep involving the club you will be banned permanently." He nodded toward the office door then. "Get out and get off Club property. Don't let me catch you back here for at least a month. And when you do decide to come back in this clubhouse, it will be with an apology on your lips for the entire club, especially Charlie, about your rude-as-shit behavior. Am I understood?"

She nodded and stood to leave. That was not good enough for Iceman though. "I asked if I was understood," he voiced sternly.

"Yes, you're understood," she answered in a hushed tone then proceeded to leave. Iceman was immediately on the phone.

"Yeah, you're to follow Carol. Make sure she leaves the property and keep eyes on her for a couple days. Report back with anything out of the ordinary." He got ready to hang up and then stopped, seeming to think of something else. "Bring her leathers to me too. I don't care what kind of fight she puts up. They no longer belong to her."

He hung up and turned his attention back to me. The guys seemed stunned by whatever that meant. I just sat there, waiting. This was not the reason I had been summoned to the office so there was still the possibility of one more shoe dropping on me today.

"Charlie," he huffed out a sigh. "Fuck! I'm really sorry that cunt got in your face. She's been trying my patience for a couple years now, and my failure to deal with my personal problems cost you today, for that you have my apology."

I looked Iceman in the eye because I wanted to be sure he heard me. "Don't ever apologize to me for another person acting out. That is beyond your control. I appreciate you handling it, and having my back, as well as trusting that what I told you was the truth. That means a lot."

Iceman smiled at me then turned to Rage. "You better lock that shit down before someone else sees what they're missing out on."

Rage smirked, bringing out just one dimple to play with the maneuver as he tossed a wink my way. I rolled my eyes at him, and the guys in the room laughed. "The best kind of sassy there is." He smiled as he glanced between the both of us and then he was looking at only me again, face growing serious.

"We called you in here, because we need to know a few things. I understand you were kept in the dark about a lot in your marriage, for obvious reason, but you knew about the connection to the Modern Saints MC, so we're hoping you might know a little more."

I thought about it and shrugged. "Feel free to ask specific questions, and maybe it will trigger something I haven't thought of on my own. All I know, off the top of my head, is that Josh was the financial backing for a supposedly legal brothel. I heard Modern Saints in conjunction with it, and honestly thought that was going to be the name of the place or something considering the longer version sounded more like a catchphrase than a brothel name." I had to take a minute where I massaged my throat because it still hurt to speak so much. Rage moved toward a mini fridge in the corner of the office and slipped a drink out to hand to me.

"I saw that woman, the one he was apparently dating the whole time, outside of our place once, and she was wearing a t-shirt with a Modern Saints logo on it. It looked like it was more about bikers than a whorehouse, so I wasn't sure what to think. I figured maybe they were catering to a rougher clientele or something."

"Did you ever see any bikers hanging around your place too?" Spinner asked.

I thought about it for a minute. "Not specifically, but we lived in a condo downtown just a couple blocks off the strip, so there was always bike traffic."

"How good are you with faces? Do you think you could recognize someone if we showed you pictures?"

"Sure, but why does it matter if you already know the Club is involved somehow?"

"That's Club Business, sweet girl," Shameless told me.

"It's also my life. I get your need to keep club business separate, and if it didn't have to do with me personally, I would be fine with you all keeping everything to yourselves. In this case, my life is literally at stake, and I need to know if I have more people out there willing to kill me for what they think I'm worth, or if this will truly all be over once Josh and his whore are taken care of." Every eye in the room deferred to Iceman.

"You're right. In this case, you get a little more detail than I'd otherwise give. We have reason to believe that only a small faction of Modern Saints is involved in a human trafficking operation. Their Prez, Davis Walker, is claiming he knows nothing about Josh providing financial backing in Wild Honey, which is the name of their brothel. It's a club business, so they wouldn't want to pull in outside investors who weren't interested in joining the club."

"So, you think his investment went toward buying girls as part of a trafficking ring since the brothel he thought he was investing in wasn't real?"

"Partly. We think Walker, he's known as DW to us, has bigger problems in his own backyard, and some of his people want to get into a more lucrative game. Buying and selling women is a gold mine, especially when they're dealing with high-end transactions that they get from rich bastards who are looking for very specific fantasies. Our brothers in Cedar Falls and Sierra High have been dealing with a rival club that have been bottom feeding, doing snatch and grabs of girls. When they were telling us about it, we had another angle to look into after DW claimed Josh had no involvement with the club. Obviously, DW has some bad apples in his cart, and he should know who he needs to weed out."

"We also needed to know, because when the hit he put on you failed, there was another put out in its place, only this one was a little different." Shameless added.

"He wants to sell me?" I asked doing the crazy outlaw math in my head.

Shameless nodded. "They have a buyer who has a particular kink for sexual violence against women, and one who makes snuff films out of it too."

"Snuff films?" I asked, and then wished I didn't when I got my answer.

"The women are abused in every way possible until they die, and it's all filmed for future sales. It's among the most expensive porn in the world, because the clients can verify that girl in the film died. After they're used for filming, the girls' bodies are strategically placed somewhere they're certain to be found." Spinner explained, and I felt as though I was going to be sick. I was certainly saying goodbye to my appetite as quickly as I had gotten it back.

Rage moved to me in a space quicker than a heartbeat and pulled me over to the couch where he sat first and then pulled me on his lap. "We are not going to let anything like that happen to you, darlin'. I promise you that."

"You're damn right we're not."

"This is why we didn't want to tell you, because I'd rather you not have this worry added to the burden you've already been carrying around." Iceman informed me. "I do have good news though," he stated, making me look back up at him. "We heard from Bishop."

That perked me up. My attention was completely on Iceman now. "He's doing just fine and checking into the people involved in the trafficking ring. Once we gave him our theories, he was able to piece some things together for us. We're closer, but we need to keep you as close to home as possible. I don't want you feeling like a prisoner, Charlie, but..."

I held my hand up in the air and shook my head. "No need to placate me there. If I have to stay locked in my room for the next few weeks or months to know I'm safe when I'm finally let out, I will. Running is exhausting, and that future you painted that they have planned for me... Yeah, I'm okay feeling cooped up here." Rage held me tighter to him when he felt me shudder.

"Well, Shame and Rage mentioned to me that you talked about possibly choreographing some dances for the girls at Rosy's. I was thinking we could bring them over a couple days a week, during the day, and have you work with them here. We have a stage – though somewhat smaller – in the commons. It has a pole too, so if you think..."

"YES!" I yelped, interrupting him. As everyone's snickering grew louder, I blushed and then calmly said, "Yes, that would be fantastic."

"Alright then, we'll get that set up for you. Rage or Shameless will keep you updated about the rest of it."

"Okay," I told them. "Thank you."

"You don't have to thank any of us for taking care of you. We look after family. We'll have some pictures for you to look over as soon as DW gets them to us, though."

13. WAKING TO A NIGHTMARE

Hot breath on my neck woke me from the sensual dream I'd been having about Rage. We hadn't done anything more than him holding me or kissing me on the top of my head. There had been no kissing, intimate touches, and no sex since I'd been recuperating, but boy did my body wish there had been. A very small part of me was still disturbed by the thought that I wanted to have sex with another man when I was still a married woman.

Yes, I know how crazy that sounds considering the man I'm married to is trying to have me killed or sold into sexual slavery so that someone could kill me in an even more horrific way than he originally planned. Yet, when I took my vows, I meant them. No, that wasn't even the part that bothered me, because I think my allegiance to those vows ended when I found out not only did my husband want me dead, but also that he had been with another woman for the entirety of our relationship. That fact still made me cringe. No, my problem with moving on to someone else was that I wasn't doing it with a clean slate. Whoever I decided to be with next, whether it be Rage or someone else, deserved to have all of me. He deserved more than me being stuck with another man's name and a price tag on my head.

While my thoughts were running wild, I remembered what had woken me up in the first place. Someone breathed heavily against my neck. The veil of sleep lifted, and I began to panic, because I had gone to bed alone.

The breath at my neck stank strongly of whiskey while the pungent aroma of stale cigarettes and cheap perfume also clung to the air surrounding me. Slowly, I began to pull away before the insane pounding of my heart gave way to my panic and informed my intruder that I was indeed awake. I got out from under the solid arm of muscle that had me pinned to the bed, and moved to the door that would lead me out into the hallway where I could scream for help.

When I opened the door, and the light from the hall filtered in, I saw that it was Rage who had crawled in bed with me. His familiar scent had been covered by all the whiskey fumes seeping from his pores and on his breath. What the hell? I moved closer, leaving the bedroom door propped open for light, and that was when I saw the lipstick marks all over his face and neck, along with a giant hickey that certainly hadn't been there earlier in the day. His pants were unbuttoned, his shirt was missing, and I had no clue where his boots or socks had gotten off to, but they weren't in my room.

"You okay, lady?" A man called from the hallway. It was my across the hall neighbor, Flint.

"Do you, um… do you know where Shameless is right

now?" I asked, trying to control the edge that was in my voice. Inside, my emotions teetered between dramatic girly hysterics and supreme anger while trying to keep calm on the outside in the wake of the absolutely heartbreaking mess I had just woken up to. Only moments ago, I'd been thinking about how I wanted to come to this man with a clean slate, and he had the audacity to climb into my bed drunk with evidence of another woman all over him? My heart clenched so tightly in my chest that it physically hurt. Flint peeked inside my room then shuffled back as he huffed, "Damn," then turned on his heels. "I'll go get Shame for you."

"Thanks." The word came out so quiet I doubt he heard me. It took about ten minutes before anyone showed up, but eventually, Shameless came crashing down the hall looking concerned.

"What's going on sweet girl?"

I pointed into my room. Shameless, not taking in the complete picture at first, smiled. "He wanted to be close to you, huh? The boy had a rough night. I don't blame him for seeking you out." He turned to me then, noticing the sick look I must have had on my face. "I thought you two were okay and working towards something?"

I grabbed his hand and pulled him into the room. "I woke up to find him draped across me, stinking of whiskey, perfume that I don't wear, and looking like that!" I almost shouted the last couple words as I let my anger get the best of me when I pointed to his neck and face.

"Holy fuck!" Shameless growled. "What did you do, Rage?"

"I don't give a shit what he did, or why he did it, but get

him the hell out of my room. I'm going to need a change of sheets too, so if you could tell me where to find those, that'd be great. If not, I'll just go read while I wash these."

The pity in Shameless's eyes when he looked back up at me, was something I couldn't stand. "I'm gonna go see if Rabbit is in his room to help you get him out." He tipped his head towards me, in agreement with me, and I left.

I knocked, loudly, on Rabbit's door before I tried the handle. It wasn't locked so I pushed it open to find him in bed. He was not there alone, but thankfully they had only been sleeping, and I didn't walk in on something I really didn't want to see.

He lifted his head toward the door and noticed it was me. "Showgirl? What's going on?" he asked as he lifted himself up to a sitting position while maintaining his modesty with the sheet.

"Shameless needs your help taking the trash out of my room."

"Trash?" he questioned. "What the fuck, Charlie?"

"Please," I begged. "Just come help!" I turned and left his room so he could get dressed. By the time I got back down to my room, Rabbit came out of his door securing the button on his jeans. As he moved, he asked once again, "What's going on?"

I pointed to where Shameless stood with fists balled up and shaking his head. "This stupid motherfucker," he started to say and glanced at Rabbit. "If he wasn't completely fucked out of his brain, I would beat the shit out of him this time."

"What the fuck for?" Rabbit turned to me wild eyed. "Did he attempt something with you that you didn't want?"

I scoffed at that. "Did I want to wake up with a freshly fucked – by someone else – whiskey factory draped over me? No, I certainly did not. He didn't touch me inappropriately though, because he had someone else for that before he crawled his sorry ass into my bed."

Rabbit's eyes flashed with murderous fury as he glanced back and forth between myself, Shameless, and the lump of useless asshole who was still passed out in my bed. Whereas Shame held himself back, Rabbit moved forward and took in all the evidence of the previous night that there was to see on Rage's body. Then, he slapped Rage across the face with his open palm. The sound reverberated through the room and was successful in rousing the bastard.

"What the fuck!" Rage roared out as he came to a sitting position with inhuman speed. Then he grabbed onto his head and groaned loudly.

"You stupid fuckwad!" Rabbit yelled at him.

"I fuckin' trusted you with my baby girl," Shameless added.

"What the fuck? Can you assholes tone it down?"

"Tone it down?" Rabbit screamed at him. "Do you know where the fuck you are right now?"

I could see Rage glance around and shake his head. "Charlie's room," he mumbled almost incoherently.

"Charlie's room, motherfucker. You crawled in her bed, spooned up to her..." Rabbit cut off his spiel when Rage smiled a big goofy smile. Then he smacked Rage across the face again before snatching him up off the bed and dragging him to the bathroom. He flicked on the light and pushed

Rage in front of the mirror. "You crawled into her bed looking like this you stupid fuck!"

Rage's eyes immediately bulged as his hand went to the nasty mark on his neck. Then moved to scrub the lipstick off his face. "What the fuck?" he growled. "How the fuck?" He turned panicked eyes to Rabbit then. "What the fuck happened? I don't... I wouldn't..." Then he smacked his own head. "I don't remember shit. Who the fuck was I with that did this? I was drinking, and then..." he just stood there blankly as if there was nothing after that. "I can't fucking remember anything beyond the commons and taking a shot with..." His hands went to his head again where he tugged at his hair. "Somebody?" he whispered questioningly.

Then something else dawned on him. "Where's Charlie? Did she see me like this?" Again, everything he said was slurred so it came out more like "whirs Chaw-wee? Id see me zis?" While slurred, the panic in his voice was still evident.

"Of course, she did, fuckwad! Who do you think came to get me to remove you from her room?"

"Noooo!" He cried. The pain in his voice almost broke my resolve, but not quite all of it. "Fuck, no! Everything was good. Who did this?"

"You did this!" Rabbit screamed at him, and I looked away then, moving over to strip my bed of the tainted sheets that smelled like whiskey and bad decisions. None of which belonged to me. "Come on, let's go," Rabbit said as both he and Shameless moved to prop up the man I thought I was falling for.

As soon as he noticed me, Rage called out, "Charlie! Fuck, Charlie, I'm so sorry darlin'! Don't know what, how, this happened." His words were slurring together even more, and he looked absolutely pathetic as his damn near limp body was maneuvered out into the hallway, his feet dragging for the most part, while Shameless and Rabbit supported all his weight.

I received one more piteous look from Flint when I went to shut my door. "Sorry, babe." He got out before I shut and locked the door behind me. I also engaged the bolt lock too for good measure, something I hadn't used in the entire time I had been staying with the Aces High MC.

A part of me had been waiting for the other shoe to drop. I figured it would come in the form of something to do with Josh though, and not another betrayal, this time by the man I was falling for. Fool me once, shame on you. Fool me twice, shame on me. What in the hell had I been thinking? These people lived by an entirely different set of rules than I did. I should have known better when I watched the way Iceman interacted with his wife, old lady, or whatever the hell she was to him.

A knock at the door startled me out of my thoughts. "Baby girl, it's me. You wanna open up?" Shameless asked me.

"No. I'm going back to bed," I called out through the door.

"Without clean sheets?" His question was laced in humor as I groaned, looking at the mess I'd made while stripping my bed and tossing the contaminated sheets in the corner. There was glitter on them. Glitter! That just made me angry all over again. I stomped over and opened the door to Shameless holding out a fresh set of sheets.

"Thank you," I told him as I accepted the bundle. He went to gather the dirty set, and I was kind enough to warn him since he hadn't been the one to anger me. "There's glitter all over them." The disgust in my voice made him hesitate in picking them up. "Do you know what glitter is, Shame?" I didn't wait for an answer and continued my rant while Shameless paused mid-way to grabbing the offensive linens. "It's the herpes of the dance world. I'll find that shit it on everything for weeks now!" I cried out, almost at shrieking level. Then I glanced around the room and sighed. "Maybe I won't have to be here that much longer."

"What?" Shameless growled. "I thought you said you'd like to stay?"

"I don't think this world is for me," I told him honestly as I sat defeated on my stripped-bare mattress.

"I'm not sure what to tell you sweet girl, because I don't want you to ever think I'm putting my brothers before you, but I don't know what the hell happened tonight. That was not the Rage we all know."

"No? Because it's not like he hasn't done something similar since I've been here. He was with Jezzie that night making a show of things while I worked the bar."

"Fuck!" Shameless snarled as he sat in my desk chair. "That wasn't exactly in character either, but I get what you're saying." His elbows rested on his knees as he tucked his head into his hands and exhaled a sigh. "I don't want to lose you because he fucked up. There's more to the club than Rage and whatever the hell caused him to end up like that tonight."

"Normally, I'd agree, but I saw the way Iceman spoke to

his wife too. What if I mess up and get bitchy with someone? Will I be treated like that too?"

Shameless shook his head. "I wish you had been around longer to know the dynamics at play here. Carol was already on the way out because she's been unfaithful to Iceman. Not to mention, she tries to pull shit with the other old ladies and BRATs on a regular basis. There's a lot of history behind how he behaved with her. I'm not going to tell you we're all angels or that we'll be perfect all the time, but you won't get that anywhere, as you well know." When he glanced back up at me his eyes were glassy and pleading. "I don't think I can lose you again, sweet girl. I had to say goodbye once when you were all dresses, bows, and pigtails. Having to say goodbye now too would kill me."

"Shame, I didn't plan on going far away. I just don't think I should stick around here and watch..."

"I swear, I'm going to kill that fucker when he sobers up," Shameless grumbled. "That's if he doesn't do the job himself when he realizes what happened."

I waved his comment off. "I have a sneaking suspicion he'll be feeling plenty of pain tomorrow. He made the decision to get shitfaced, whatever happened as a result is on him and he can live with it. We weren't anything anyway."

"Now, that's a load of shit," Shameless scoffed. "We all saw it. Iceman even called him out on it and told him he better step to it and lock you down as quick as possible."

"Mmm, and the same night he gets blitzed and fucks around with some glitter-bomb wielding whore. So, like I said, we have nothing. Even if we were working towards something," I swallowed hard. "There's nothing left now. He destroyed any chance of that tonight. I forgave him the first time and gave him the benefit of the doubt that it wouldn't be how he would react every time something bothered him, but tonight proved I was wrong." I anxiously twisted my fingers up in each other.

"Sweet girl, I wish I could fix it for you. The one damn night I turn in early, and shit goes down that defies fucking logic. I don't get it. He had no reason to act out of jealousy or anything else. So, I just don't get it." I gave Shameless the look that said I didn't care for the speculation game. He raised his arms in surrender. "Okay, I'll get out of here and leave you to it, but please, know you are loved and wanted here, baby girl. Don't let stupid shit run you off."

I nodded and gave him a weak smile. He gathered me up in his arms and hugged me tight. Just as quickly he released me, gathered up the nasty, glitter-infected sheets, and left quietly. I moved to go throw the lock behind him when my door slid open once more. "Did you forget the pillowcase?" I asked thinking it was Shameless. To my surprise Spinner stood there.

"Spinner?" I questioned. He quickly moved into the room and shut the door, locking it behind himself too. It was the first time since our first meeting that I'd been nervous around the man.

"I need you to sit down and listen to me for a minute. Rabbit came to me wanting to kill Rage. I had to explain to him what I'm about to tell you, and if you don't believe me, I'll take you down to see the video Rabbit and Iceman are going over now. Carol wasn't the only one who didn't realize we'd installed new cameras recently. Rage was set up, Charlie. He was drugged, made to look like he cheated, and then brought to your room. We know who did it, and I think there may be more to the story than just the setup. I think it was done to make you run from us."

"To make me run?" I asked. "What in the world for?"

"We're working that out, but what I can tell you is that I think some of the people who were recently removed from our club have gone to the enemy."

"The enemy?"

"Josh and whoever he's working with to find and kill you."

"Son of a..." I started to say. Spinner nodded, but then cut me off.

"I don't have all the details to finish playing connect the dots, but from what I've seen, it looks pretty obvious to me. I won't know more until we finish going through all the footage, but now we'll know who we should have been watching all along. I just wanted to let you know something so that you wouldn't..."

It was my turn to cut him off. "So that I wouldn't run like they wanted me to?"

"Exactly."

"I was never going to do that." I sighed. "I'm not stupid. I may have been uncomfortable here after what happened with Rage, but I'd rather be uncomfortable than dead."

Spinner smiled widely then. "I'm happy to hear you're thinking with your head instead of letting your emotions rule your actions."

"Don't give me too much credit. I just told Shameless

that I wanted to move out of here as soon as my issues are cleared up."

Spinner's smile disappeared. "I hope you'll rethink that now that you know it was a setup."

I frowned at him. "You can tell me it was a setup, and you can even show me the video, but it's going to take some time to forget what I woke up to tonight. They had a solid plan considering how things went down with Rage and that skank bitch the last time. It automatically made the whole scenario they cooked up easier to believe. It's... well, I need to wrap my head around everything. This world, my world, it's all so crazy right now that I honestly don't know how to process everything that keeps being thrown at me."

Spinner nodded. "If you need to talk," he started and sighed. "I know you have a friendship with Rabbit, and Shameless is like a father figure to you. I haven't been around as much, because I'm trying to keep Rosy's on track after having to get rid of our previous piece of shit manager for lining his pockets with club money. I need you to know though, if you need someone else, I can be there for you too."

"Thanks, Spinner, I appreciate that."

"Well Showgirl, my brother's an idiot on the best day so I figure you'll need a friend with a brain eventually." He worked his magic, and did what he intended, making me laugh.

"I think you're more like your brother than you like to admit. That sounds just like something he'd say about you."

"Yeah, but in my case it's the truth though. With him it's all lies!" He chuckled as I laughed again.

14. DANCING IS THERAPY

SWEAT POURED DOWN MY BACK AS I SPUN OUT, KICKED HIGH, AND dropped straight into a split. The girls from Rosy's who had been brought over this morning, more than likely as a distraction for me, started to clap.

"Holy crap, that was insane," Mel told me as she tossed her hand out to help me up.

"It's a simple combo, just fast paced. It will be perfect for some of the hardcore music you ladies dance to." One of the women scoffed at my statement. "What's the matter?" I asked, calling her out.

"You keep referring to us as ladies," she stated evenly.

"And?" I asked not seeing what the problem was.

"We're strippers, sweetheart. That's just about as far from a lady as we can get."

I marched right up to her, and while she was shorter than me, I managed to look her in the eye anyway without acting like I was looking down my nose at her.

"You are dancers. You earn money showing off your beautiful bodies and your amazing moves. There is no part of that description that says you can't also be a lady. Even if you go out with your man afterward and have the wildest, kinkiest, dirtiest sex in the history of sex that does not mean you can't be a lady. You deserve respect for being a human being. You deserve it for taking the initiative and doing what you must in order to survive, get by, or get ahead. So, don't let anyone tell you that you are defined by the job you do, the clothes you wear, or the things you like. The only thing that defines you is how you allow others to make you feel. Today, you are all ladies because that is what I see. Either keep the title or feel free to show me why you deserve something with less respect. I'll follow your lead."

Her eyes were glossy, but she just tipped her head in respect and moved back to her position instead of arguing with me. Mel, on the other hand, ran up and gave me the biggest hug I think I'd ever received. In fact, her legs were wrapped around my waist as she hugged the absolute shit out of me. That is the position we found ourselves in when the guys came out of their meeting.

"Hot damn! We've been missing out on all the action!" Rabbit called out from across the commons.

"What in the absolute fuck?" Someone else asked.

"I'd like to be the cheese in the middle of that sandwich," Flint shouted. Then, "Ouch, motherfucker!" Someone had apparently slapped him in the back of the head. When I glanced over, I noticed Rage was standing right behind him. He looked away quickly when he noticed I saw him though.

It made me wonder if he had really been drugged or just seduced, because that was the reaction of a guilty man.

Mel climbed off me. It didn't hurt that she was only four feet, ten inches tall and weighed next to nothing, so her jumping up on me was like getting attacked by a small child. Although, she had more boobs than I did, which was why the guys were drooling so hard.

"Okay, ladies," I emphasized the word, "I think we can wrap this up for now. Practice tonight and tomorrow, and then when we meet up the day after, we'll work on nailing the whole thing down."

"I'd like to do some nailing, myself," one of the guys muttered as he passed by us to hit the back hallway to the main kitchen area. The girls giggled and flounced their wares as they gathered all their things together.

"It must be really cool being able to live here with all these sexy beasts," the girl who called herself Star said to me as she stuffed her extra clothes into her bag.

"It's interesting, I'll give you that," I told her; not really knowing any of these girls well enough to reveal any of my ongoing drama.

"Rage!" Sasha, the woman who questioned me for calling them all ladies yelled when she saw him. She ran over, squealing like a stuck pig, ready to pounce on him when Rabbit stepped in the way to block her. She stopped mid-run and pouted at being shut out that way.

"Aw, baby, come on. You know one of these days you're going to give in and forget the rules so we can finally get together."

"I'm taken," Rage said as he sidestepped both her and Rabbit.

"Since when?" she asked with an indignant tone.

Rabbit chuckled. "Since that one showed up and swept him off his feet with her sweet-as-sin smile," he announced pointing at me.

Jaws dropped. Sasha narrowed her eyes at me. Then she flounced back in Rage's general direction. "Her teaching us new routines makes her an employee of Rosy's too. So, if we're off limits, she is too."

Rabbit laughed. Rage stared at her like she was stupid. Spinner came over and stood directly in front of Sasha. "Stop while you're ahead. Charlie is family first here, and she doesn't work for Rosy's. She's doing me a favor by helping you girls get some new material to liven the place up. I'm warning you now, you give her any shit at all, and you will find yourself without employment. No questions asked."

Sasha poked her lip out in an even more exaggerated pout before turning back to the stage Mel and I were still before she came to grab her things. She didn't even make eye contact with me, so she must have been at least a little smart. Once she walked away, Mel snagged my attention. "Don't worry about Sasha. She's been crushing on Rage forever, and he's never once reciprocated, so don't think, because she acted all familiar that he has. That's just wishful thinking on her part."

"Thanks, but Rage is not mine, so it doesn't matter," I stated simply.

Mel's eyes grew larger as she stared at something over

my shoulder. "Might wanna tell him that then," she whispered as she grabbed her stuff and hauled ass out of there. I knew who would be there when I turned around, but I wasn't necessarily ready to face him.

"Can we talk for a minute?"

"I have to clean up out here, and then go get a shower." I started to tick off a much longer list, but he stopped me.

"The prospects will take care of this mess," he said as he looked around taking in the nothing that cluttered up the stage now that the girls had taken all their belongings with them. "Go get your shower if you need to. I'll wait, but we're talking as soon as you're done. We should have talked after the first incident, and it's my fault for blowing it off after what happened with Beaver. We will have that chat now though. I won't knowingly make the same mistake twice."

I sighed, not really having a choice since I lived and worked near him. I glanced around the room, but no one looked like they would be on my side either. Too bad, because honestly, I could see the black and purple hickey ridding up from under the collar of his shirt and it made me sick to my stomach. Instead of trying to find someone to help me out, I nodded my head and took off up the stairs toward my room. I had the feeling I was about to take the longest shower in the history of showers.

Thirty minutes later, I realized I couldn't actually stay in the shower any longer. First, the water had started to go cold. Secondly, I was pruning up worse than an old lady left in a swimming pool too long. Thirdly, well, avoidance had never been my thing. Granted, I'd been on the run from my murderous husband for nearly a year, but that avoidance was about self-preservation rather than not wanting to deal.

Josh's cousin was FBI, his close friend worked for Vegas PD. I really didn't feel I had anyone I could trust to turn to for help. At least, not until I was reacquainted with my estranged motorcycle family. That thought brought me back around to the man I was avoiding still. As I towel dried myself and started in on my hair, I thought about our situation.

We really weren't anything other than touchy-feely sort of friends. Even if he had gone out and fucked someone last night, I couldn't be mad. We never had a talk about being together, let alone being exclusive. Sure, it was assumed in a way with how he was so intimate with me and how the other guys assumed he'd want me for his old lady. The fact was that those words never came from him though. They were just that, assumptions. We'd never been more intimate than me sitting on his lap fully clothed, or him laying half naked with me in my bed while I was drugged up and healing from being attacked. We had never even kissed, so I was confused about why I felt the way I did. Just because I wanted more with him, just because I felt like my world was on fire when he was around, didn't make it a something real.

Knowing all of that didn't help take away the hurt and betrayal I had felt at finding him in my bed the way I did. It certainly didn't help to add in the confusing layer that it was something that had been done to him, and not something he'd set out to do himself. Then, there was the added layer of guilt I carried over being mad at him, because essentially, he'd been a victim. I couldn't even imagine how he was feeling about that right now. He had to be ashamed, angry, hurt, and a whole slew of other emotions just knowing someone incapacitated him and did things he had no control over, and probably didn't remember. Ugh.

Finally, I tossed open the door to my bathroom, heading into my room for fresh clothes, when I noticed the man sitting on my bed staring at me slack-jawed, eyes wide, and unable to look away from my very naked body. As soon as I got over the initial shock, I screeched, threw myself back through the bathroom door, and grabbed one of the large bath sheets with my shaking hands. Holy hell, Rage had just seen every little piece of me. How in the hell had he gotten in my room? I could have sworn I'd locked my door.

A knock sounded on the bathroom door then. "Charlie?" he called to me.

"What are you doing in my room?" My voice was pitchy as I squeaked out the question.

"I came to talk. You said you were showering first, but you left the room unlocked. I assumed you wanted me to wait here. I'm sorry. I can... um, shit."

I wrapped the bath sheet around myself. It was a long, fluffy slice of heaven that stretched above my boobs down to my knees like a good towel should. Once I had everything tucked in place, I opened the door again.

"I wasn't expecting you to wait in my room, and I'm not sure why the door was unlocked," I told him as I moved to get around his bulk while attempting to get to the closet, where I grabbed some clothes before scurrying back into my bathroom to get dressed.

Rage stood there scowling at my door, as I'd done a

moment before, and it made me wonder. How in the hell had my door been unlocked? I knew for absolute certain that I'd thrown the lock. I could hear Rage through the door talking to someone. "Check the cameras and let me know. If someone tampered with it, we need to move now rather than later. I won't put her at risk any more than necessary to ferret these bastards out." He was quiet for a moment, then "The cabin, maybe. Only if I have to though, because I still think she's safer with all of us around."

I opened the door and stood watching him. He didn't shy away or try to hide his conversation from me. "Yeah, just let me know who did it. If it's someone different, we'll have another person to question. If not, maybe that's a good indicator that our infiltration is on a smaller scale than we thought." Rage glanced at me, his face a mask of whatever emotions were boiling below the surface.

"Yeah, okay. I'll be in Charlie's room for now. Come find me when you know." With that he clicked off the conversation he'd been having, then turned his back, walked to my door, and threw both the regular lock and the bolt lock on my door. "I want you using both from now on while you're here. You got me?"

"Yeah, I will. What happened? Did someone unlock my door? Were they in my room?" I asked suddenly nervous about what they could have possibly been doing in there. "Oh God, I was in the shower for a long time. How long have you been out there?"

"Just five minutes or so before you came strolling out. When you didn't come back out right away, I came to find you."

"What was someone doing in my room during that time? Nothing here is mine, or at least not before I got here. I have nothing to steal. I have..." Then my whole body froze just before the trembling started. "You just saw me naked." I rasped as the tremors in my body grew.

"Hey, now. If it makes you feel any better, once we get our shit straight, I plan on being the only one who ever sees you naked again. And baby, I will be seeing you naked again. Every damn day of our lives, if I get a say in it."

Normally, his proclamation would have been a balm to my frazzled mind, considering I'd just been fretting over whether I was anything to him, but the implications of someone having been in my room was too much to bear.

I pulled him close to me, as if I was hugging him, and I whispered in his ear. "What if someone put cameras in my room?" His whole body stiffened at the implication, and he tucked me even closer to him as he moved us back into the bathroom. He turned the shower on, the sink too, and then he picked his phone up. "Charlie just asked a really fantastic question about why someone was in her room." He waited a moment, listening.

"We need to know if cameras were installed in here, and we should probably figure that out without tipping off the person who may have planted them." There was another pause as he listened. "Nah, man, she was really smart about it. Pulled me in for a hug and whispered in my ear all quiet like. We're in her bathroom now. It'll look like we're making up in the shower if there's anything being seen." He listened a moment longer and then hung up.

"You think I'm right, don't you?"

"Better safe than sorry. Obviously, we can't talk out there so just listen quickly, and I promise you will have more detail later."

I stopped him there. "Spinner already gave me a very abbreviated rundown of what happened last night, because he was afraid that I might run and that it would have played right into what they intended." Rage looked hurt for a moment before his mask of indifference slipped back into place once more. "You wouldn't be anywhere near me if I thought what happened was the truth, but please, understand I needed a minute to wrap my head around everything and come to terms with it. Last night was a complete mind-fuck for me."

"And have you?"

"Wrapped my head around it?" I asked to which he nodded. "Yes," I replied all hesitancy leaving my voice.

Rage nodded again and then wrapped one hand around the back of my neck, the other around my waist, and then tugged me closer to him in the matter of a heartbeat before his lips were suddenly on mine with surprising ferocity. I opened to him immediately allowing our tongues to glide together and mingle as one. Flashes of heat erupted throughout my body sending shockwaves of lust and supreme need coursing through me as my panties grew wetter. My hands explored Rage's solid chest, up under his kutte and shirt, layers of clothes that were suddenly very much in my way.

Sadly, as I tried to pull at Rage's shirt, he took a step back. "As much as I wish you were still wearing nothing more than that towel, we have people headed our way." I hadn't realized someone was on the way to my room, but as if his words conjured them out of thin air a loud banging sounded on the door followed quickly by Rabbit yelling, "You two better not be fucking in there, because we're coming in!"

"Bolt's thrown, good luck, fucker!" Rage called out after opening the bathroom door so he could be heard loud and clear. I didn't miss the fact that he was scanning my room. Most likely, he was looking for something out of place, but as I did the same thing, I already knew where to look. I leaned in, over his shoulder, and whispered in his ear again. "Lamp's been moved on the nightstand. Alarm clock too." He didn't acknowledge what I said, and instead walked over to the bedroom door and threw the locks open to let the guys in. He held a finger up to his face, so they knew to watch what they said.

"Sweet girl," Shameless called out as he pushed past Rabbit and Rage. "You doing okay?"

"I'm fine, Shame. A little startled by having someone sitting in my room when I came out of the shower, but I'm over it."

Rage mumbled, "I'm not." Rabbit snickered at the man then focused his attention on my blushing cheeks.

"Were you naked when you came out of the bathroom, Showgirl?" He wiggled his eyebrows up and down in a comical gesture that was meant to be lecherous. Rage smacked him in the back of the head.

"Stop picturing her naked."

"So, she was naked?" Rabbit continued, grinning like an idiot.

"For fuck's sake, can we stop talking about my baby girl

being naked?" Shameless yelled at them. It was all normal, playful banter that we might have any other time. In the meantime, the guys were no doubt cataloging things to check out in my room. I moved to go sit on the bed, picked the alarm clock up, glared at it as if it offended me, and then set it face down on the nightstand.

"That clock piss you off, sweet girl?" Shameless asked.

"Time is pissing me off. I have things I want to do and every time I look up it seems like hours have slipped by. Days, weeks, and months have slipped by too," I grumbled. He came over and sat next to me pulling me into a hug as he whispered in my ear, "Clock a problem?"

I nodded at him and then said, "I hate that lamp too," Since there was only one light in the room besides the overhead lighting he knew right away. "Anything else seem off?"

I made a point to look directly at him before I glanced around, acting frustrated. "I don't know, Shame, everything seems so off lately. Those clothes in my closet aren't mine, and I don't have anything to fill that dresser, I nodded my head toward the only piece of furniture between the bathroom and closet doors, because it had been disturbed. Drawers were off kilter that shouldn't be, because I never used it since there were shelves in the closet. I tried to think back to when I came out of the bathroom in the towel and went into the closet to retrieve my clothes. Had it been opened? Closed? I honestly couldn't remember now.

"Okay, well, let's go see Iceman, because I think he has some news for you. Apparently, your dad left you some money that you weren't aware of." Shameless laughed. "It was club money that he was paid for jobs he did for us. He kept it in one of our accounts, and he's accrued quite a large sum over the years. I guess his intention was to make sure it all went to you if he passed." I wondered if he was setting something up, knowing he was being recorded, or if it was the truth. I guess I'd find out when we got somewhere secure.

15. PLANNING IS EVERYTHING

I WAS NERVOUS ABOUT SPEAKING IN ICEMAN'S OFFICE TOO, JUST IN case someone had broken in there, but the guys assured me it was impossible since only Iceman and Rage could access the biometric locks. Apparently, they had body part scans in place that made it impossible to get into the room undetected. It was also, as I was made aware, soundproofed.

"We pulled up footage of the hallway from the time Charlie went back to her room, until Rage showed up." Iceman glanced up to take us all in. The office was overfilled with bulky, muscular men dripping testosterone, and if they hadn't been there to protect me I would definitely be intimidated. "No one got near her room."

"What the fuck? She said her alarm clock, lamp, and dresser looked as though they'd been fucked with," Rage told him.

"Yeah, well, luckily I'm smart enough to remember that while we were all busy in Church, Charlie was out teaching Rosy's girls to dance." Spinner laughed at everyone's shocked faces. "We backed the camera footage up further and saw this."

Iceman had already turned the monitor to face us, and we watched as one of the guys who transferred in with Beaver after their old, dismantled club was absorbed by Aces High, walked into my room after jimmying the lock. We couldn't see what he did while he was in there, but it took him a good fifteen minutes to do it.

"If he did this while no one was in the room then..." I started to say as my eyes began to overflow with tears. "The bathroom," I choked out.

"Motherfucker!" Rage yelled out. "I want that room swept, now. I don't give a fuck who finds out. Obviously, we know Parker didn't work alone getting Jezzie in here for that setup. That was Bramble in Charlie's room."

"Is it just me, or did their club have the worst road names ever?" I attempted to joke. Rabbit chuckled, and Shameless pulled me into a one-armed hug while everyone else just gave me the look that said my joke wasn't appreciated right now. "So, what now?" I asked.

"You will stay here with a guard on the door, and one in the room, while we go do a sweep for all the brothers who patched over when their club went under."

"You think they're all in on it?" I asked, knowing it was about six men that had patched over with Beaver. They'd been pointed out to me when I first started working the bar, and Rabbit had warned me that they were heavier handed with women than the normal Aces High crew, and not to be afraid to tell one of the guys if they tried anything.

"Since we can't be too sure, we're going to pull them all

for questioning. Two, we know for sure, are about to go down after we make them sing." Spinner announced as his fists clenched tightly with his obvious disdain.

"Did you get Jezzie locked down like I asked?" My head snapped up then because I wasn't aware she was still around.

"She's here?"

"Prospect caught her trying to sneak out after she participated in that little setup last night. He snatched her ass up, and we've had her held downstairs since."

"I wasn't aware there was a downstairs."

"We usually use it in emergencies. If there is ever a natural disaster, or if the clubhouse were ever to come under attack, we have escape tunnels built in down there, but we also have heavy duty, blast proof panic rooms. She's being held in one as we speak. Only three people have access to open them from the outside." Iceman informed me.

"Thank you," I stated, suddenly feeling gracious of the fact that they were trusting me with so much. "I know you're giving me more information than you normally share. I just wanted you to know I appreciate it." All the men in the room smiled at me then.

"All right, we have some work to do. Charlie, you're staying put with Rabbit. We need Shameless on this one. We'll have a prospect outside, not that anyone can get in, but just in case someone tries, they can let us know immediately."

"Before we run off," Rage stated as he walked back over to stand beside me. "I just want to make it clear that I'm claiming Charlie, if she'll have me." He glanced down at me, and then kissed my forehead before walking to the door of the office. "She's not going to answer that right now though, because I know what she's going to say, and I'm not about to hear that shit."

He probably did know what I was about to say, because he seemed stupidly in-tune with me. If given half a chance I would tell him that I couldn't accept until I was no longer married. He deserved that fresh start with me. I deserved that fresh start with him. We could discuss that later when we were alone though. The rest of the guys did nothing more than glance between us quickly and head to the door as well. Rabbit was smirking in my general direction as they left and pulled the door shut behind them.

"So, what happens now?"

"Now, we wait." Rabbit had moved so that he was sitting behind the desk, no doubt watching the security footage as the guys went about the business of rounding up the men that may, or may not, be responsible for trying to get to me so they could turn me over to my husband. Ugh. I really needed to stop calling him that. He was never a husband in the real sense of the word. We were two people tied together by a piece of paper that I certainly had no intention of honoring any longer. As we sat there, waiting as Rabbit watched me fretting about my life and how far down the rabbit hole I'd travelled, the office phone started to ring. It was strange to see a landline in the place, and even stranger when I watched Rabbit's face contort upon seeing the caller ID.

"Hello," He stated as he picked up. Then he put a finger over his mouth to hush me as he placed the call on speakerphone. He also pointed to the camera in the corner of the room to let me know why he was making the call audible. I nodded.

"This is Sheriff Davis Mitchell. Who am I speaking with?"

"This is Rabbit. What can I do for you, Sheriff?"

"Is Iceman around, son?"

"No sir, he's off dealing with unruly bikers. You know how these boys are. A little too much drink, a little too much testosterone and the big boys have to play bouncer and sort shit."

"It's not even 4pm," the man on the other line stated as if that meant anything to bikers.

"And?" Rabbit asked. "Did you call to make Iceman aware of the time, or is there something I can help you with?"

"I was just calling to give him a head's up. It's come to our attention that a young woman who has been missing for the better part of a year is said to be in your clubhouse. We've had a tip here that she's being held there against her will, and the boys are on their way to pay a visit to the place as we speak."

"And do these boys have a warrant they're bringing with them, because I'd be really curious to know how that was procured without evidence."

"Well, here's the thing, we were e-mailed video evidence of her being there just about an hour ago. Not all of it was flattering. The video was of her in the shower, and I'm fairly certain she had no clue there were cameras in there."

Rabbit's face turned colors as he attempted to tamp down his fury. He was also busy tapping away at the keys on his phone.

"Well, I can assure you we do not have any missing girls held against their will here, Sheriff. Feel free to send your boys out to check if you must though. Actually, I'd really appreciate if you'd come yourself since I don't trust half your boys, and this may turn into a pretty delicate situation."

"Are you saying the girl is there?"

"How can I say that when I don't know who we're talking about?" Rabbit snipped back.

"Fair enough. I'll be there momentarily since I was calling from the car anyway."

"We'll have the welcome mat out, but do me a solid, and come in and listen to what I have to say before you turn those boys loose with a search warrant."

"I can do that, but fair warning, I have an FBI agent on the way into town as we speak who is very interested in getting to that girl."

"And that is why we need to have this chat ahead of time." Rabbit told him before hanging up.

Rabbit looked at me then, completely serious. "I'm giving you two codes, sweetheart. When I get back to this door with the Sheriff, I will call that phone and tell you 'watermelon is delicious' if I want you to open that door. If something is wrong, and I think you're in danger, I will tell you, 'remember to feed the fish.'" He made eye contact with me and didn't release it. "You got that?"

I nodded. "Watermelon is good. Fishy means danger. Got it." He tossed me a quick smile then.

"That's my girl. Don't forget the codes. I'll be back in a few minutes."

"Rabbit," I called out to him as he opened the office door. "Please, be careful."

"I will, and everyone else knows what's about to go down too. They're underground dealing with our problem people, and don't worry, even with a search warrant they won't be found down there." He winked at me and took off out of the office, making sure the door latched shut behind him as he went.

The wait seemed to take forever. I tried to sit behind the monitor and watch security footage as Rabbit had been doing, but he'd done something to the monitors before he left that killed the feed. At first, I was pissed, thinking he was hiding things from me. Then I remembered he was going to collect the Sherriff and probably didn't want him nosing around in our security feeds when he brought him back to the office. The phone rang, startling me out of my thoughts.

"Hello?" I answered.

"Watermelon sure is good to have on a hot day, sweetheart. I hope you have some in there with you." I laughed at Rabbit, hung up, and went to open the door. He entered along with a man wearing a sheriff's uniform.

"Mrs. Cooper," the sheriff said as he tipped his hat toward me. Rabbit closed the door behind us.

"I'd really appreciate it if you didn't refer to me as Mrs." I told him, causing him to cock a brow.

"Well, now I was under the impression you were married to a Mr. Joshua Cooper, who has been frantically searching for his wife for going on a year now."

"Sheriff, I need you to really hear what I'm about to tell

you. I don't trust too many people anymore, and I'm going out on a limb trusting you."

"Okay," he told me as he took a seat on the couch. "I'm all ears." Then he pulled out some sort of device and tipped his head to it. "Do you mind if I record this?"

"I don't care." I waved his concern away. "In October of 2016, I lived in an unhappy marriage. I knew my husband was cheating on me, but I had yet to be able to catch him in the act."

"Your husband being former NFL running back, Josh Cooper, correct?"

"Yes, that is correct." I sighed. "It was October 24th, the two-year anniversary of my dad's death. I was headed to the cemetery to place flowers and pay my respects. When I got there, a man I'd never seen before took me by gunpoint and ushered me quickly into a brown mini van that had been sitting down on the path near where I was parked. He put me in the van, tied me up, and drove us out of there. We were on the road for hours." I took a deep breath as I remembered how completely freaked out those events made me. "It was dark by the time we arrived at a pueblo revival style home in the middle of nowhere. I later found out I was near Phoenix, about fort-five minutes outside of town."

I continued, delving deep into the memory of my abduction. "The man who took me carried me into the house, sat me in a chair, and told me he had a story to tell me." I looked up at the Sheriff then and made sure he saw the sincerity in my eyes. "I'm not going to give you all the details of his story, because I will preserve his identity with my dying breath."

"Why on earth would you do that? The man kidnapped

you at gunpoint, drove you across state lines, and you want to protect him?" He was shaking his head.

"Do you want to hear the rest or not?" I asked.

"Of course, I do."

"Then hold your questions, they'll be answered as I go." And with that I dove back into my past. "This man, we'll call him Blackhawk, sat on a chair opposite mine, made a show of putting his gun down on the floor and kicking it out of reach. I wasn't stupid; I figured he had another one on him somewhere that I couldn't see. It was obvious he was trying to gain my trust though. He pulled something out of his pocket and held it up so I could see. It was a picture of him with a deceased family member of mine. They had served together a long time ago." I sighed. Remembering the moment when I realized the man who had kidnapped me was standing beside my father in the photo brought back the same pang of pain that I had the first time. I remember feeling so heartbroken and hostile in that moment.

"The man explained that he heard chatter about a murder for hire scheme and that he recognized my name. When he made contact, the person providing the information turned out to be a blond woman about 5'2" with blue eyes and big, fake tits. She had a sparrow tattooed on the cleavage of her right boob."

"That's pretty descriptive," the sheriff muttered, interrupting me again.

"Yes, it was, and for reason you'll understand momentarily. The description he gave sounded familiar immediately. It sounded like a woman I'd seen around my husband before. I had suspected she might be the one he was having the affair with, but he had assured me she was just a business partner in the whorehouse he was funding for a biker club in Nevada." The sheriff leaned forward in his seat then, completely enraptured with my story now.

"The woman gave Blackhawk a picture of me, and told him Josh wanted it done quickly, but that she wouldn't mind if I suffered a bit before I was taken out." I clenched my teeth through the last bit, so I had to unclench to finish.

"Blackhawk accepted the hit, took half the money up front. It was something like $10,000, and the rest of the information that he needed. She informed him that my father's death anniversary was in two days, and that he could find me at the cemetery at some point that day."

Both Rabbit and the sheriff were watching as I continued telling my story. "Blackhawk has video evidence of the transaction. He played it for me when I didn't believe him."

"Are you in possession of this evidence now?"

"No. Two days after he took me, Blackhawk went back to Josh with photos he had of my faked death. He was supposed to make sure Josh knew that my body would be found in a public place in the next few days, and that it had no way of linking back to him. That was the plan, anyway. He was supposed to come back to get me and take me to his friends for safe keeping once he was done with that meeting, but he never returned.

"I don't know why, or what kept him away, but I stayed in that house for a month living off of what was there, before I ventured out. Then I found a job at a strip club, dancing to make money because I didn't know what else to do and I wanted to stay as far off the radar as possible. The club owner took me on without identification and paid me under the table. I stayed there for 6 months until one night a guy Josh and I had both gone to high school with rolled in and recognized me.

"He called my name out in front of the customers, and I knew I couldn't stay there. I was already listed as a missing person then, since no one had discovered my body yet." I continued with my story. "Before I left, I checked my e-mail at the local library. There was a message, which I assumed was from Blackhawk. It was months old already, but I had avoided all electronics since I'd been taken captive. Anyway, the e-mail was a quick video of Blackhawk's interaction with Josh the day he went to meet him."

"Do you have that video?" The sheriff asked.

"Yes, if I can see your phone, I can pull it up for you."

He handed the phone over immediately, and I pulled up my e-mail account, not caring that the Sheriff would probably have access to it from there on out, or that it could be tracked since everyone already knew where I was anyway. Once it was queued up, I handed it back to him and he and Rabbit watched as Josh spilled the beans about how he couldn't pay the rest of the money until the body was found, because the insurance money had to come through first.

He explained that the Biker Club known as Modern Saints, in specific a man named Hammer, could vouch for him, and that they would make sure Blackhawk got the rest of his money. Blackhawk slyly asked a few questions through the conversation, made Josh just comfortable enough to tell him all about his plan.

Josh looked at the pictures we had faked of my death. "I

can't believe she's gone. It's so weird. She was an okay girl when we went to school together, and I hate that she had to die, but she had no one. No one will miss her or mourn her, because she was all alone. Honestly, I did her a favor by marrying her, so she at least had a little taste of happiness before she died," he told Blackhawk callously.

Blackhawk, as I'd been calling him for the interview with the sheriff, stood and left the scene, but as he left, fiddling with his phone, was hit and fell to the ground with a grunt. The video ends with him being dragged away. Both men glanced up at me then. "Holy fuck, Charlie! Why didn't you show that to Iceman right away?" Rabbit asked.

I shrugged. "We weren't sure until recently that they were tipped off by the background check you guys ran. I didn't want to take the chance of accessing the e-mail account in case it was compromised."

The sheriff stared at me, slack-jawed, and wild-eyed. "I just saw Josh Cooper admit to trying to have you killed. I watched him dismiss images of you supposedly dead like they were trading cards."

"Yes," I agreed.

"You had this video, why didn't you go to the police?"

"I didn't trust them. Josh's close friend works for the Las Vegas Police Department, and I had already witnessed him fixing smaller incidents for Josh's buddies before. The FBI Agent on his way here is more than likely Gordon Cooper, correct?" Sheriff Mitchell nodded at me.

"The surname Cooper didn't ring any bells for you? That's Josh's cousin. I can't tell you if he's dirty or clean, but what I do know is my husband tried to have me killed. His buddy is a dirty cop, and I wasn't about to take any chances where his cousin was concerned."

"I need to make a quick call. I told the boys to give me twenty minutes. That time is just about up. I don't want them storming in here." Sheriff Mitchell picked up his cell and dialed out to the men waiting to serve the warrant to search for me. Then he paused and looked at me. "There was a video of you in the shower that was sent in today as proof that these guys had you here."

"We realized someone with a grudge about their buddy getting kicked out of the club, for attacking me, set up cameras earlier today. Unfortunately, we realized it after I'd showered in one of the rooms he rigged," I stated. "The boys of this club had nothing to do with that. They are my family."

"One more question, before I put this call through. Mr. Cooper seemed pretty sure you had no family beyond him. How is it you found yourself out here in South Dakota with the Aces High Biker Club?"

"Divine intervention for the most part. A dancer told me about these guys when I was on the run, and when I got here, the guys informed me that my dad was a nomad in their club, and that I'd been brought up in it when I was a little girl."

"And you believed that?" he asked.

"Well, they have plenty of pictures to prove their story," and they did, because Shameless had shown me a couple albums he had in his room one night when I was in need of some cheering up.

"Okay." The sheriff made the call, sending the guys away, and told them to inform him when the FBI agent got here."

Iceman and Rage came back up to the office after Rabbit sent them a text.

When they came into the room, Rage moved straight over to me and pulled me into his arms. "You doing okay, darlin'?"

"I'm fine. Sheriff Mitchell has been very gracious in listening to my story."

Rabbit interrupted and asked Mitchell if he could show the guys the video from the e-mail. He also forwarded a copy to a general club email address for safekeeping. The men watched, and as they did Rage pulled me even closer, not wanting to let me go. Then he turned to the sheriff. "So, what are we going to do about the FBI agent that happens to be the cousin of this bastard who attempted to murder Charlie?"

"We are going to welcome him here for a little chat, if you don't mind." He pointed up at the cameras positioned throughout the room. "I assume those are running at all times?"

Iceman smiled. "They are."

"And you wouldn't have any issues with handing over the segments of video pertaining to this case, correct?" Sheriff Mitchell asked.

"We'd be happy to," Iceman told him.

"Good. Then I'll have my men re-direct the agent out this way when he gets here, because I have no control over whether your cameras are running as opposed to the ones at the station." I smiled at Sheriff Mitchell then.

"Thank you, Sheriff."

"You don't have to thank me for doing my job. People

tend to forget that part of the job is to protect. Seems you need some protection that your boys can't offer without borrowing a whole heap of trouble."

"No, but I feel that it's necessary considering how I couldn't count on other law enforcement to do their jobs." He nodded at me and grumbled about that being a damned shame.

"You boys did a good thing here," he tipped his head towards me. "I wish you'd come to me sooner, but I understand why you didn't."

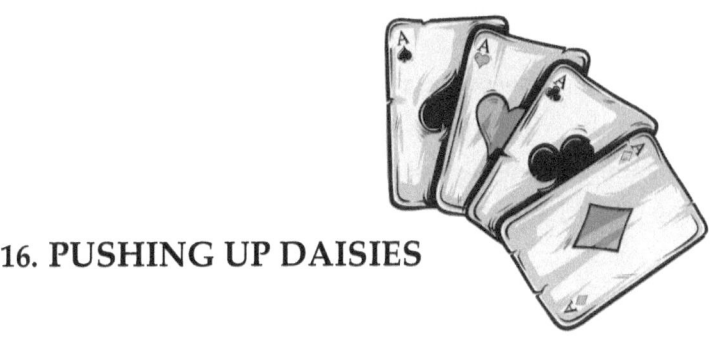

16. PUSHING UP DAISIES

We sat inside Iceman's office for more than an hour waiting for Gordon Cooper to show up, and when he finally did, we were met with shocking news.

Spinner, who met him at the exterior door, escorted him into the office.

"Charlie," he greeted. Spinner stayed out of the office, off on a mission to take care of the people they had to question downstairs, no doubt.

"Gordon," I offered back. We had only met the once at our quickie wedding. He had been in town visiting his mom when Josh decided we should get married so Gordon served as one of our witnesses.

"I know we didn't know each other beyond that first meeting when you got married, but I wish you could have trusted me enough to come to me if you were in trouble." I nodded at him, and then sat back as he listened to the recording Sheriff Mitchell made of my version of events earlier. Then he watched the video of his cousin with absolute disgust written on his face.

"I already had the video in my possession. It was sent to us by your friend, the one you referred to as Blackhawk. I've been part of the team investigating my cousin."

"How is that possible since you're related?" Iceman asked what we were all wondering.

"It was possible, because they needed me undercover to get more information. Trust me when I say that I was being watched like a hawk. Not that it was necessary since I would never get behind what my cousin attempted to do. I had a hard time believing my cousin was capable of any of it at first, but when he thought I was dirty and willing to help him out, I got a lot more details out of him. He was planning on offing the girlfriend too, because she knew too much, and he didn't want to part with half the money he knew would be coming in. He asked me to do the job since I'd know exactly how to cover it up." My mouth dropped open.

"A regular male black widow, huh?" Rabbit asked.

"Precisely. It sickens me to think that this was my family we're talking about." His head shook back and forth, the disgust he felt evident for all to see. While I wanted to feel bad for the position his cousin had placed him in, I couldn't. At least he didn't have a choice in being Josh's family. I had stupidly walked into a marriage with him. As if feeling my misery, Rage pulled me closer to him, and held tight. I was already perched on the man's lap, so I allowed my head to rest on his shoulder and soak in his heat and comfort. Gordon noticed and smiled weakly at me.

"Looks like you found a much better match, Charlie." He

finally said as he continued watching the interaction between Rage and me. "I know I was only around the two of you for a couple days, but considering you were newlyweds, I never saw that level of interaction." I nodded, agreeing wholeheartedly. Josh would have never held me like this. He would have just told me to get over whatever was bothering me. God, I was such a damn fool.

I didn't really say anything to Gordon to acknowledge my seemingly new relationship. I watched him and waited for whatever news he brought us. "I hoped that you would be okay when we finally found you. The message we received with the e-mailed video included the line," he looked down at a notepad he pulled out of his pocket. "She's still alive and well." Gordon sighed. "My cousin, not so much," Gordon finally revealed.

"What?" To say I was shocked by his statement was, well, an understatement. That also seemed like information he should have opened the conversation with. He reached into the briefcase he'd brought in with him and handed me a piece of paper. We were interrupted by a knock on the door that Iceman answered, allowing Spinner into the room with us, and shutting the door behind him again.

"Sorry," he told everyone, "I needed access to the computer in here for a minute," he claimed as he moved behind Iceman's desk and angled the monitor back towards himself.

Gordon didn't hesitate to continue with his news. "Josh was found a week ago with a bullet lodged in his skull. He was in the apartment the two of you once shared, and it appeared that a woman had been staying there with him recently too."

"Do we want to know how you came to that conclusion?" Iceman asked.

"Used tampons in the trash, lipstick on a glass in the sink, birth control pills in the cabinet that did not have Charlie's name on them. Then there was the security footage we went over for the building's entrance where we watched the two of them enter and leave together quite often.

"My cousin was an idiot. If anyone had been looking, with any seriousness, into his claims that Charlie had disappeared, and he was a distraught man awaiting his wife's return, he would have given them enough evidence to suspect foul play on his part in her disappearance. You were right about his buddy in the Vegas PD though. He, and a couple others, were taking point on your case, and since you had no other family to raise a stink about how long it was taking to get results the case was left to fall through the cracks.

"Except for the fact that the FBI were already involved with our own sting operation and investigation into the corruption and suspected cover-up," he added with a wink.

"So, he's really dead?" I asked to clarify one more time. Gordon nodded, and I let out a sigh of relief.

"That doesn't mean you're out of the woods yet. The woman he was seen with, Sheri Lynn Michaels, was last seen coming out of the apartment near the time of death with a man dressed in biker gear. His patches did not indicate he was a member of either Aces High or Modern Saints. Instead, he is a member of The Tribe." A series of cuss words rocketed out of nearly every man's mouth in the room, including Rage's.

"The Tribe are not some cursory worry," Iceman interjected.

"No, they are not," Gordon agreed. "Our gangland taskforce has them slotted as the number three one-percenter organization in this country. They deal in drugs, weapons, and human trafficking. We have yet to nail them down and obliterate them, because every time we try serving warrants on their properties they are beyond squeaky clean."

Spinner laughed. "That's because you're serving them on the wrong properties, no doubt. They are notorious for their ghost properties."

"We are aware of that." Gordon agreed.

"What does this have to do with me? Surely, the insurance scam won't work now, because the woman was implicated in my murder for hire already. I'm assuming this Sheri Lynn lady matches the description I gave you from the first video I saw. She's the one who hired Blackhawk."

"Blackhawk?" Spinner asked, and I blushed.

"The codename for the man who helped me escape their plot," I informed the guys who weren't there for the initial interview. Spinner smiled at me and nodded.

"Yes, she matches the description, down to the sparrow tattoo, but the problem is without the video you spoke of seeing, we have no way to connect the dots. Granted, she'd land herself in the middle of a ridiculous investigation as to how she became the beneficiary, how Josh died under more than suspicious conditions, and how she ties to the both of you. It's enough to keep things tied up, especially since they still have the small problem of not having a dead girl to claim insurance on."

"What about Josh?"

"What do you mean?"

"Is she able to claim anything belonging to him? Technically, I'm his wife, and everything would go to me unless he left a will or something stating otherwise, right? So, what about his part in the whorehouse, club, or whatever that he was financing with the Modern Saints?"

"Well, we found no evidence that he was working with them beyond an initial deposit of interest. It's safe to say, he strayed into the The Tribe's territory instead, and ended up dead for it."

I remember the guys saying something about how they thought Josh was buying into human trafficking instead of the Modern Saints' club before. I didn't mention it, because none of them did, and I didn't think they were ready to share all with Agent Cooper, no matter the story he was spinning.

"There was some chatter a few times when I was around about inheritance you should have come into from your dad. Do you know anything about that?"

"No," I stated honestly, because I was only just finding out about any money that may have been saved away for me in a club account. "My dad had been dead for two years before all of this started. Why would they suddenly think I was about to come into money form my dad?"

"Josh was informed by someone recently, that you had ties to Aces High MC. I think they just assumed there was more money that you didn't know about when your dad died as a result."

"So, their plan to get a hold of me now and sell me to this guy who makes snuff films is what? Part B of the plan after they somehow trick or force me into signing over whatever insurance money and accounts from my dad that they think I have access to?" I asked the questions while still unsure as to how they thought that would play out in their favor. "I'm just stumped. I have no clue what in the world all that means."

"So, I'm assuming you heard the latest threat against Charlie then, since she mentioned being sold?" Gordon asked. Iceman tipped his head to indicate he had. "For some reason this Sheri Lynn woman thinks she will be entitled to anything you leave behind, and that it's just a matter of having you killed off with proof of death before she gets what she considers her money."

"Why the hell would she think-" I started to ask but was cut off by Spinner.

"Fuck me runnin'" he grumbled as his eyes scoured over something on the computer in front of him. "I think I just came across the 'why' of it all."

"Did you ever see that woman, like really see her from close up, Charlie?"

"Not really," I admitted. "I only ever saw her from a distance."

Spinner turned the monitor around so we could all see what he was looking at. It was the picture that Gordon had, no doubt, been discussing that showed Sheri Lynn with a biker from The Tribe leaving my old condo. I gasped slightly when I finally got to take in the woman's features that were so like my own.

"Are we certain that Lulu had a boy that died all those years ago?" Spinner asked while looking directly at Shameless.

"Son of a bitch!" Shameless yelled out as he stood and moved to get closer to the screen. "That's definitely the bastard Luanne was cheating on Brazen with too. You don't think..." He started to say, but then glanced back at me.

"That is my sister?" I asked, aghast. "You're telling me that my own sister has been trying to have me killed for over a year, plotted my death well before that even, and that she's still gunning for me? Does she know we're sisters?" I shook my question off. "Never mind, that was dumb. Obviously, she knows because she thinks she can gain access to anything I leave behind. That means she thinks we're family, right?"

"Her dad certainly would have known who you were, so yeah, she probably did too."

Someone spoke those words, but they were somehow disembodied as my entire world seemed to flip in on itself once more. Not only did I recently find out my mom was apparently a cheater, and that I would have had a sibling if they hadn't died due to complications from a car accident, but apparently my sibling had not died. I had a sister, and she looked a whole lot like me. She was also in on a plan to kill me for money they thought I would bring in. Oh yeah, and she was willing to sell me to some sick fucker who wanted to rape me, do other unspeakable things to me, and film my death too.

Yeah, that was a comfort. Learning you had a sibling out there who wanted you dead in the most horrific way possible sucked. Knowing that same sibling was the person your own husband had been with on the side, or more to the point that you had unknowingly been the side piece in the scenario even though you had the marriage certificate... Ugh, I couldn't wrap my brain around this shit.

A tug at my ribs pulled me from the swirling thoughts that were eating at my insides. "Darlin', I need you to come back to the-here-and-now with us." The words were whispered into my ear, and I turned to see the concern written all over the face of the man who was still holding me close to him. "You back now?"

"I never went anywhere," I admitted, the words barely a whisper from my lips.

He tapped on my head lightly. "You were gone in here for a little while, darlin'. We were trying to ask you questions, but you were checked the fuck out. Not that anyone blames you for that, all things considered. This has all been a hell of a shock."

"I think 'hell of a shock' is an understatement at this point." I explained as I glanced back around the room at all the faces watching us, and the sympathy etched in each of them. "What do I do now?"

"We can try a few different approaches. The best option would be to use you as bait to lure them out and see if they try to pull a snatch and grab on you." Gordon started to say but was abruptly cut off.

"Fuck no!" Rage snarled at the FBI agent. "All they need is one fucking open shot at her. I get that they want her for this trafficking business, but let's be real, if it comes down to selling her off, or just letting this bitch sister of hers inherit the money after her death, what do you think they're going to go for?" he paused for a moment to let that sink in. "Kidnapping her out from underneath an MC she's protected by would be the harder of the two options. Waiting for a quick headshot wouldn't be that tough."

"Jesus," Gordon hissed at Rage's forthrightness.

"It don't sound pretty, but he's right," Shameless put in.

"I know he is, and this is why there's Plan B. I was going to meet with the woman under the guise of selling her fake identification, so that she can access the insurance policy. I'm offering her the money from that in exchange for your life."

"How much was the policy on Josh, because the only one I knew of was only a million dollars. It wouldn't have been enough to pay off his damn condo." I sighed. "Plus, they think I have some huge trust fund left to me from my dad. I still don't know the details about that beyond the fact that something might possibly exist."

Iceman coughed then. "We can discuss the logistics on that when there aren't more ears than necessary in the room, but I will say it's a healthy sum, and sure as fuck beats a payout from the insurance policy. The real question is how they knew about it, because only a select few inside the club knew. It was part of the reason Shame tried tracking you down after your father died."

"How did my sister manage to find me when you guys lost me?"

Shameless shook his head. "I told you before, I was off on business when your dad passed. We got the news a little slowly, and when business wrapped, and I went to find you..."

"I was already gone." He nodded.

"She must have already known about you, and followed along, or had someone in The Tribe on you all along."

"We need Ghost up here," Iceman stated quickly. "What happened with him when you called previously?"

"He had some shit going down with his daughter and the club there. Said he'd be along as soon as he could. I think there was a grandbaby involved," Rage informed him.

"Jamie had a kid?" Iceman asked.

"Nah, it's a complicated situation, man."

"Okay, well, whatever it is, we need Ghost here ASAP. Probably wouldn't hurt to have Hopper with him, because those two will know a fuck of a lot more than we do about The Tribe."

"What if there were an option C?" I asked.

"What do you mean?" Rage's voice when tight when he spoke while he tightened his grip on my body once more.

"Well, what if you use me as bait, but in a way where they think I'm already dead anyway?"

"What the fuck, Showgirl?" Rabbit asked, just as confused as everyone else in the office seemed to be.

"It worked once before when," I glanced at the two LEOs still in the room before using the codename I had developed for Bishop. "When Blackhawk faked my death and took pictures, they believed it. Why don't we do the same thing? Only this time, we have the local sheriff come to collect my body and take me to the morgue or wherever you take the dead around here. Then we can set a trap when they come to verify that I truly am dead.

"Gordon can play his part by putting word out that my body was found." I smiled big, because I knew I was on to something when I saw a few eyes light up in response to my plan. "My sister can't claim shit of mine unless she comes to identify the body and prove somehow that she's my blood relative so that will put her in arms reach. Then all we have to worry about is finding whoever the hell her father is."

All eyes were on me, and I thought Rage would cut off my circulation if he squeezed me any harder to him. No one said a word for a solid few minutes. Iceman finally broke the silence.

"Can we have people on standby, watching? We could tap into some video feed to the room where she is taken and the whole nine yards beyond? If not, then it's a no from me. We'll be putting that cunt too close to our girl without any help, and I won't trust in that. We'll also need someone inside the transport that comes to pick up her supposedly dead body, because we don't know if there will be eyes on the ground before the Fed makes the announcement about her death. Obviously, they already know where she is."

"How do you know they know where she is?" Gordon asked.

"We had a few rats in the nest. There were a couple of folks who were ousted recently for their shit attitudes and decided to take tidbits of information with them when they went."

"How much information was given, how many rats are

we talking, and are you sure you flushed them all out?" Gordon asked in rapid-fire succession.

"Considering the video I received this morning; I'd say you still had some close."

"It's handled," Iceman explained.

"I need more than that," Gordon began, but was cut off by Iceman.

"You don't need shit about our club business. We'll take your help, but I don't fucking trust your story. You may be telling the truth, but then again, you may be working with the enemy. We have no way of knowing. So, you'll get what we give you, and we'll be watching."

Gordon took his ball cap off and slammed it to his knees in frustration. "This is the kind of shit that will get her killed," he stated angrily while stabbing one of his fingers in my direction accusatorily.

Surprisingly, it was the Sheriff that jumped in then. "Hey now, let's tone it down." He looked right at the agent before telling him. "Remember, you were invited into their house today to try to solve a problem, and not the other way around."

"If we don't trust one another here, someone dies." Gordon spoke in his no-nonsense way.

"If we trust you, and you're lying, someone dies," Iceman stated coolly.

17. SETTING A TRAP

KNOWING THE DAY THAT YOU ARE SUPPOSED TO DIE IS UNNERVING, even if it isn't real. A week went by as the guys made plans, and things were set into motion that would eventually make it appear as though I died in an accidental overdose. I wondered why we had to wait, but as the guys informed me, it would look suspicious if we flushed out the rats from the club who were gunning for me only to have me turn up dead the next day. The plan was that I should die three weeks later. I wasn't sure I could wait around on edge for three solid weeks. One down, two to go, still sounded like two too many.

"Charlie, I need to introduce you to Savannah. She's going to take over Sasha's parts and needs to learn her routines." Mel, the little pixie of a dancer from Rosy's explained to me, pulling me out of my morbid thoughts of my impending fake death. Fake or not, it sucked to think about.

"Sure, why is she taking Sasha's choreography?" I asked

just as the front door opened and Rage came barreling in with the woman in question behind him. She had her bags with her, and a prospect followed behind them with even more bags.

Sasha glanced over and noticed me watching the strange processional. "Thanks so much for coming to get me, baby," she cooed at Rage. He immediately turned on a dime and faced her. His finger flew in her face quick as a flash to point out the seriousness of what he was about to say. "You don't fucking call me anything but Rage, ever. Are we clear?" He gave her a moment to respond with a hesitant nod. "You will stay the fuck away from me. You won't talk to me unless it is absolutely necessary. We will not tolerate any bullshit drama. Tallie and Jezzie were just tossed out for that shit recently, and I won't hesitate to do the same with you.

"My vote on you moving to the clubhouse as a BRAT was a firm and decisive no, but other brothers here wanted a chance at your pussy for some fuckin' reason or other. *They* are the reason you are here. Not me. You don't fuckin' come near me. You don't start drama. You suck dick and fuck when you're asked – and make no mistake, it will never be me asking – and maybe you get to stay. You fuck up, cause unnecessary drama, I will be the one to boot your ass out."

The dumb bitch reached out to touch Rage's arm, but he stepped out of her way while scowling down at her. "I thought you only left me alone because I worked at Rosy's." Her voice was low, and unsure.

He laughed, but it was a cold sound. "If I ever wanted you, I would have taken you from Rosy's and either moved you here as a BRAT or something else. I didn't do that. The thought never once crossed my mind. Get this infatuation you have with me out of your head now, because it won't be tolerated by me, my woman, or my club." Sasha looked up at him, with hurt clear in her eyes before she shifted them to me and nodded. I kind of felt bad for her being so publicly humiliated by a crush, but she really brought it on herself.

"Get her set up in the BRAT's wing. Tallie and Jezzie's old rooms have been cleaned down, and either should be ready for her." Rage ordered the prospect that was still standing there with her luggage.

Rage sauntered his fine ass over to the makeshift stage the guys had set up in the corner, complete with a pole for when the dancers came to the clubhouse to entertain. He hopped right up on the stage and zeroed in on me like I was the only person around.

"Hey, babe," he called out just before his arms wrapped around my waist and pulled me into the thick wall of muscle that he called his body.

"Hey yourself," I tossed back at him in a seductive tone that had him quirking a brow at me.

"You ladies about done here?" he asked, again while looking at me as he did so.

I smirked. "We were just starting actually." He heaved out a heavy sigh and rested his head on my own then as he whispered into my hair, "That's a damn shame, darlin', because I was going to whisk you off to the bedroom and get some personal instruction to how you move."

Holy hot flashes! My body was suddenly doused in the unforgiving flames of arousal. "Damn you!" I huffed and slapped my hand against his very firm pectoral muscle. He chuckled in response.

"Looks like I get to pregame with a show. I'll be over there," he pointed to the bar where several other men had also gathered. "Watching," he added as he glanced down into my eyes with a heated look that almost forced me to cancel practice with the girls today. Had it not been for the new girl, I certainly would have.

How in the hell was a woman supposed to concentrate on teaching an exotic dance routine to someone when the man she wanted to have sex with was there to take in the show? I glanced over, watching his tight ass in those body-hugging jeans move across the expansive room, away from me, and my resolve was set. I was going to use this opportunity to tease the absolute fuck out of him, and then maybe I'd get what I'd wanted since the first day I watched that same tight ass moving in front of me at Renegade Rosy's.

I started working with Savannah through the slowest, most seductive dance I'd probably ever choreographed for a strip routine. It was stunningly beautiful though, the movements in tune with The Way You Look Tonight by Adelita's Way. Savannah picked it up quickly, worked through the routine, and incorporated some of her own signature pole moves into the seduction. That girl worked the pole like it allowed her to defy gravity. I was in awe until she came back down, and we moved through the last few moments of the dance that would transition into the far more upbeat Notorious, also by Adelita's Way. We moved, swayed, shimmied, and shook our asses across the stage, and worked up a sweat while doing it.

"Fuck my life!" One of the guys called out. "Please, tell me they'll be together on the stage like that at Rosy's tonight!"

"Get your eyes off my woman, Fox!" Rage called out as he moved across the room, hopped on the stage, and announced that practice was over as he tucked his shoulder into my belly and slung me up and over. It was a complete caveman move that was cheered on by all his brothers. Hell, Mel and Savannah were cheering me on too. I didn't waste the opportunity presented to me either with my head slung down over his back I reached out and smacked my hands into the globes of his firm ass, and latched on, digging my fingers in.

"Woman, you need to stop now, or we won't make it back to the room before I strip you down and take you."

I didn't listen to the warning, and instead dug my fingers in deeper to the meaty part of his ass while his brothers hooted and hollered from behind us. The man sprinted across the rest of the floor to the stairs that led up to the bedroom he'd been sharing with me for the past week. Then he managed to climb the stairs two at a time all the while with me draped over his shoulder. I was truly in awe of his strength, because even though I was in excellent shape, I would have been winded running up the stairs like that without carrying the weight of another person.

It didn't matter though. The man took me straight back to my room and set me down on my bed none to gently before he moved back over to lock the door. He hadn't even turned back to me before his kutte was off and being draped over the chair in the corner. Once his eyes locked with mine though, I became a puddle of hormones begging him to take me in any way he wished.

"Strip!" He ordered on a growl, and I obliged.

It wasn't as though he hadn't seen me totally naked just a week before. Granted, it felt like a lifetime ago, and that was an accidental viewing of me in all my glory. So, I decided to give him a bit of a show instead. I slowly began to remove my shirt, teasing tiny little peeks of flesh momentarily before raising the shirt further up my body. When my bra-covered breasts were finally exposed, I pulled the shirt over my head and sat up on my knees on top of the bed. My bottom lip was pulled seductively between my teeth as I discarded my top and ran my hands slowly back down my chest, stopping to slowly rub around the taught nipples that were trying to peek out from behind the satin cups of my bra.

While I was putting on my little show, Rage was watching as he tugged off his boots, socks, and unbuttoned his pants. As his zipper came down, I tugged the yoga pants I'd worn to practice down my own legs. His shirt came up and off, giving me the beautiful view of his sculpted chest and abdomen along with the dusting of hair that ran across his chest and trailed down his belly into the pants that were now sliding down his thick, well-muscled legs.

To my surprise a pair of black boxer-briefs held his impressive erection snuggly as he did so. I'm not sure why I always pictured him going commando, but seeing that he wasn't, made me giggle.

"What the hell is that about?" Rage asked with a smirk on his face. I shrugged.

"Just never pictured you as a boxer-briefs guy," I replied

honestly while I reached behind my back to unclasp my bra strap.

"And what did you picture, darlin', silk boxers or something? I am a biker, you know." He stalked toward the bed, and me, before I could answer.

"I pictured you with nothing underneath those jeans. Maybe it was just wishful thinking for ease of access." I winked as he came down on top of me, knocking me flat to my back, as he helped pull my arms free of the bra since the clasps holding it there were released.

As he dropped the bra to the side with one hand his other came down, trailing his fingers gently across each of my nipples causing them to perk up even more than the slight chill in the air had already done.

"You're so damn perfect, darlin'." His voice came out a hoarse whisper that sent chills dancing across my skin. "So fuckin' perfect," he managed to mutter before his head dipped down and our lips met in the sweetest of movements. A slight brush of flesh on flesh, a quick flick of his tongue, and then his hand moved to the back of my neck and pulled me toward him where those sweet kisses flamed into passionate, uncontrolled, torturous dips of our tongues into each other mouths.

We took turns chasing and relinquishing control for a time before I noticed his hands were kneading my breasts too. Yes, the kisses were that hot that I didn't notice all the other stimulation going on at first. The pull and tug of my nipples between his finger and thumb brought a yelp from my lips just as he tugged on my bottom lip with his teeth.

"Just the beginning darlin'. I'll have you screaming for real soon enough." His fingers trailed across my ribs, down over my belly, and lower to the little satin panties that were the only layer of clothing left between us since he'd ditched the boxers at some point before tackling me to my back on the bed.

As Rage moved further down my body his mouth stopped periodically along the way to taste a trail of my skin as he went. First, it was with little nips and sucks of my neck, then my collarbone. Then his licks and nibbles landed on the soft fleshy part of my upper breast before he locked on to first my right and then my left releasing both with an audible pop that had me flooding my panties just a little bit more.

Rage dropped lower and began planting kisses along my belly button as his fingers grasped hold of my panties near my hip bones and began sliding them down my thighs. I raised my hips a bit to make the task easier on him, which also earned me one of his full dimpled smiles before his mouth went back to work tasting its way down my lower abdomen and into the space my panties once occupied.

He traced the trail of my landing strip's worth of pubes straight to my juicy center, first with his fingers and then with his tongue. Sweet, fiery heaven. That tongue on my body was a thing mere mortals should never be allowed to experience. It was heaven, nirvana, Valhalla... Just as those thoughts rolled through my mind, Rage lifted his head from between my legs and rumbled out, "Nectar of the fuckin' gods, darlin'."

Apparently, we were on the same divine wavelength. He

didn't hesitate to dive back down and take from me every-thing he wanted and I was willing to give. Then he took even more. Fingers searched, touched, and left a trail of want in their wake as his tongue and mouth devastated me in the very best of ways. It didn't take long before I crashed back down to earth from heaven on a ride consisting of rippling muscles, and a rush of wetness that had the man before me rambling out obscenities as he climbed his way up my body and thrust deep inside me without any hesitation.

"Rage," I moaned out as he slammed to the hilt inside me. He was a large man in body, stature, and personality. His manhood matched it all and then some. I had never felt so damn full in my life. The sensation was just this side of discomfort, as he stayed still while completely sheathed in me, giving me a moment to catch my breath and adjust to his size. As soon as he felt my hips twitch beneath him, he growled, "Hang on, darlin'," and pulled out to just the tip before slamming back inside.

"Fuck, fuck, fuck," he hissed out with each pump back into me. "The way you grip me, darlin'."

I could see the strain on Rage's body as I felt the sweat dripping off his brow that fell to my chest and neck. His hand moved down so his fingers could strum my clit and get me closer to my second release. Then he let go, pulled out of me, flipped me over onto my hands and knees, and rammed back inside me. I didn't even have time to wrap my head around what was happening before his rhythm held me in his thrall.

Strong fingers gripped into my hips pulling me just as hard as he was slamming into me, doubling up on the force, and hitting something inside me along the way that I swear had never been touched before. I knew, in the back of my mind somewhere, that it was my cervix he was bumping into. The bite of pain with each hit mixed deliciously with the ecstasy every time the head of his cock rolled across that sensitive patch inside me that already caused my insides to quiver, just shy of my orgasm rolling through me.

"Almost, oh my God, Raaaaggee!" His name flew from my lips as my body convulsed beneath him. My pussy contracted around his shaft, and he seemed to be having trouble moving beyond my involuntary grip.

"Sweet fuckin' Jesus, darlin'. Never felt anything so goddamn good in all my life!" He continued moving in and out of me twice more, slamming home the final time as hot release coated my insides. The warmth of his body covered my own as he attempted to catch his breath kept me from becoming chilled in the air-conditioned room as the sweat began to dry on parts of my skin where he wasn't in contact with me.

Rage gently nipped at the skin between my shoulder and neck as he rolled us so that we could collapse on our sides. He was still inside of me even after our move and I relished the feeling of him being there even as I felt him growing softer post-release. "I can't believe we've been missing out on that experience all this time," I finally managed to get the words past my lips as he chuckled behind me. The movement of his chest against my back sent sweet gooseflesh dancing across my skin.

"I'm not regretting anything, because we are free and

clear of a lot of drama that would have overshadowed what we just shared. This way, you didn't have anything holding you back, darlin'." I knew he was right as his words sank in. If we had attempted this before I found out Josh was dead it would have been tainted by the fact that I was a married woman and technically belonged to someone else, even if that bastard had tried been trying to have me killed.

"You're right. It was better this way." His arms squeezed tighter where they were wrapped around my middle with one coming up to tuck between my breasts and clasp my shoulder, pulling me back as tight to his body as he could get me. "I have a question for you though. Hell, I probably should have gotten the answer to this long before that just happened."

His brows knit together in confusion as he studied my features.

"I don't know your name. I just know you by Rage, but surely you have a real name somewhere too that you go by."

He smiled at me, dimples popping through the stubble that covered his cheeks. "In another life I went by Ryder Lancaster. I suppose I still do every year when it comes time to file taxes or whatever, but no one has called me by that in a long damn time, darlin'." My jaw had slackened and Rage reached over with a finger and tipped my mouth closed again. "What about my name is so damn shocking to you?"

I giggled then. "It's not your name that has me awestruck. I didn't realize you paid taxes," I joked.

"Ha, ha, funny lady. We have to be as legit as possible on paper so we don't trip too many trips to see us from the feds. I have a real job too, so yeah, I pay taxes."

I was puzzled then, because other than the first day I showed up to Renegade Rosy's I hadn't seen Rage go off to a normal 9-5 job. Hell, that day, I thought maybe he was a bouncer at the bar, but he certainly didn't spend enough nights away from the clubhouse for that to be true. "What exactly is your job?"

"I hold part ownership in both the auto shop and Renegade Rosy's.

"Oh, I guess that makes sense then. I didn't realize you were part owner."

"What did you think I did, darlin'?" he asked with humor in his voice.

"I don't know, at first I thought you were a bouncer at the club since you were the one to escort me back to the office to see Spinner. I figured he ran the joint." I shrugged my shoulders up and down.

"At first? Why just at first?"

"Well, then you were around too often in the evenings and at night here, so I figured there was no way you were a bouncer there. I guess I just assumed the club was your only job then."

He smiled, kissed the top of my head, and pulled me closer. "Well, now you know pretty much all there is to know about me. My name, and the fact that I'm not some club slacker with no real job under his belt." I felt the fact that he was laughing more so than heard it. So I smacked a hand down on his bare chest that had finally cooled off after our round of heated sexcapades.

"Whatever. At least its better than me, seeing as to how I am currently an unemployed stripper with a pity-bartending job. Hey, that reminds me," I said to him as I looked into his warm amber brown eyes. "Almost everyone here, except Shameless calls me Showgirl now, why don't you?"

"Rabbit gave that name to you, it's a name for them to use. You're my woman, my darlin', my Charlie. I get more of you than they get of Showgirl. They get that side of you only. All the rest is mine, so what I call you will always be just mine too, darlin'."

Well, hell, I definitely wasn't going to argue that point.

"As for the rest of you said prior to that, you need to knock that shit right out of your head now. You're a fucking dancer, and I don't mean the kind that takes her clothes off for money. You only did that shit out of necessity because you were on the run and in hiding. Now, you bartend for the club, but you're also a choreographer for the girls from Rosy's. Both of those positions help support our club, and that's important as fuck, darlin'. Do not ever sell yourself short." He huffed and then squeezed me tight. "Besides, there are plenty of women who would have shown up here in hysterics, crying for our help, and never offering to lift a hand to help themselves or us. That sure as fuck ain't you. From day one, you looked to earn your own keep, and not by doing it on your back like the BRATs either. Me and the rest of the guys here have crazy respect for that, darlin'. Don't ever think otherwise."

"Okay," I managed to breathe out as he kissed me once more and I snuggled in deeper to the warmth his body provided as he wrapped himself around me. I was just about to drift off into a post coital nap when a knock on the door startled me. "Hey guys, hate to disturb whatever kind of quiet fucking you have going on in there, but Iceman needs to see you down in the office." I recognized Rabbit's voice and his chuckle as Rage grabbed one of my shoes from beside the bed and chucked it at the door.

"We'll be there in a 15."

"It hasn't been three weeks. Do you think its time anyway?" I asked, worry apparent in my tone. We had planned for three weeks, but it was with the knowledge that we might have to speed up the timeline if it became apparent that there was just too much danger in waiting.

"Maybe," he answered back. "You know, you don't have to do this."

"I do though. How else are we going to draw them out? You have had people searching for them all week and there hasn't been a trace since the image that was captured by security footage that Agent Cooper showed us."

"Fuck if I don't know that, but I still think it's too dangerous to use you as bait." His gruff voice was laced with frustration as he spoke.

"They'll think I'm dead already though. How dangerous can it really be for me?"

"Considering Bishop had you play dead once before, pretty fucking dangerous. They may be more inclined to be certain you're not breathing as a result." Rage scooped me up from the bed where our combined fluids were starting to leak out of me. It was only then that it really dawned on me that we'd just had unprotected sex. I had never had sex without a condom before, not even with Josh. Rage and I had talked about birth control and the fact that we were both clean, but it still took a leap of faith to believe in that, especially after seeing how the club members were with the easy pussy around the clubhouse. I knew that Rage used to participate in that lifestyle at some point. Just the thought sent a shiver through my body.

"Sorry, darlin', I'll have the water heated up for you in just a sec." Rage thought my chill was because of the air temperature and I was willing to let him keep believing that for now. No use letting him know that I didn't fully trust him. Hell, it wasn't even that I didn't trust him. I didn't trust myself, or my ability to see the truth when it was right in front of me. I had married a man that had never been mine. How long had it taken me to see that? How long had it been before I suspected Josh was meeting up with another woman? What the fuck had been wrong with me that I hadn't put two and two together much sooner? No, it wasn't Rage I was questioning at all. It was me. Not that he would see it that way though.

"You still with me, Charlie?" The use of my name brought me out of my thoughts. He never called me anything other than darlin' so it was startling.

"Yeah, sorry. I just got lost in thought about every-thing..." I left what my thoughts were vague, because he really didn't want to know where my mind had wandered.

He smiled down at me as he guided me into the large shower and under the spray of hot water. "Don't worry, darlin', we'll make sure you have plenty of guys watching out for you while you're vulnerable. I won't have it any other way. Now, let's get you cleaned up so we can go meet up with Iceman and see what's doin'. With any luck, he'll have news that the assholes have been found, and none of the smoke and mirrors we planned out will be necessary."

I scoffed at that. "I could only be so lucky," I huffed out. He tipped my head back as he made sure the water saturated every strand before he started shampooing my hair for me. I moaned out loud without any thought, because his fingers running over my scalp, massaging there, felt amazing.

"I do love those noises you make," he told me with a laugh. "But maybe save them for later when we have more time."

"You might want to let me take over then, because if you keep your hands on me like that you're either going to drive me back onto your cock or into a pleasure coma."

"Fuck, darlin'! The things that come out of your mouth!" He leaned in and took my lips harshly with his own while pushing me back into the stream of warm water as he washed the suds from my hair while taking what he wanted from my mouth. Finally, he pulled away, but not before his cock had fully hardened between us again. He glanced down into my eyes with a look of sheer disappointment. "We definitely don't have time for what I want to do to you right now, but later, before any plans can take place..." he grinned big so that his dimples popped out on his cheeks. "I will have you riding me like a wild fuckin' cowgirl, darlin'." I giggled at the thought of me bucking on him while slinging a cowboy hat around above my head in circles. Then I finished washing up, and moved out of the way so that he could take care of himself while I dried off.

I was hoping like hell I would get another shot at showering with Rage, because soaping him up and making sure every single inch of his body was cleansed by my hands and mouth was a dream I definitely needed to come true. It didn't take long for the two of us to get ourselves ready and within twenty minutes – not fifteen – we were down in Iceman's office waiting to hear how our lives were about to change.

18. TAKING THE BAIT

'WE HAVE A PLAN IN PLACE.'

'We have a plan in place.' I chanted those same words on repeat, like the mantra they were quickly becoming, as the van the hospital sent out to transport my 'body' rolled and bumped down the pothole laden drive from the clubhouse.

'We have a plan in place.'

This was part of the plan. Too bad I was freaking the fuck out, because thanks to being stuffed into a black body bag, secured to a metal gurney, and it felt like I was suffocating on the stale air inside. Panic overtook me a little bit as I continued to be jostled by the van's movements while the little shit who had come to collect me had zero fucks to give about it. I guess he shouldn't since he assumed I was what I was pretending to be, a corpse.

I was being transported to the hospital as the victim of an overdose. I had never had a drug problem before, but word had been spread in advance of my death notice that I'd picked up a new habit while on the run bouncing from gentleman's club to strip club to titty bar working my way northeast. Iceman told us two days ago, in our little meeting of the minds, that Macy, or Cutie-Pie as the guys knew her, was questioned by some bikers wearing Tribe patches.

She informed them that I'd been fired, because I was caught doing blow in a backroom with a client. It wasn't normally an offense worthy of letting someone go at such a fine establishment, but I had also apparently caused drama and beat one of the other dancers when she attempted to offer a lap dance to said client a little while later.

None of that sounded like me, but then again, people go crazy, and act out of character when they're on the run for their lives. Macy set the groundwork for our plan with her little lie and gained some favor from the Aces High guys who had turned her out several months before after she broke their rules. She even confirmed what The Tribe already knew. I was more than likely in the Dakotas somewhere, because that's the direction Macy had pointed me in for employment when I took off.

I'm not sure how the guys pulled it off, but The Tribe was given similar stories of my erratic behavior and drugged up state as they checked in with other places I had been along the way. Now, supposedly, I had overdone the party favors and checked myself out of this game called life without my sister and her fucked up family having to do a damn thing to make that happen. The guys still hadn't been able to flush out the perverted asshat who was attempting to buy me so that I could star in his latest snuff film, but whatever. We could deal with that dickwad after we tricked my sister into thinking she'd won, and that I was deader than dead.

Another bump, this one far more severe than any of those along the path to the clubhouse, had the gurney I was strapped to tipping up on one side for a moment before I heard the driver yelp out, "Holy shit!"

Well, that did not sound like things were going to go according to plan. Damn. I had about a solid minute more, probably less, to contemplate what could possibly be happening before the van tipped up on two wheels again, knocking my gurney off balance. How the fuck does something like that happen?

The van didn't just tip up on two wheels, we were rolling, downhill it felt like as the van tumbled and I was slammed – gurney and all – to the roof of the van before being tossed back down. I ended up back on the floor, I think. The gurney was supposed to be locked into the van so that it couldn't tumble around that way, but the moron driver didn't seem to give a rat's ass about what happened to the corpses he went to collect.

Fuck.

We *had* a plan in place. The sinking feeling in the pit of my stomach, and the aches all over my body from being tossed about begged to differ.

That plan just got sucked right the fuck out the busted windows of the corpse transport van that had been driven off the road by a moron. Rage wanted to use a prospect, at the very least, to drive the van, but Iceman and Agent Cooper had nixed the idea of having anyone club affiliated inside because it would be too easy to figure out that it was a set up. It didn't seem to matter now, because I smelled smoke, and if I didn't get the hell out of this body bag soon, I might just end up burned to death. Warm liquid trailed down into my eyes as a reminder to me that I hadn't escaped the accident unscathed.

As if the blood were a cue to my dazed brain, a fierce sort of throbbing began in my head, near my hairline as pain sizzled down in an arc toward my ear. A searing pain burned in my shoulder, leaving my left arm useless as I struggled to use the right to grasp onto the zipper that Rage had tucked toward the inside of the bag just in case I panicked and needed to get out. I was pretty sure the liquid that dripped into my eyes was blood since it felt like far too much to just be sweat, but it could have been sweat too, or a combination of the fluids, because the panic and suffocating feeling from before the accident had definitely done a number on my anxiety and my body's responses to it.

I couldn't hear movement from the front of the van. No telling what happened to my driver. Finally, I got the zipper unstuck and it started moving at just about the same time that I heard voices. "Is she in there?"

"I don't know, but if she wasn't already dead in there, she definitely may be now," a male voice called out in a joking tone.

"You better hope this wasn't a ruse, and that your little stunt didn't just kill her. My parents want her alive, if possible, and dead as a consolation prize only."

"Since when do you care about them getting the girl intact?"

"I'd rather gut the bitch, personally. She's been a thorn in my side my entire life. Mommy dearest has been crying about getting her back for years, and my dad promised she could have her. So, she'll get to talk to the little bitch before she gets sent off to that sick fuck who wants to buy her."

"Why in the hell would Lulu agree to send her to him if she's been trying to get her daughter back for years?"

"You're an idiot. Lulu isn't going to know. She'll be led to believe that the bitch ran away."

Metal clanking close by let me know they had moved a bit closer. "Well, this fucker is dead," the woman huffed. "That probably doesn't bode too well for his cargo, Spark."

"Eh, it was the quickest way to deal with the situation. Fucking sue me."

"You're going to be lucky if Crank doesn't kill you for this."

The zipper pull being inside the body bag with me wasn't the only comfort Rage had left me with. I palmed the gun he'd tucked in here at the last minute too. Thankfully, it hadn't been dislodged from where he'd tucked it under my thigh when the van went tumbling. It was just luck that it happened to be under the one strap the moron driver had tightened up pretty good to keep my body from moving off the gurney when he took the sharp turns. I knew this, because the sick fuck had talked to the body bag, like he had to walk the presumed dead person through the steps he was taking to insure it got to the hospital in one piece. Clearly, his plan hadn't worked out to well though. Not for me, and especially not for him.

As soon as I heard the male voice coming from right above me, I held my breath, listening for my opening.

"Where's the zipper on this thing?" He asked. I tipped the gun up and shot in the direction I'd heard his voice coming from. Two taps. I thanked all the merciful angels in the world for the silencer that had been placed on the gun, because there's no telling what would have happened to my hearing if it hadn't.

A heavy pressure immediately fell upon my chest making it more difficult for me to breathe as a woman frantically shouted.

"Spark? What the fuck is going on in there?" I could hear her panting breaths before she spoke again. "Fucking hell. So, you are alive in there, you little cunt. Well, guess what? Today is the day of your reckoning, and now you gave me a way out. I can blame Spark for your death, and mommy dearest never has to know it was me that took her precious lost daughter from her. I bet you didn't know that she tried to have you kidnapped after she supposedly died and lost her baby. She did though. When she couldn't get to you, it devastated her. I was never enough. Who cares about the child you have when the one you're missing can't be obtained, right?"

I tried to point my gun up so I could shoot again, but the dead weight on top of me prevented the movement needed. The sweet tang of blood filled the air along with the acrid scent of urine. Most likely it was from the dead man who lay draped over me. My useless arm that hung limply at my other side wasn't helping any as I moved and wriggled beneath the body. The words that my sister – at least that's who I figured it was since I was still trapped in my body bag – had said were echoing inside my brain. "Mommy dearest, mom, Lulu." It couldn't be. Everyone, including my dad, told me she died when I was five. Shameless told me we lost her and my baby brother that day. What the hell was going on?

Before I had a chance to think things through any further a pop hissed through the air above where I was trapped under the dead dickwad who had been trying to kidnap me. A feminine shriek of pain reverberated through the van just behind it, letting me know my sister had taken the bullet. Meanwhile, I was wriggled and struggled to get out from under the dead weight that had fallen on top of me. It was not going in my favor since my legs were still strapped down tight, and they were strapped from outside the fucking bag while I was trapped inside it.

Never in my life – even in all the running from Josh – had I felt so helpless. A whimper escaped my lips as I attempted once more to shift the dead guy off enough to move my hand and make any shots from my gun count.

"Drop it!" I heard yelled by a male voice I was all too familiar with. "Drop the fuckin' gun now or I will end you where you lie." A metallic clank rang out which probably indicated that my sister wanted to live rather than make a last stand.

"Make sure you check that cunt for more weapons before you toss her in the transport." Rage bellowed into the night air. "Darlin'? You with me in there?" he asked hesitantly.

"Get this fucker off me. He's nothing but dead weight." I am a complete fool and started giggling as I announced that fact.

I heard laughter ring out then that didn't belong to Rage. "Damn, she has a sick sense of humor," Rabbit called out in between chuckles. The body above me was yanked off and hit the floor of the van with a sickening thud as the body bag was cut away from me while the straps holding my legs down were released.

"Why the fuck was she strapped down to the gurney? We fuckin' told him not to do that shit." Rage yelled at no one and everyone.

"Well, it's not like we can ask him. This guy is deader than dead. He's half out the driver-side window and the van's on top of him." Doc – at least I think it was Doc – stated coolly. "You hurt under there, sweetheart?" he asked, letting me know that yes, it was Doc.

"A little. Blood trickling into my eyes from somewhere and my arm is useless."

"Okay, sweetheart, just stay still until I can get over there to check on you." There was a pause, a grunt as something shifted in the front of the van and then Doc spoke again. "No!" He shouted. "Do not move her yet. We don't know why her arm is useless, and with blood trickling into her eyes too, she could have damage to her spine. Keep her still. I'll be there in a minute."

More grunting sounded, and then Doc was beside me. "I'm going to pour some water over your face to help wash the blood away," he warned. "Hold on to her so she doesn't move." He addressed someone else. Hands grasped either side of my head and held me immobile as Doc slowly streamed a bit of water over my face and then used some-thing cloth-like to wipe at me. I hadn't realized before, because there was no way to see through the body bag anyway, but my eyes had been sealed shut with the amount of blood that had congealed around the edges. Gross.

"There, you should be able to open your eyes now, sweetheart," Doc informed me. The first thing I saw was his smiling face, and then I looked up to see Rage standing over me too. My heart thumped a bit harder, and relief flooded my system as I laid eyes on him. "You have a nasty bump on your forehead, scalp laceration that will need stitches, and judging from the way you've been wiggling your entire body around the whole time since I told you not to move, I'm guessing the dead arm isn't from a neck injury," he added while shaking his head disapprovingly.

"Sorry. It was harder being trapped in that bag than I thought, especially after I shot that asshole and he fell on top of me."

"Looks like you may have a dislocation. We'll fix it for you back at the clubhouse." He glanced over his shoulder at someone who lingered near the door of the van. "What's happening?"

"Molly just rang. Says the x-ray machine in the basement is working just fine now, so you'll be able to use it if needed."

Doc's smile beamed. "Fuck yeah! I knew getting our hands on that facility would pay for itself in the end. If any of that other equipment works, it will be like living in a gold mine when you fuckers get hurt."

"Do I want to know why there's an x-ray machine in the basement of your clubhouse?" I asked with trepidation.

"Haven't you ever noticed how sterile looking our joint is?" Doc asked with a waggle of his brows. I nodded my head thinking back to the hallways that hadn't been given as much concern to décor as the main areas had. They were sterile looking and reminded me of a hospital in a way. I had always thought maybe it was some sort of medical office structure before, but now I was reassessing my initial thoughts.

"Our place used to be some sort of research and treatment facility." Rage finally clued me in on what it all meant. Don't know why it went belly up, but we were there in the end to scoop it up when the money backing the program shut it down. They left some of their toys behind when they vacated. That's why we have that crazy security on the doors too. It was in place already. We just had to take it over and make it ours."

"Um, okay." My body ached and my head was throbbing with an increased ferocity. I squeezed my eyes shut to keep the dizziness at bay that came in the wake of nausea triggered by the pain I was in.

"Let's get you out of here, darlin'." Rage leaned in and scooped me up into his arms and took me to yet another van. I started shaking a bit when he went to put me inside. "It's the only way to get you back. You can't ride with that busted arm and head of yours." I knew what he wasn't saying too. He would not be riding with me, because he couldn't leave his bike behind at the accident scene either.

I glanced inside, noting my sister was also in there. She was bound and gagged, but that really did nothing to give me warm fuzzies about having to ride anywhere with her. She may have been a blood relation, but the dishonorable bitch had been trying to kill me for over a year now. Who knows? Maybe long before that. She was bound and gagged, but that didn't stop me from leaning over and punching a bitch in the face. If I had it my way that wouldn't be the only time that I got a hit in on her.

19. MEETING MOM

I SAT BACK AND SHOOK MY HAND OUT, NOT HAVING REALIZED HOW much it could hurt to punch a person in the face. Next time, I'd punch a bitch in a softer spot, for sure. Ouch.

"Maybe you should leave the brute force to the brothers?" The prospect, who I'd heard a few of the guys refer to as Flicker, told me from the front of the van. When I just stared at him and said nothing he continued to speak. "It's just that you're down one arm, you know? No use in fucking up the other one."

Well, hell. He certainly had a point there. Sadly, he was a little late on the delivery. "Not that I'd want to take the hit back, but it's a little too late to think logically about that now," I informed him while trying to shake the pain from my knuckles again. Flicker chuckled in answer while staying ever watchful and vigilant. He would probably make a hell of an asset to the club one day as a fully patched brother.

Shaking the pain from my knuckles didn't work, so I leaned against the back of the driver's side seat and studied my sister who glared daggers at me from where she had fallen over on her side after taking my hit. Much to my satisfaction, I noted the red mark on her cheek darkening as we waited. It took a few minutes more before Doc made his way from the little pow-wow the guys had been having after I was placed in the van. Once he was inside, we took off, headed for the haven of the Aces High clubhouse. I honestly couldn't wait to get there.

Riding in yet another van, after what just happened, wasn't exactly the cure for the anxiety I'd faced on the initial ride. I took solace in the fact that I was able to see while for this trip, even if I was bogged down by alternating physical pain and emotional numbness. My body was battered, bruised, and a little bit broken on top of the fact that I had killed a man. Granted, he would have killed me if I hadn't gotten to him first, but still the idea that I had taken a life started to worm its way into my brain. It worried me, in the abstract, over what type of nightmares I could expect once everything settled, and I was able to rest.

The only saving grace to the whole experience had been that I was trapped in that body bag and never had to see the man I killed. He would always remain a faceless nobody. Maybe that would help me sleep at night. Maybe it wouldn't allow me to sleep at all. Time would tell in the end, and I had a feeling tonight would be the test of how things went for me.

It didn't take long to get back to the clubhouse, because as it turned out we hadn't gotten that far away from it before my sister and her cohort waylaid us. They must have had brass balls to think about ambushing my "corpse transport" that close to the Aces High property, but I suppose they didn't think the guys would care what happened to my body if I had truly been dead. These were all things I was certain the guys would attempt to glean from my sister eventually.

The familiar rumble of motorcycle engines died off as Flicker parked the van. For the first time since I'd been able to see her since this ordeal started, my sister's eyes filled with fear. Her jaw set stubbornly, even around the gag they'd placed in her mouth, but I could see the muscle working where she was trying to psych herself up for whatever was supposed to come next. If only her eyes hadn't given her way, I'd have never known she was worried.

I hoped like hell she was shitting her pants. I really didn't know why I continued to call her my sister either. This bitch had never been a sister of mine, no matter the DNA we might share. The side door to the van slid open just as the back doors were wrenched free. My sister, no, the cunt known as Sheri Lynn Michaels, was ripped out of the back too quickly for me to process.

"I want to be there when she's questioned," I called out as Rage's face peeked in the side door looking for me. He nodded and reached in to carry me to the clubhouse. We had not pulled out front, and instead were in the back of the building in a part I had never seen before, complete with a loading dock and bay doors. I had forgotten just how big this place was since I was only ever in the upper portions of the building.

"We are going to get you checked out and x-rayed first. Don't worry, they're just putting your sister in a holding cell until we're ready for her."

"Not my sister," I argued. "She's Sheri Lynn Michaels, a pain in my ass for the past year or so of my life, and nothing more." Rage smiled down at me as I tucked my head against his chest and listened to his heart beating while he walked me down a very sterile-looking, hospital-like corridor. The guys had done a lot to make the upstairs look less like a hospital and more like a home-base if this area was what they originally had to work with up there too.

"This place is kind of spooky looking," I commented.

"Yeah, you should hear the stories about what went on here before they got shut down," Rabbit's voice called out from just behind Rage.

"Don't go telling her that right now. It's all fucking town lore anyway."

I grimaced. Great, I'd been staying in Spearfish's very own house of horrors all this time and didn't even know it. What if there were ghosts? As if the thought conjured the sound, a feminine shriek bit through the hall and echoed back to us from somewhere just ahead.

"They just took her gag off, and she's trying to make noise, is all. I promise, no one is questioning her yet." Rage's words were also a comforting rumble coming through his body and seeping straight into mine.

"I believe you," I told him. "I saw the fear in her eyes before she was yanked out of the van."

"Did it bother you?" he asked.

"No. She planned to kill me. Hell, she's been plotting my death for a long time. She was jealous. She mentioned my mother being alive and trying to kidnap me when I was younger." A strange look passed between Rage and Rabbit when I admitted to hearing that much.

"That's good to know," Rage stated.

"Sure the fuck is. No one was aware that your mom was alive." Rabbit turned and pulled his cell out of his pocket. "I've gotta bring Shameless in on this since he knew Luanne personally."

"Maybe get Ghost the fuck up here sooner rather than later too, yeah? I get that he has a new grandbaby, but this is club business that can't wait any longer."

"I'll make sure he's updated, and travel arrangements are made."

The radiology room in the basement of the clubhouse seriously made me think we'd taken a special trip through a wardrobe to a hospital-like Narnia-esqe world. I was completely blown away that something like this had existed right beneath my feet when I'd been working the bar upstairs this whole time. It also made me curious to see the rest of the facility, but I wasn't sure the guys would ever allow that. They did seem to enjoy their secrets.

NOTHING WAS BROKEN, thankfully. It felt like they were trying to rip my damn arm off when Doc did something with weight, tension, and general medical fuckery to pop my shoulder back into place where it should be. The minute he did though, the relief that coursed through my body was like sweet surrender, even if only temporarily. Having the pain disperse from my shoulder made me more aware of what was going on in the rest of my body.

My left knee hurt like a bitch, and was bruised and swollen, but otherwise okay. Then there was my face. I'd hit the top of the van at just the right spot to end up with a nasty gash damn the middle of my face at my hairline all the way over to my temple. Doc stitched me up, and I'll be honest, I refused to look in the mirror afterward. I did not even want to know what kind of Frankenstein look I'd be rocking.

Yes, I was aware that my looks were the least of my worries, but even on my yoga pants, flip-flops, and baggy t-shirt kind of days, I still wanted to look more like a woman and less like a monster. Once I was done being put back together, Rage managed to get me up to the room we'd been sharing in the clubhouse. He had moved into the one they'd put me in, because I refused to move into the room where he'd been fucking God knew how many women before I got there.

I wasn't into the new world, paranormal mumbo-jumbo, but I felt like that kind of energy left a vibe behind. It was an invisible taint on the air. I knew that others had used my room, but that was fine, because I wasn't with them. I was with Rage, and just like I'd wanted to give him a clean slate with me no longer being married; I needed him to give me a clean slate too. Especially when I remembered that day that Jezzie had come prowling out of his room.

By the time we made it to the room, I was completely wiped out. Either that or the pain meds doc had given me finally kicked in. It was probably a combination of both. Whatever the case, Rage tucked me in, made sure there were pillows propping up my injured side, so I didn't accidentally attempt to roll that way in my sleep, and the last thing I remembered was the way he gently kissed the uninjured part of my forehead before I slipped into a deep sleep.

WHEN I AWOKE, it was to someone yelling, which caused me to jump up too quickly from the bed. The movement jerked at pretty much every wound on my body. Ouch was an understatement. The drugs had officially worn off.

"I say the cunt doesn't get to see her!" Rage yelled. "What the fuck was he thinking bringing her here?"

"He was thinking with his head. We aren't getting answers from the girl. Chances are, we can pull the heart-strings of the woman a whole hell of a lot easier, but we need your woman's cooperation to do that." That voice belonged to Spinner.

"The fuck you do!" Rage roared again. "You see what happened to her after the last time we needed her to lure someone, or something, out?"

"How about giving Charlie the choice. It's not like we'll force her, asshole. I just want to…"

"You want to ask because you know she won't say no. Don't bullshit me."

I tossed the door open, wincing as I did so, because hello pain – my new friend. "I hate to interrupt the dick measuring competition you guys have going on, but can someone get Doc for me?"

Rabbit was apparently on standby in the hallway and busted a gut laughing at me.

"Texting him. He's just downstairs, so it won't take but a minute." Rabbit managed to answer as his fingers flew across the phone keys while his shoulders continued to shake with laughter.

"What's wrong? Are you okay?" Rage asked, voice thick with concern.

"Pain meds wore off, everything hurts, and you guys screaming outside the door startled me awake, which didn't feel too damn good," I complained. "So, who wins?"

They all looked at me like I'd lost my mind.

"You assholes were out here comparing sizes, and startling me out of bed when I feel like I could vomit from this pain at any moment, I at least get to know who has the bigger-"

"Oh sweetheart, it's me with the biggest cock. I didn't enter the competition though, because you know, didn't wanna shame these fuckers." Rabbit laughed as he answered.

"Shut the fuck up Rabbit!" His brother spat out.

"Darlin' you better not be worried about the size of any other man's cock," Rage grumbled.

"Then keep it down out here!" I huffed at them. Relief flooded my eyes as I saw Doc come down the hall carrying his magic bag.

"Sorry, Charlie. I was on my way to see you when I got sidetracked by the company who came through the door."

"About that," Spinner started.

"I will beat you to within an inch of your life, Spinner!" Rage roared.

I put my good hand out to touch Rage's heaving chest. "Stop." Then I directed my attention to Spinner. "What the hell have you done to rile him up?"

"Ghost brought your mom with him. He," Rabbit pointed at his brother, "wants you to go talk to her in the hopes of getting more information since your sister won't talk." He pointed to Rage then. "He doesn't think you're up for it and refused to ask you."

I rolled my eyes, because both men were now glaring at Rabbit who was getting things done with his forthrightness.

"Okay," I started before turning my attention back to Doc. "Can you give me something a bit milder that won't land me in a drug-induced coma? I just need to take the edge off the major bite of pain."

"I'll bite your ass!" Rabbit joked.

Rage growled.

Rabbit laughed.

I couldn't help when I started chuckling too. Of course, karma is a bitch and my chuckling ended up causing me to wince in pain.

"Dammit. That hurt. Why does everything I do have to hurt?" Yep, I was whining. Nope, I didn't care what any of the big, burly bikers thought about it. Doc handed me a couple pills, a coke, and told me to go ahead and take them before I got distracted again. "I did mention I wasn't too keen on being put in a coma again, right?" I asked as I eyeballed the three pills he placed in my hand.

"One is an antibiotic. One is an anti-inflammatory, and the other is a low-dose pain pill. I'll be able to stack a different type on top of it in a bit if that one doesn't work well enough for you." Doc explained as I gulped my chemical cocktail down.

"Great, now let's go get some food in you while everyone fills you in on what's happened so far and what needs to happen in the near future. You're going to want the food, so none of that shit I just gave you upsets your empty stomach."

"Yeah, because I'm pretty sure puking would feel less fantastic than normal right now."

"Exactly. I think Boxer's old lady, Tamara, has something made for you downstairs."

"I hope it's ice cream," I told them as we walked. Well, they walked. I shuffled along until Rage stopped and gingerly picked me up into his arms. I wasn't even going to complain, because those meds hadn't kicked in and I just felt like giving up and going back to the soft, fluffy warm cloud of a bed I had been in before everyone's drama woke me.

Rabbit was still giggling over my ice cream comment. "At least she knows what she wants."

Rage settled me at one of the tables near the bar that had a comfier looking chair than some of the others. I ate some homemade chicken noodle soup that was to die for. Seriously, Boxer's woman could cook her ass off. I also wolfed down a grilled cheese sandwich and sat there staring at the guys, waiting for whatever was supposed to come next.

That was about the time Iceman walked up with a gorgeous older man on his heels. The man had to be at least a couple inches over six feet tall. His sandy colored hair hung loosely around his shoulders and his eyes were a stunning turquoise color that should have held a feminine beauty to them, but instead maintained a fierceness that both captivated and intimidated on sight.

"Charlie," Iceman tipped his head toward me. "Good to see you up and about. Sorry things went down the way they did last night, but damn glad we didn't lose you in the process."

"Me too." An involuntary hiss of breath escaped me as I tried moving around to get comfortable in the chair.

"I'd like to introduce you to Ghost, he's the Aces High National Prez, but also the President of the Cedar Falls crew your dad used to belong to."

That got more of my attention. "So, you knew my dad?"

"I did," his deep baritone seemed to reverberate through the room. "Knew your mom too, and much to my surprise, she was waiting for me on my doorstep this morning before I left to come here."

My eyes snapped around to the people who sat with me. Rabbit, Spinner, Rage, and a guy named Flyboy who I had never met before. Then I glanced back up at Ghost. "I thought I'd heard wrong a bit ago when Rabbit mentioned my mom. The pain was doing funny things to my head, so I didn't question it.

"You really brought her here?"

"I did. Not sure why she showed up on my doorstep begging me to take her to you, but that's how things went down this morning, and I never look a gift horse in the mouth. She's locked up downstairs in the room across from your sister."

Ghost came closer and knelt in front of me, so I wasn't

straining my neck to look up at him. "I know this is going to be difficult on you, Charlie, but we could really use your help."

I simply nodded. "What exactly do you need from me? I don't know if you're aware, but I thought my mom died in the hospital after a car accident when I was five, along with a baby that was supposed to be my brother, and apparently wasn't."

"There seems to be some confusion in the timeline, but I was there when the baby was lost, Charlie. It was a boy. Not sure how the other girl came into play, but that's part of what we'd like you to find out for us. I have a suspicion about your mom at this point, and if I'm right, she's been playing traitor with our family a lot longer than any of us suspected."

"You think she was a traitor to your club?" I asked. "I mean, it's pretty obvious that she became one when she cheated on my dad, but..."

"She wasn't cheating on your dad, girl. If I'm right, she was sent to be with your dad by her real old man."

My nose twitched up in pure disgust then. "What are you saying, exactly?"

"I think she was with The Tribe the whole time, feeding them intel she would either overhear or garner from your dad somehow."

"But she was with him so long. They were together for a year before me, and then until I was five!" My shock caused my voice to squeak with the built-up emotion. "You're saying all that time was just a game to her?"

Ghost nodded. I felt sick to my stomach, which wasn't good considering I'd just filled the damn thing. "Do I have to talk to her? I'm not sure I can be anything but hostile after hearing all this. I'm sorry, I just... I loved my dad. I miss him every single day, and to find out that such a huge part of his life was a lie." My words were a whispered hush by then. "My heart is breaking for him, and he isn't even here to hear this."

"I think your dad knew. It's why he went mostly inactive and turned nomad. He thought he'd hurt the club, and didn't want you anywhere near this world. I think he was mostly trying to protect you from the truth, and from her. He told me a few years ago about a kidnapping attempt that had been made on you by a Tribe member. He killed the man, and took his kutte, but never got any answers as to whether the man just wanted to kill you for revenge or to take you."

"Sheri Lynn talked about a botched kidnapping attempt yesterday when they were trying to get me out of the van, before I shot her little buddy," I confirmed.

Ghost nodded again. "We need as much information from Luanne as we can get, so that we can take The Tribe out once and for all. Sheri Lynn hasn't been very cooperative and judging from all the scars that girl is sporting, I don't think anything we can do to her will make her talk."

I winced, wondering what kind of life my sister had lived. I wondered what would have happened to me if that kidnapping attempt had been successful. Jesus. What a fucking mess. "My family is completely dysfunctional, huh?"

"Nah, girl. The family that counts will always have your back and your best interest at heart. Don't ever doubt that. I owe Marcus Kinkaid a life debt. That transferred to you the moment you were born," Ghost explained. I'm sure it was a story for another day, but today there were more pressing matters to address.

"Where is she?" I finally asked just as Doc walked up with a wheelchair in front of him.

He smiled widely. "I figured we'd give Rage's hulking muscles a break. This sweet ride was hanging out in one of the rooms downstairs. Your chariot awaits."

"I'd like to be stubborn and refuse, but my knee hurts like a bitch, so I'll accept this so-called sweet ride for now. To the dungeon, James!" I announced with my finger in the air, like the big ass dork that I was.

Rabbit laughed, of course. He and I were on the same wavelength when it came to humor. We were really eight-year-olds trapped in adult bodies. Rage shook his head, but he couldn't hide the fact that his dimples popped out on his cheeks as he tried to bite back a grin.

20. IN THE END

'HELLO MOTHER!'

The thought rumbled around in my head as I was wheeled downstairs in my mobile chariot, on the way to see the woman who had given birth to me. I couldn't even give her credit for taking care of me for those first few years because I didn't remember any of it. Truthfully, she could have been a horrible mother to me when my father wasn't around to see it. The place in my heart and memories where a mother should have been, was always a blank.

What the hell was I supposed to say to her? How was I supposed to feel about this situation? I had no clue, because all I felt was numb. Oh, and there was a huge side helping of *'I wish I didn't have to do this'* rolling around in my noggin too.

The door in front of us opened to reveal another sterile, white-walled room. An older lady was strapped down to an uncomfortable looking exam table, complete with stirrups for your feet. It was the kind typically used at gynecological visits. A shiver ran through me as I, once again, let my mind wander to what the hell this place had been before the guys took over the building. There were two other chairs in the room, both plain utilitarian pieces that did not look the least bit comfortable. It made me thankful that Doc had found the wheelchair for me.

I glanced at the woman again, starting at her feet that were strapped to the stirrups, then up to her waist that was likewise tied down, and finally to a face that looked far too much like my own for me to be comfortable with.

I cringed as I took in the fact that we had the same hair color too. At least, I supposed we had once had the same color before hers started to grey. The woman's eyes were much the same as my own, only they seemed dulled and life-less in comparison.

"It's you!" The woman cried out. She couldn't do more than attempt to pick her head up to get a better look at me. "Oh my God, I've waited so long to see you again, sweet pea."

That nickname triggered a memory. I remembered a warm, loving woman with her arms wrapped around me telling me, *"Sleep tight sweet pea, when you wake things will be different."* It was the last memory I had of my mom before her accident.

"Let's get something straight, right now." I announced in a no-nonsense way. "You will not blather on with endear-ments of any type to me. If you must address me at all, you will call me Charlie, and only that. You are not to call me your daughter, sweet pea, or any other name that makes it seem like I mean something to you, because I don't."

"Oh, but you do," she rushed to say. "I've been trying to get to you for all these years, sweet..." I rolled my eyes and moved like I was about to leave when she attempted to call me sweet pea again. "Sorry. Sorry. I meant, Charlie. Sorry, it's hard for me. You must understand that I never stopped loving you or wanting you with me, but your father hid you away from me."

"And that came as a shock to you? You live with a monster, and your other daughter became one too. Do I have more siblings out there trying to kill me too, or was she the only one?"

"Oh, no. I promise, Sheri Lynn wasn't trying to kill you. She was just trying to find you for me, so we could all be a family."

I laughed. "You are delusional. She literally said she was trying to kill me last night, and that's if her dad didn't get his way. Her father, your old man, has a buyer he plans to sell me to." I could tell by the way her features broke that she knew about that. "You knew though, didn't you?"

"I found out a few days ago," she admitted. "I overheard him making the plans. That's when I knew I had to escape and get to Ghost so he could help me make sure you weren't sent there. Other girls..." she choked on a sob. "I knew other girls that were sent to him. Crank showed me the films they were in after..." Luanne swallowed hard. "I couldn't let them do that to you."

"You tried to have me kidnapped from my father before, correct?" I asked without a hint of emotion in my words.

"I tried to get you back with me, with your momma,

where you belonged," she told me as tears built and shimmered in her eyes.

"What exactly did you think was going to happen to me if you got your way?" I asked.

She looked at me as tears fell from her eyes. "You were my daughter. I just wanted you with me. You were my heart, and it was missing."

"Are you fond of having your heart stabbed out of your chest?" Her head flinched back from my question, and the glazed look in her eyes told me she didn't understand where I was coming from. "What did you think would happen to me if your old man got a hold of me? Me – the daughter of his enemy," I clarified.

She shook her head back and forth violently. "No! It wasn't like that. You were *MY* daughter!"

"I am Marcus Kinkaid's daughter. That is what I know. But in your world, I was Brazen's daughter. He was the enemy of your old man. I was the embodiment of the fact that you did more than gather information from Brazen. I became the proof that you weren't careful with what you were doing with another man. I am sure that was an insult to Crank's ego, wasn't it? How could it not be?"

She was full-on crying. "So, Luanne, what did you think Crank would do to me had been successful in taking me from my father? Were you that selfish that you wanted me to endure torture at your old man's hands just to have me near you? Or perhaps it would be your other daughter who was allowed to torture me instead of him, because she hates me. You fed her hate by constantly moaning about missing your daughter, your heart. You had another child though, one that was there with you already, and belonged to that world. Why did you need me too?"

"Because she was born of evil, and so she became evil!" Luanne spouted rather vehemently. I wasn't sure if the rooms were soundproofed, but if not, Sheri Lynn had to hear the words her mother yelled, since she was being held in the very next room. "She learned from her father. You learned from yours. You were everything sweet and pure that a daughter should be."

"And you wanted me in the same environment that tainted your other daughter?" I asked incredulously.

"I would have done better protecting you," she stated, though it was clear she didn't believe her own words.

"How old is Sheri Lynn?" I asked, changing the subject, because that line of questions was getting me nowhere. It was evident my mom had a few screws loose. Whether she had always been like that, or had it beaten into her, remained to be seen.

"Sheri is thirty-two. I was seventeen years old when Crank found me walking home from school. He took me, put me on his bike, and drove away to his clubhouse. He kept me there for sixteen days, raped me repeatedly. Brutally. I had been a virgin when that happened." Luanne stared at the ceiling as she told her story.

"Nothing I said made him stop. If I cried, it was that much worse. When I fought..." her voice cracked. "He liked when I fought back. It fueled him somehow. He took me again and again and again. The only thing he didn't do was allow his other men to have me too. He said I was his alone.

Since I was a virgin, I was safe pussy, and he didn't have to wear a rubber."

Okay, the thought of my mother having unprotected sex with her rapist made me want to vomit, but I swallowed back the bile and continued to listen to her story. If I interrupted, she might never finish telling us what happened to her and where everything went wrong.

"What didn't click for him was that I was a virgin and had no reason to be on birth control. He took me out one day to go get me some clothes since he'd shredded the last decent thing that he'd had there for me. When he did, I was able to slip away. I made it home."

She wiped her wet face across her shoulder before continuing. "I told the police. I told my parents. I did everything I was supposed to do when bad things happen to you. It was a month later when I found out I was carrying the monster's child. When my parents found out, they were devastated. They were also terrified. They made plans to send me away, but it didn't matter. He'd found me by then. He murdered them. He did it right in front of me. The man just put a gun to my dad's head and pulled the trigger. Then he made me watch as his guys raped my mom repeatedly before putting a bullet in her brain too. I had a sister who hadn't come back home from school yet.

"He promised to leave Janine alone if I just went with him. So, I did. I couldn't save my parents, but I could save my sister. I made him prove to me that she was okay periodically. He did. Janine went to live with our Aunt Nancy, and she grew up happy and healthy. She's married now and has four kids of her own. I traded my life for hers that day, and I have never regretted it."

I seriously regretted ever eating today. My stomach roiled as I listened to her story. She wasn't done yet though. She looked past me into the room, into the eyes of the man that could never be forgotten.

"I know what you really want to know."

"And are you going to tell us?" Ghost asked. He didn't seem at all phased by her story except for the way he worked his fingers in a tighter fist then released, then clenching again.

Luanne nodded. "Crank came up with a plan to destroy your club. He wanted the guns and drugs he thought you guys were running through Cedar Falls. The Tribe usually operated out of Richmond, Virginia, but they were trying to branch out west at the time and it seemed like one little MC in West Virginia was killing his hopes of running a straight line through to Louisville, Cincinnati, and Columbus. They already had a charter in Indianapolis too. It just made sense to go through West Virginia rather than around. Every time they did, your guys hit their shipments. It was as if you had a man on the inside telling you exactly where and when to be."

She looked at Ghost for confirmation, but he gave her nothing, so she continued. "When he couldn't figure it out, he started prepping me. I was to go in and get close to you. You were the original target, but you had Celia. Crank hadn't done his homework well enough back then. He thought she was just some club slut. He didn't realize some men value their women. When it was obvious to me that you were not going to be pulled away from Celia's attention, I focused on

Brazen. He was the one paying me the most attention anyway, so it seemed like the easiest in."

"How did you pass information to Crank?"

"He would meet me at the grocery store. I went every Tuesday and Thursday like clockwork to give him updates. After a while, he must have worried that I was falling for Marcus, because he started bringing pictures with him of my sister and her new boyfriend. Later, he brought me pictures of her children, to keep me in line.

"When I ended up pregnant again, and after Marcus proved that Charlie was his, that's when Crank decided I wasn't useful there anymore. I had that test in the fifth month to check for abnormalities. Crank had them draw enough for a DNA test when I went. The boy was his. He wanted to pull me out of there to keep the boy for himself.

"He staged the accident, but it didn't go the way he had planned it, and I lost the baby. I came close to losing my life too, and some days I wish I had."

"What do you get out of this little visit?" Ghost asked. "What do you get out of telling us the truth after all this time?"

"I got to see my Charlie one last time. I knew I was a dead woman the moment I went to you. Crank already has a new girl, a younger one. Hell, she's younger even than his own daughter. He doesn't need me around for anything anymore. I'm a traitor to your club for what I did to save my sister. I'm a traitor to his for coming here. Either way, I'm dead. I just hoped that I could see my girl one more time. I still hope that you'll kill the bastard, so my sister stays safe." Luanne shrugged. "She's lived a long, happy life already. I can't keep suffering for her any more though."

I had heard enough. I didn't know if I should feel bad because this woman selflessly gave her life over to the monster who stole her innocence to save her sister from the same fate, or if I should hate her because of how she tricked my father and stole a piece of his life away. My brain swirled with confusion, and the need to get out of that room for some fresh air overwhelmed me. I glanced over my shoulder at Rage, who had stood at my back rubbing circles there the entire time my mother spoke. He was a comfort, but right now it wasn't enough.

"Get me out of here," I whispered to him. He nodded and moved to push my chair out of the room.

"No! Wait!" My mother shouted; desperation evident in her voice. "Please, don't go. I just want to know that I'm forgiven. If I could have chosen my life, I would have given anything for what I had with Brazen to have been real. He was a good man. I wanted nothing more than our family to have been the real one." Tears streamed hot rivulets down her face, and my own were a matching force to be reckoned with.

"It's not my place to forgive you. That's up to my daddy wherever he is now. Thank you for telling us your story, and I am very sorry that happened to you." I tapped Rage's hand to let him know I wanted to leave now.

"Please, Charlie, don't go," she pleaded as we left the room. Was it heartless after hearing her story? I didn't know. She was still the same woman who had wanted to willingly kidnap me to put me in the middle of that hateful world she described. So, I didn't have too much sympathy for her. I'm sure her warped sense of the world around her was a product of being trapped in that environment for so long, but that just wasn't my problem to have to sort through.

"That was a lot to take in," Rage finally said to me as he pushed my chair up the ramp that led to the main floor. "How are you doing?"

"I seriously need some ice cream with lots of chocolate," I sighed.

"Let's go see what the women have hidden away in the kitchen then." Rage wheeled me in there, made me the biggest damn ice cream sundae I'd ever seen and then sat with me to help eat it.

"Do you want to talk about it?" he asked.

"I don't know what to say," I offered with a shrug as I scooped another spoonful into my mouth. I moved the spoon around to indicate the food we were eating.

"I know this seems weird, but my dad used to give me ice cream whenever things didn't go my way. He said, *'I don't know how to deal with girl tears, so just eat this, it will make it all better.'*" I smiled through tears that welled up with the memory. "He was completely clueless about what to do with teenage me, when it came time for my periods, but he tried in his own way. I loved him even more for it."

Rage smiled as I remembered my dad. "I don't know how to reconcile the life he thought he lived with the reality. A part of me understands the gun my mother was under, but then I can't condone her ruining other people's lives either. You know? How do I wrap my head around the fact that her reality is so warped she would have taken me to that environment as a young child, or even now as an adult woman? She had to know what would happen to me."

"Darlin', I don't think your mom is all there. From the sounds of it, she hasn't been for a long damn time. I can't regret the way she played your father because you're here. I don't think he'd regret it either, because it would mean his life would have been emptier for the lack of you."

I turned my watery smile up at my man. "I guess you're right about that part, but I don't want anything more to do with that woman, or her other daughter, if it's all the same."

"I will make sure no one even thinks to ask you to speak to them again, and if anyone does, you let me know so that I can explain where they went wrong with my fists."

"I don't think that will be necessary," a man said from just behind me. I turned to see turquoise eyes staring down at me. "You mind sharing that? I could use a bit of a sugar rush after that absolute shit show of a history lesson."

I pushed the bowl further over on the table and nodded my head back toward the drawer where the spoons were.

"Spoons are in there, help yourself." I glanced up at Rage. "I think he thought he was feeding an elephant when I asked for a bowl of ice cream." Rage grinned at me.

"Ah, he's just doing right by his woman. I would have done the same for my Jamie too. I was a lot like your dad after my wife died. Well, scratch that. I was a single parent with one daughter too, but I checked out for a long time after I lost Celia, and Jamie suffered for it. I'm man enough to own that. But on the few occasions I bothered to be a decent father, I would shove ice cream at her problems too." Ghost informed me with a wan smile.

"Did you learn from your mistakes though?" I asked, sensing sadness in him when it came to his daughter.

He nodded. "Still learning every day. Your dad did right by you, girl. I should have followed his example."

That made me smile. "My dad was amazing. I'm sure you'll make up for whatever shortcomings you had while you were grieving. You already admitted the problem. That's the first step, right?"

"Sure is. Hopefully, you'll be able to meet my Jamie some time. She's close to your age, a couple years younger. She was just a little thing when everything happened, and your dad took you away. I have a feeling the two of you would have been best of friends if you and your dad had stuck around the clubhouse. She could have used that too."

With that parting lament, Ghost took one more spoonful of the swiftly melting ice cream mess and then smiled at Rage. "You keep her safe and love her fiercely. Her father wouldn't have put up with anything less from her old man. You hear?"

"You have my word, brother. She will never know another bad day if I can help it, and when she does, I will be there with ice cream to pull her out of it." Rage winked at me as he spoke, and my heart melted a little more. If this man kept it up, I would be in puddles, boneless at his feet. With that said, Ghost and Rage cleaned up the mess while I sat there, and prayed Doc had ESP and would come to me with more pain meds. My head, shoulder, knee, and ribs all seemed to be throbbing in time with my every heartbeat. "Rage, can you get Doc?" I finally asked as he finished toweling off the bowl he'd washed.

"Yeah, darlin'. I'll have him meet us upstairs that way you can be comfortable when he gives you the good stuff."

That was an idea I could get behind. As much as I didn't want it earlier, sweet oblivion was calling my name now. Part of me wanted to escape the pain aching through my body, but the other part of me just needed to shut down and process the lifetime of suffering my mom spelled out for us. When this was over, I was going to find my aunt and go have a sit-down chat with her about my grandparents, about her life, and about how her sister sacrificed so much for her. She should at least know that much. My mom was right about one thing, no matter how you cut it, she had screwed over two MCs. One of them certainly deserved her wrath while she hurt the other one to save her family. Either way, she was a traitor to both, and I didn't see how any of them could grant her mercy.

WHEN I AWOKE, it was to the men scrambling around with a plan in place. While I had been tucked away in my chemical cocktail coma, life had continued without me. Agent Gordon Cooper called to give the MC the heads up that Crank and his crew were on the way to the clubhouse to demand the release of his daughter. He apparently wasn't aware that we also had his wife. Either that or he really didn't care about her, but I honestly don't think he'd make it that easy for her to get away even if he had replaced her with a younger model already. I'm pretty sure that my mother seeing him with another woman was supposed to be part of her torture.

At any rate, the man made demands, and was apparently ready to huff, puff, and blow the house down. Our job, or the Aces High MC's job, to pay Agent Cooper back for all his help was to stall The Tribe out front of the clubhouse long enough for them to set up a secure net around the place so they could be sure to pick each and every single one of those bastards up and hopefully bury them somewhere deep in the criminal justice system.

"I still don't like it. I get that the fed did us some favors by providing intel and setting up that giant clusterfuck to fake Charlie's death to get them to come out of hiding, but they're asking us to let that fucker live and be tried by the system." Rage argued when I got downstairs.

"I get that you're angry, but you know as well as I do that The Tribe hasn't made many friends in the MC world. None of those bastards will last long on the inside, no matter where they put them." Iceman countered.

"Fuck man," Rage glared over at Ghost then. "You can't tell me that you don't want a little personal fuckin' justice considering Brazen was your man, and it was your club that was infiltrated."

"I'd love nothing more than to get a piece of him, especially after hearing what he's been doing to Luanne all this time, but son, I've been around this world probably twice as long as you have, and I promise you sometimes you have to play the long game to find peace and satisfaction. What happens if we shoot, miss, and he is the one who slips through our fingertips? Your woman will be looking over her shoulder the rest of her life. I dare say she's probably tired of being cooped up in this clubhouse, even if it is a giant fucking monstrosity built on a house of horrors."

Ghost had a point, and once again reminded me that this place had been creepy as fuck before we attempted to turn the main club area into something more hospitable. All the motorcycle memorabilia and bits of Americana hanging from its walls helped, but there was always an undercurrent of something else, especially when we had to go downstairs for anything.

"Okay, fine, but you know if we use them as bait the chance that they'll live through an exchange are slim. Luanne came to you of her own free will this time and not as his pawn. He won't think twice about offing her. Can't say for certain what he'll do with his own daughter." Rage posed the questions to the audience at large that consisted of Iceman, Ghost, Spinner, Shameless, and Rabbit.

"Why don't you give the two of them the choice to be used as bait? Obviously, they don't have to know they're bait. Just that Crank is here and you're either offering them protection from him or turning them over to him. It will be their choice. Then, whatever they choose is on them and not on anyone here if things go wrong." Everyone stopped and stared at me as if I had two heads. "Sorry, I know this is a boys club, but since I share DNA with the people in question, I figured I should get a say."

"You're fine girl," Ghost stated. "If we didn't want your opinion, you wouldn't be sitting in on this meeting." He glanced around at the other men. "I think she made a mighty fine point though. Let's allow it to be their choice."

And that was how I ended up sitting in the security room watching the monitors with Rage while the front security door was opened, and Luanne and Sheri Lynn Michaels stepped out into the waning sunlight as the day lingered just this side of disappearing for the night. Luanne asked to say her goodbyes to me. A request the guys were willing to fulfill, but I was not.

I understood her motivations, but that didn't mean I could forgive the things she'd done or attempted to do. Thank God I had a good daddy who kept me safe from her and the craziness she tried to bring me into. Thank God I was my daddy's daughter, and not the monster we were sending these two women to.

Sheri Lynn had not asked to speak to me. No surprise there, as she had all the reasons in the world to both hate and envy me and the life my father had given me over the life hers had given her. I understood her too. That didn't mean I felt like falling on my sword to help either of them though. They'd made their choices. The two women stepped further outside of the vestibule that was used as a secondary security measure when entering the building. Once they were free and clear of it and walking down the pathway to the parking area a voice boomed out for them to stop where they were.

"Sheri Lynn why were you in there?" That same voice boomed out.

"I was captured while trying to retrieve the little bitch," she stated clearly.

"Did you hear anything useful inside?" The disembodied voice asked.

She glanced to her left where her mother stood. "I heard this disloyal bitch tell stories about how you raped her to make me, and how you kept her in check by threatening to kill her sister and the rest of her family. She had them all convinced it was the truth."

Laughter boomed from the evil man. "Those weren't lies. Your momma told the truth baby girl," the voice stated simply. That was when I saw the first cracks in Sheri Lynn's visage. She hadn't known her own mother's story even as she grew up with her. The girl turned wide, surprised eyes on her mother.

"It was true?" she asked. She didn't have time to get an answer as a bullet ripped through Luanne's head before she could give one. "Noooo!" Sheri Lynn screamed and moved to dive down and help her mom. Our mom. There was nothing she could do though. I was certain my mother had been dead before she hit the ground. Bright lights flashed, illuminating the entire space, making clear where The Tribe members had been hiding in the shadows. It didn't matter. Another shot rang out and Sheri Lynn dropped with her body half draped over Luanne's. Both women were dead as the ATF and FBI agents surrounding the building started rounding up all the men that were lying in wait. We watched as they got seven men and thankfully Crank was among them.

Rage's arms circled me in their warmth and comfort. "Darlin'?" he questioned when I sat there staring blankly at the screen that showed the two women slumped together. I continued to watch as the teams moved in and began assessing both women and calling for body bags. "Why didn't they move in before they were shot?"

"I don't know, darlin'. I do not know." Rage sighed, his frustration evident. "That's not on you though."

"It's not on you guys either. They were given a choice. I think Luanne knew what her fate was, but Sheri Lynn went out there with complete faith in her father. It astonishes me that she still had faith in the man who abused her. How could that be possible?" I stopped myself from going down that road of endless questions that would never have answers. "Never mind, I don't want to know."

It took hours for the mess outside to get cleaned up. Rage moved me from the security room, so I didn't have to watch it all take place. Instead, we went to the kitchen, grabbed some drinks and snacks, and hauled ass up to our room. Rage put me in the shower and washed every bit of my body, my hair, and then wrapped me up in one of the soft, fluffy towels he'd brought me. When he took me to the bed and had me lie down, he went back to the bathroom and retrieved a bottle of lotion I used on my skin.

"What are you doing?" I asked.

"I'm making it all better for you. I didn't think your stomach could handle ice cream right now. Instead, you get me pampering you for a bit. Doc left some pills there," he nodded to the side table where there were indeed a few bottles of pills. "He meant to leave them here before, but with everything going on he kept getting called away before he could get you full prescriptions together."

"Doc deserves an award. Do you guys have a champion doctor patch he can add to his kutte?" I asked in jest.

Rage laughed. "He already has something like that,

darlin'. That man is cool under fire, for sure. Now just hush that mouth of yours unless it's to moan in pleasure."

"Yes sir," I hummed as he gently took my sore leg in his hands and started massaging lotion from toes to the tips of my thighs. I wasn't sure how I was meant to relax when his fingers brushed over my mound as he moved a tad too high on my thighs, but judging from the devilish glint in his eyes, I didn't think he cared whether I was relaxing or strung out on a sexual high. So long as my brain was turned off to life's realities, he was happy with the result. Either way was fine with me, too.

EPILOGUE
FIVE MONTHS LATER

"What do you think?" Tango asked me as the grin that exploded across my face answered him before my words could.

"It's perfect! Now, get it on my body!" The demand was full of so much excitement that Tango chuckled and got to work, shaving the area where my new tattoo would go, without any further encouragement. A couple weeks ago, I took a picture of Rage while he was playing poker with the guys, and it was such a perfect image that I knew exactly what I would do with it.

Rage had been sitting in a chair that was turned around so that the low-back faced the table they were playing cards on. His full back was exposed as a result, giving a perfect shot of his kutte and his long, curling dark hair that I wanted to run my fingers through.

The best part of the shot had been the way Rage held his cards off to his left side, up and away from Rabbit who had been trying to peek at them before placing his bet. Rage had all four aces in his hand, and they were visible in the picture I took. Part of me wanted to keep Rabbit's pouting profile in the picture too because it was adorable, but I didn't think Rage would agree with another man's face being placed on my body, unless it was a memorial to my father.

"He's going to flip his shit when he sees this, Charlie," Tango said bringing my attention back to the present.

"I know." I clapped my hands together and squealed like a giddy little girl. "I can't wait. Thank you for doing this."

His eyes grew serious once more. "Normally, I wouldn't do it without him here. It's tradition that the club brother brings his woman for her property ink. You're lucky Iceman agreed to this."

"It would have ruined the surprise if he was here to see it before you inked me."

"I know it," he agreed. "He's one lucky fucker," Tango added in a mumble.

"So am I."

We got started, and after a few hours, the image of my man's back from the waist up, with his club insignia in the middle of his kutte had been inked onto my skin. The only changes to the picture, besides the obvious cropping, were to the top and bottom rockers on the back of his kutte. Instead of "Aces High MC" being at the top, Tango wrote in a beautiful scroll: "Property of" at the bottom, instead of "Dakotas Chapter" mine read: "Rage."

Just as Tango cleaned me up and got ready to wrap my tattoo, the door to the shop slung open and in walked the man of the hour. I suppose now was as good a time as any to show off what I'd done.

"Darlin'?" The endearment was more question than anything as he moved closer. I glanced back over my shoulder at the delicious man that was all mine. "You didn't tell me you were getting ink. I would have brought you. There's something I planned on getting for you anyway."

My response was a nervous giggle, which only cause his hackles to rise. "Tango," Rage spoke the man's name as if it were a curse. "What the fuck did you do to my woman to cause her to giggle like that?"

"What can I say? She loves my tool!" He teased his club brother, to both of our amusement, as the resulting growl from my man caused us both to laugh harder. "Why don't you come take a look at what your woman asked me to ink on her back? I just cleaned it up, so you can get a good look before I wrap it." Tango stood in the way and held his hand out first. "I'm going to give you some privacy for the reveal, but you need to remember it's fresh ink, brother. No touching."

Tango patted my arm. "Thank you for the honor of inking that into your skin, Charlie." He walked away as I glimpsed over my shoulder once more to watch as Rage took in the fresh ink displayed across my right shoulder blade.

"Charlie," his voice shook as he spoke with complete reverence. "You took a picture of my hand?" he asked. His eyes drifted over the picture I had printed out, along with the original sketch of the image that Tango had created.

"I did, and the minute I looked at it again after printing it, I knew exactly what to do with it." Nervousness set in as he continued to stare at the image now inked into my skin. I might have told him that I wanted to wait on the whole marriage thing, considering the first time around for me was so damn traumatic, but that didn't mean that he wasn't mine to claim just as I was his. This was my promise to him.

"Charlie," he whispered my name and when I glanced back up into his eyes, they were glassy. Rage moved closer and leaned in to kiss my shoulder, just north of where the ink stopped. "Darlin', I don't even have words. You were already amazing, but this..." He traced his fingers around the angry skin where Tango had inked his image. He then kissed closer to my neck while careful not to touch the inked portion of my skin.

"This is a gift I will treasure forever." He stared again for a bit and swiped at the tears that fell down his face. My tough man, being brought to tears by the tattoo I had inked for him, made my heart flutter in the strangest of ways.

"I wanted to get my property patch on you, but darlin', this is better than anything I imagined there."

I turned, which removed the tattoo from his line of vision, but that didn't matter. He pulled me out of the chair and into his arms. "I love you, Charlie."

"I love you too, Rage, with all my heart."

"Now, I have to figure out whether the tattoo I get to embody you will be of your beautiful body swinging around the pole at the clubhouse or decked out in your showgirl attire."

"Don't you dare!" I teasingly shrieked while slapping his chest. "If you get me inked on you decked out in showgirl feathers and plumes, I will never get rid of that damn name Rabbit slapped on me."

"I have news for you, Charlie, Showgirl is the name on your kutte."

"I don't have a kutte," I reminded him.

"Yeah, you do, darlin'. I just haven't presented it to you yet. 'Bout time to remedy that though."

"Does it really say Showgirl?" I asked while wrinkling my nose in distaste.

He chuckled in response. "It does."

"Dammit!"

That response only worked to ramp his chuckling up to full-on belly laughter. The man was gorgeous on a normal day, but when he let go of the seriousness, threw his head back and laughed, he was even more magnificent than my heart could handle.

"I love you so much," I told him.

"You, Charlie Kinkaid – soon to be Charlie Lancaster – are everything to me. My love, my lover, my woman, one day my wife, and hopefully the mother of my children too."

I didn't miss the fact that he deferred to my maiden name and left Cooper out of the mix. My man was considerate and smart.

"I still can't believe I only learned your legal name a couple months ago. It feels like we did parts of our relationship backwards."

"Nah, we did it just the way it was meant to be done."

"You do know that if you add your first name after your road name it sounds even more badass, right?"

He laughed again, and that time, Tango joined in as he had come to clean up the mess he'd made while inking me.

"Rage Ryder," my man said contemplatively. "I guess so."

"I won't call you anything else now," Tango teased him.

"Come on, woman. Let Tango wrap you up so we can get out of here. We have plans."

"Oh yeah? Where are we going?"

"To our bed," he deadpanned while Tango laughed.

"Get comfortable with doggy style while she's healing, brother."

My face bloomed with heat at Tango's suggestion. I wasn't a prude, but sometimes, the way the men were so open about discussing their sex lives in mixed company still had an effect on me.

"Darlin', that blush just makes me want to do more naughty things to you," Rage leaned in to whisper against my ear while Tango got the wrap ready.

A month later

"Are you sure you want to do this, darlin'?"

I had never been more certain of anything in my whole life. "She should know. I bet she's been wondering about her long-lost sister for years now. Wouldn't you want that closure?" I looked up at him and saw the answer in his eyes. If it were me, he would want to know what happened.

"Okay, let's go."

We had called ahead and let the woman, my aunt, know that we were coming. When we got up to the door, we didn't even need to knock as it was torn open and a lady, who looked so much like a healthier version of my own mother, burst through and wrapped her arms around me.

"I can't believe it. I can't believe she survived, and that you are a part of her." The woman blubbered into my shoulder as she spoke. I hugged her hard, because I knew this was bringing back all the horrible moments from her past. She had been the one to discover her dead parents, when she arrived home later that day, after my mother was taken for the second time by Crank.

I sat down with my aunt and her husband and told them the entire gruesome tale, stopping when she needed a moment, and starting again as she got herself together.

"Thank you," she finally told me when I was done. "Thank you for coming to let me know. I've always wondered. I always thought maybe she'd been a part of our parents' death." She shook her head, looking remorseful over the fact that she had doubted her own sister in such a way.

"I knew something bad happened to her before, but no one wanted to tell me anything, because I was too young to hear it. Knowing that she had to watch... That she was taken... That she went willingly to spare me..." A hiccupped sob tore from her. "I owe my sister a debt of gratitude, even if the rest of her life was some big game, and she was a piece that the bastard moved around, she always looked out for me."

"She did," I agreed.

My aunt eyed the kutte that my man was wearing once more. "Are you all right though?" she asked. Pretty ballsy of her considering Rage was sitting right beside me. I offered her a genuine smile in response.

"I've never been happier. The men of the Aces High MC are not like those degenerate Tribe members. They're good men. My father was the best person you could ever know. He saved me from my mother and the man that warped her into what she became."

"You think your mom would have hurt you?" she asked in disbelief.

"Not on purpose, but she wanted me to live in that environment with the man who raped her, killed her parents, abused her other daughter, and eventually wanted to sell me into slavery to an evil man who would have done far worse. She was so far gone down the rabbit hole, she didn't even realize what would have happened if she had gotten her wish and been able to take me from my father." I glanced over at Rage and then back at my aunt. "I thank God every day that my father was the man he was. He took care of me, loved me, and put me above everything else. Then, even in death, he led me home to the family he left behind in order to keep me safe."

My aunt wiped away a few more stray tears. "Do you know what happened to the man who killed my parents?" she finally managed to ask.

I nodded my head. "I do. He was taken into custody the day Luanne and Sheri Lynn were killed. While in a federal holding facility awaiting trial, he was stabbed to death by another inmate."

"Good. He didn't deserve to rot in jail." Her words came out firm and honest. "You're sure?" she asked once more.

"Absolutely. It was verified in person," Rage explained.

What he didn't tell her was that he knew the man who

had shanked Crank. He was an Aces High brother who had been hauled in for some scam he had been running, on his own outside of the club, with counterfeited money. Taking out Crank was part of the penance he had to pay for bringing down the feds on the Tallahassee Chapter of the Aces High MC.

We stayed and chatted with my aunt and her husband for a while before we had to leave for the airport. Rage and I had a wedding to get to in South Dakota.

No, it was not our own nuptials. I wasn't ready yet, even though Rage had asked. We were taking our time in getting to the altar. I was his old lady and had my gorgeous property ink to prove it. Everything healed nicely over the past month, and I had grown fond of wearing off the shoulder shirts or tanks that showed it off to everyone. The men envied that I had done something so awesome for my man. The single women grew more jealous of the fact that he was mine. My Rage didn't play their games though. When the women around the club tried to challenge our bond, he put them in their place immediately, and much to their chagrin, with no remorse in the things he said to them

Even though I loved my old man enough to not only get his name, but his image, tattooed permanently on my body, I just couldn't bring myself to get married again. Being part of a marriage for murder scheme to bankroll someone's foray into the human trafficking world was not an easy thing to get over. So, my image of marriage was slightly tainted.

We'd get there eventually, but for now, we were both happy with the way our lives turned out. We were together, and each day we made sure the other knew exactly how much they were loved. That was all that really mattered in the end.

THE END

THANKS FOR READING Dancing with Danger, book #1 in the Aces High MC - Dakotas Series.

Please read/review the book, as this is how other readers find the books you love.

Don't forget to check out the other books in the Aces High MC - Dakotas Series.

- Whiskey Tango Foxtrot
- The Restart and the Remedy

Don't forget to sign up for my newsletter, so you never miss a new release!

https://christineandanne.myflodesk.com/newsletter

ALSO BY CHRISTINE MICHELLE

CHRISTINE MICHELLE

Kings of Anarchy MC: New Mexico

Property of Bigfoot

Aces High MC – Dakotas

Dancing with Danger · Whiskey Tango Foxtrot · The Restart and the Remedy

Aces High MC – Charleston

The Other Princess · A Love So Hard · The Princess and the Prospect · The Killing Ride · A Twist of Fate · Everlasting · A Year and a Day ·The Broken Beginning – Part One ·The Broken Beginning – Part Two

Aces High MC – Tallahassee

Crushed

Aces High MC – Sierra High

Walker · Trouble

Aces High MC – Cedar Falls

Redemption Weather · Proven · Smoke and the Flame · Redemption Duet Box Set

S.H.E. MC

Angel Girl · JoJo · Keys

Robeson Family Novels (standalones)

The Forgotten Wife · When the Last Petal Falls · A Different Husband

Standalone Novels

The Groupie Journal

Letters to Lily

His Bittersweet Regret

Bad at Love

TFO

The Fortunate Ones

T.I.E. Series

The Infinite Something · The Infinite Beat

Valhalla Rising

Revived

Dark Leopards MC (paranormal)

Ridden by Darkness · The B Team

Mirage Island Mates

Into the Grasslands · Beyond the Grasslands

Seasons Pack Series

Winter Wolves

The Ancients Series

Shadows of the Ancients · Falling into the White · Branches of the Willow · Bound by the Moon

Vukodlak Brew Series

Entwined · Enraged

The Awakening Series

Birthrights · Revelations · Incarnations

Death Viewers

Breathless

Upper YA Titles

The Voodoo Follies (PNR)

Catch a Falling Star (Dystopian Romance)

ANNE STORM

Savage Vipers MC

Wait For Me · Devastate Me · Surprise Me · Baby Me

Loved for the Holidays

Cupid Broke My Heart · Ghosted by Texas · Resolving Rumors

Cheating Hearts Series

The Homewrecker's Fate · The Regrettable Mistake

ABOUT THE AUTHOR

Christine Michelle runs on coffee and giggles as she writes
her angst-fueled romance stories (motorcycle club, rockstar,
paranormal, college, & other contemporary as well as
women's fiction and marriage in trouble novels).
She is a mom to four humans (2 girls, 2 boys – all grown
now).
When she's not writing books, she enjoys reading, drawing,
hiking, or feeding her soul with live music at concerts.
Christine is a traveler and has lived all over the USA (and

other parts of the world). She currently lives in San Antonio, Texas with her two fur babies.

Universal links to everything
(website, social media, book links, and more)
https://linktr.ee/christinemichelle

facebook.com/M00nlitDreams

instagram.com/christinemichelle_annestorm

tiktok.com/@christine.michelle.books

www.ingramcontent.com/pod-product-compliance
Lightning Source LLC
Chambersburg PA
CBHW030655260626
47157CB00007B/2658